the untitled

Gayathri Prabhu

First published in India in 2016 by Fourth Estate
An Imprint of HarperCollins *Publishers*

Building 10, Tower A, 4th Floor, DLF Cyber City, Phase II,
Gurugram Haryana – 122002, India
www.harpercollins.co.in

P-ISBN: 978-93-5264-060-7
E-ISBN: 978-93-5264-061-4

2 4 6 8 10 9 7 5 3 1

Typeset in 11/14.2 Adobe Caslon Pro by
Manipal Digital Systems, Manipal

Printed and bound at
MicroPrints India, New Delhi

BOOK ONE

Seventeen Ninety-Eight

His feet struggled to steady on the burning sands and hands slid off the slippery back of the nearly naked man who had lifted and carried him from the boat. Richard could hear the captain calling out his name, wanting to know if he was fine, but words were turning into silent bubbles on his lips. The taste of fear that had rushed into his mouth and through his head as the surf had thundered and foamed around them was still fresh. He had felt the captain's large cloak come around his shoulders while a tower of water rose several feet high above their eyes, spraying violently in their faces, filling the boat to the ankles despite the swift arms of the man bailing out water. He had heard the voice of the figure at the stern shouting, stomping his feet above the roar of the surf – 'Ya-lee! Ya-lee!' – and the ten rowers echoing in gusto. Not once during the months of being entirely at the mercy of miles of salty water had he felt this kind of terror.

The anxiety had begun gnawing at his nerves even before they left the ship. Endless were the tales of those who had sailed safely for nearly a year over treacherous seas only to be dashed to death while making the landing in India. 'Captain! This is no boat! These are just planks of wood tied together by rope!' he had exclaimed in horror.

'With good reason, Mr Dawson! These ropes are going to protect our lives. If they were nailed to ribs like any old boat, the surf would surely dash it to pieces against the shore. Come, come, there is nothing to fear. The catamarans will ride alongside to fish us out if we do chance to overturn.'

He had looked around to see four narrower boats, barely more than floating logs, adroitly manoeuvred by dark men wearing only a thread around the waist that held a small piece of cloth against their loins. They were frightful-looking saviours, especially for a man who was a poor swimmer. He was grateful to be making this trip ashore with Captain Singleton and sat close to him. It was only months later that he would remember that day and realize that he had never really thought of the native men as naked. He could not even honestly claim to have thought of them as being men. In that moment of uncertainty, he could barely think beyond his clenched heart and the tense breathing of the captain at his sleeve. At each wave barrier the boatmen had waited, knowing the exact moment when the break of the surf happened, running the boat to the very edge without encountering it. The rowers worked the oar backward till a strong wave curled up and swept along with thundering violence. Every oar was then plied forward with vigour to prevent the wave from taking the boat back as it receded. Twice, it worked with mathematical precision. The last line of surf was the lowest and the fiercest, tossing the captain and Richard against each other as they bent low and held on tight. The boatmen shouted at each other. The sun burst over their heads into a white watery flame. Richard opened his eyes and saw they had been flung straight into the shallow water lapping the edge of the beach. The sternman jumped out even as the boat hung in air before the landing and turned the broadside to the waves while the rest of the crew joined him with ropes in hand to drag the boat away from the luring sea.

Richard wanted to collapse on the sand, even at the risk of being scorched, just to gather his breath, but there was neither time nor opportunity. A rush of people, all jostling against one another, swamped them. Voices mingled, some even thrown at him, but he could scarcely make out a word. He shakily dug out money for the boatmen's outstretched hands, not bothering to count as the coins slipped through his fingers. Floating figures in white swallowed him up before he could thank the rowers whose teeth flashed back in gratitude. He thought he was going to faint. The sunlight was now dazzling off the sand, making his eyes smart. The heat radiating from every object and person around was unendurable. The world began to blur. He felt the captain's firm grip steer him by the arm straight through the crowd. He noticed with bewilderment that the figures in white were native men who spoke English, for the captain was conversing with perfect ease, though barely a word said by the others was intelligible to him. What did they want?

'Dubashes, Mr Dawson,' the captain explained, 'local stewards who take care of every single need you can imagine, from house to servants, all arranged even before you show your papers of introduction to anyone in Madras. Very efficient, but mind you, just as shrewd. They think every white man is made of unlimited fortune that he must necessarily be parted from.'

They cut through the crowd and past a small gathering of Europeans, traders and Company men expecting a consignment on the *Absalom*. The captain was still speaking. 'Ah! Here comes Anthony, my personal dubash. I think this is where we part. You can collect your luggage after you meet your host. I am sure we will run into each other fairly soon in the Fort. Good day to you, sir.'

Watching the captain stride away, Richard felt orphaned. He was finally in India, two years after he had first thought of it, following months of planning and living at sea, but now, more than anything else, he wanted to stay close to the captain and get back on the decks of the *Absalom*.

Richard plodded through the sand in the direction that the captain had pointed out, keeping his head so low that figures and voices smeared around him, as in a clinging nightmare.

'It is the heat, the heat, that's all,' he muttered to himself, trying to shake off the despair – that is what it is. 'The heat. I will be get used to it soon ... soon...'

Men of all shapes and sizes walked in and out of the clumsily constructed tent without looking up. A little board beside the tent said 'Customs House' and for the benefit of any visitor who might raise an eyebrow in disdain, another hand had scribbled beside it 'Temporary'. Richard stopped at the entrance and peered into the dark interiors. It was a clutter of gigantic proportions, harassed-looking men bent over shaky tables stuck into the sand, swamped by packages of all kinds and piles of paper that they diligently kept counting.

'Mr Cole!' someone shouted. 'Are you finished with your list? Mr Sullivan is asking for it again.'

The man nearest to the entrance, his shirtsleeves rolled above the elbows, smiled vaguely at Richard as he continued to run his quill over a roll of paper.

The tired man turned to Richard and shrugged a weak smile. He could not even remember the day.

'April. The twenty-seventh,' Richard offered.

Cole extricated himself from his seat, held out a hand with a broad smile that instantly wiped the fatigue from his eyes.

'I might be expected to remember that!' he introduced himself, 'Jonathan Cole. Have you come in on the *Absalom*? Can I be of any assistance to you, guide you to your regiment, perhaps?'

'Thank you, but I am no good with bayonets.' Richard smiled back. 'Except to draw them. I am an artist ... Richard Dawson.'

'Ah, an artist! We have been lucky to be graced by quite a few of those, all doing very well we hear. Welcome to Fort St. George!'

A flock of coolies panted over the sand dunes, approaching them with a majestic piano of grand proportions. Richard blinked hard. A roving piano on an Indian beach, headed straight towards a grand buggy standing by itself, complete with harness and missing only a horse or two.

Cole noticed his expression and explained. It was nothing out of the usual for them. These were wedding presents from Mr Preston for his new bride. She was the same age as Preston's daughter, so the ladies would probably enjoy sharing it.

Richard nodded. He wished he were not feeling so utterly helpless and faint. 'I'd be grateful if you told me where I could find Mr Gilbert Forbes, member of Council.'

'Ah! An excellent choice for a host. Mr Forbes likes to be well stocked on the wines.' Cole smiled genially. 'He also likes to keep a close watch on the happenings at the Exchange and I suspect you should find him there at this time of the day. But it might make more sense to first check in at the Factory House since that would come up first as you go in through the Sea Gate over there...'

'Mister Cole!' A voice boomed from behind them.

'I'll find my way.' Richard hastily stepped back. He wanted to get into the Fort before any of his fellow passengers landed. In his present state of disarray and discomfort, he could not bear the idea of being around anyone familiar.

After seven months of being tossed around by endless water that capriciously changed colour, temper and momentum, the land constantly talked about was finally under their feet. Not long after the *Absalom* had pushed away from the Trincomalee port with fresh supplies of water and food, the Coromandel Coast had not only been anticipated but often glimpsed through the hot vapours that crushed their lungs. Passengers had repeatedly warned each other of the Indian summer. All hearsay of blistering heat and pestilence in the approaching land had been generously passed around. In the confines of their stuffy quarters, at the captain's table where they told harmless lies about themselves, during the evening walk on the deck to soak up yet another crimson sunset, writing long letters in solitude to people they ached to see the very next day but couldn't for years, there had been a simmering anxiety among the travellers. The tension abated only when a fellow East Indiaman, the *Dover*, had sailed alongside them for a while. The shared meal had sizeable contributions of fresh poultry and lamb from both pantries, cooks vying to boast of the better-fed ship, wine sloshing over heaped plates, and the chatter exploding into energetic music and dance. Someone had started to talk of India with enthusiasm, of the wealth and the grandeur and the unlimited potential for a man of enterprise. Soon the whole company had been roused into the same optimism. Hadn't they all seen living examples of this back in London? Men who had returned from the east, their trunks dripping with secrets and treasures, the same men who had only seen coal come out of mines now pinned diamonds in the hair of delighted ladies. Oh those nabobs, living in oriental splendour in the heart of England, suggesting those who had opted to stay in India were even more flamboyantly rich. What was there to doubt or be fearful of? The British were safe in India except for occasional threats from terrors like Tipu Sultan, reportedly contained within his Mysore territories. Good times, the travellers had agreed, awaited them all. For the remainder of the journey, not one had cared to speak of death or disease or bankruptcy or the reality that few of them would ever return home.

The polished columns of the Government House peeked above the fort walls, shaky through the waves of heat rising from the sands. Richard's feet dragged up the curving pathway, past the dark faces that blinked at him from the shadows of the fort as they carried packages up and down from the sea roads, through the colonnade and into an open square. Although of average height, he towered lankily above them, sandy brown hair plastered with sweat, the hint of a stubble across a square jaw. Everything was different, unreceptive of him, almost unwelcoming.

'I will never fit in here,' the voice in his head was saying, 'this is a mistake, a very bad decision, a monumental error, one there is no escape from. I am going to die here in India. I should have never left home...'

An hour later, he was still disoriented, wandering up and down wooden staircases of the trading house, smiling vacantly at curious glances, peering into rooms filled with papers and tables, finally settling down to mop his clammy face on a bench beside a window covered by Venetian blinds. A cool draught swirling across the high ceiling brought some relief and momentary calm.

The name Richard most wished to avoid was the one that he sought now with the utmost desperation, attached to it in ways that could not be erased or forgotten. Gilbert Forbes. The name had been uttered alongside his name nearly all his life.

'Curse him!' his father had growled many times when the business shared with Forbes had been folded. They had shared an envied business enterprise, Forbes in India and Dawson in Britain, both purses growing heavier with the expanding sea traffic. Forbes then decided to break away and suddenly there was nothing in the books for his partner to salvage. 'Curse him!' were his father's last words.

'Gilbert,' his mother had whispered to herself when she was combing her hair, her eyes glazed with a faraway look, unaware of the name having slipped out. He did not miss the longing in her voice nor did he ever ask her about it. They were forbidden to mention the man's name in the house. But Richard had to endure the name again and again when the box of papers in the safe had been opened to reveal bundles of letters exchanged between his dead father and the distant associate, dated from even before he was born. He knew then that it was not just friendship or business at stake but two men with destinies twisted crudely together, as much in survival as in success. He could not have imagined such a thing possible; both men matched equally in temper, accusations and justifications, confessions and consolations, sins and blessings, all mashed into one another. Several of the letters carried his name, his welfare and future discussed. They had agreed he was their joint heir but almost seemed to wish he did not exist between them.

When his father died, Richard had considered himself free to abandon his two part-time jobs, as bookkeeper to a trader and as assistant to a draughtsman, to become an artist. He was sixteen, and one of the dozen apprentices to Thomas Lawrence, London's celebrated portraitist. He often asked his mother how she managed to get an introduction to such an important man, but she avoided the matter and he knew why. There was again that name they did not wish to say aloud. Just as she did not wish to explain the money she was beginning to receive to run her household of many children.

Richard had burrowed into his work. After months of merely cleaning the studio, he was allowed to help fill colours in the portraits, mostly into the background or clothing, under the strictest instructions and supervision. He painted long hours but not a single line or shade of colour was his own. There came a time when he simply could not go on enslaved to another man's imagination and decided to try his luck as an independent artist. He confidently announced his intention to be a portrait painter. His mother had moaned that there just wasn't enough money. He had insisted he would make his own. For a month he bravely returned the meagre allowance she spared him out of hers. He hung around taverns to make charcoal drawings on sheaves of paper for men who wished to give their sweethearts a keepsake in exchange. It fed him, not regularly but frequently enough to keep soul close to body. But it did not give enough to buy paints or paper and at the end of the month he was back in his mother's kitchen. She had been strangely smug, smiling while she poured out both tea and polite conversation, slightly funny and modestly wise, as if he were a treasured social acquaintance. He waited for the words and they emerged before he had drained his cup. Gilbert Forbes. As soon as the name was out between them, the evening froze and turned hollow.

'Why doesn't this Forbes pay back the money he owed Father if he is such a gentleman and as wealthy as you claim?'

'Because,' Mother bristled indignantly, 'he did not owe your father any money. It was all a misunderstanding.'

Richard thought it pointless to repeat the accusations of his father. He watched cagily as she launched on a long discourse: there was a fortune to be made in India. They had all the soldiers and merchants and administrators they could use and now they needed artists. There was tremendous demand for portraits. The gentlemen in the presidencies had enough money to commission paintings and the Indian princes were just as eager to acquire European art. Their dear friend Forbes had sent her a letter assuring support and guidance in Madras for dear Richard. All that remained to be done was the required permission from the Company and that would be managed because Gilbert had offered to write a letter as well.

Richard had nothing to fall back on – very little money, hardly any contacts and shaky career prospects. It was a gamble, this trip to India, and a desperate one. Having taken it, there was nothing to do now but to push the past out of his heart, think not of Mother or her Gilbert, but somehow survive. Taking this man's help, he had determined, would be a purely professional move, a detached association, nothing more than an introduction, a helping hand...

From amidst the chatter of scurrying people, he heard the footfall, clearly set apart. He turned. A middle-aged gentleman in an elegant waistcoat and elaborate white wig was walking towards him with stiff measured steps. It was a face he had seen before on a man he had never met. He continued to stare as the stranger moved closer and in his mind he saw the same face in its youth, just as grave and fierce. This time the image was trapped within a miniature portrait that sat on the dresser beside his mother's bed, a face he had always thought belonged to one of the many brothers that she claimed to have lost over the years. Instead it had been Gilbert Forbes all along. And suddenly, the long-suffering eyes of his mother, the contemptuous smirk of his father whenever she tried to speak about their old friend, the lonely nights on the busy streets of London, the frothy evenings on the ship's deck when the stars dipped low enough to be reached for, the sapping air of this strange land and the dry paintbrushes in his bag waiting to shape his fortune, all came together in the cold grip and smug smile of the man who now shook his hand.

Two palanquins strutted through Fort St. George, one closely behind the other. The sun was directly overhead and an undulating shimmer rose from the fairly deserted roads. Richard had never seen such wealth in white pillars and arches, domes and minarets beneath a uniform wash of shiny plaster.

'I am in India,' he whispered softly and sank back in the cushions as if that thought had never crossed his mind until then.

Richard had been reluctant to be folded into the little covered seat and be hoisted on the shoulders of six men. He tried to tell his host that he preferred a horse carriage or even to walk but was dismissed with a laugh. Within minutes of being borne away, it was easy to forget the muscles that carried him so effortlessly. A young boy, face averted and holding a large painted umbrella, walked by the side of the palanquin to block the sun from Richard's face.

Forbes did not own a house within the fort and his explanation had been brusque. There was a house there during the old merchanting days when a man thought less of the heat and even less of pleasure. Now a man of means lived in garden houses in the Choultry Plains, a charming little place, a bit like one of the provincial towns back home, you know, like Bath.

It was nothing like that. Richard knew from the angle of the sun that they were travelling to the west, beyond the river that ran its intricate channels around the fort walls, to an open plain where a lofty customs post rose awkwardly above rows of pale houses. They crossed open fields where the brown of the land lay bare, and then through a wave of foliage infused with the deepest green and brightest flowers. A brief rush of sea breeze, heavier with the worries of inland fever and humidity, rustled the curtains of the palanquin.

Not a cloud in the sky. Only a dourly trailing kite. Flashes of rust orange and white. A laburnum dripped gold blossoms into the thirsty earth. The bearers chanted to keep in step and occasionally called out to passers-by to make way. Richard wiped his face on his sleeve and slumped deeper into the cushions, knees folded high. He closed his eyes and submitted to the rhythm of six pairs of feet that walked as one. The earth became glassy bottomless water, the wooden frame his head leant against was the vibrating railings of the ship; in the distance a blurry horizon suggested lush islands and the fear of the approaching mystery rushed in, all turbulent, churning, boiling, till there was an inexplicable stillness and calm.

'Hullo! Ho there, you Boy! O, Boy!'

Richard woke up in panic. The sea had frozen into a slab of jade under the *Absalom*. He then realized his cramped perch was planted firmly on earth. At a distance, two of the bearers were squatting to peer at him. On the other side he could see an imposing pair of stocking-clad feet against a white wall. He clambered out and propped himself against the palanquin. Mercifully, he was not the boy that Forbes was yelling at and soon he would find out that all native servants were thus summoned. It was a shock nonetheless to find he was in the midst of a crowd.

Dear Lord! We have fallen into an anthill!

Servants poured out from every opening in the house, fussed about, picked up orders even before the words had completely fallen out of their master's lips and escorted Richard from the cushioned palanquin to a bright central hall with open raftered ceilings. This kind of bustle around one lone man might have felt incongruous anywhere else but right here it was an experience of the most natural kind. Isn't this what he had heard and imagined life in India to be like? To live like a nobleman, fawned upon and feted, to have a social station that London would never condescend to confer upon the son of a trader.

He walked in to be confronted by bare walls. Gilbert Forbes was the model of austerity but for a few pieces of furniture the house was nearly empty, not a painting in sight. Richard hoped other residents of Madras were different. If not, he might be forced to travel to Bengal from where there had been more reassuring reports of artists making a comfortable living, but that would however entail another journey, more expenses and a much longer wait to make any income. No, he had no choice. This was the man to help him, even push him ahead.

Forbes was pointing to a figure bent so low that Richard barely saw his face. Ramaswamy, the head steward of the house, was curtly introduced. Luncheon was to be served at two o'clock and that gave him enough time to wash and rest. Forbes had turned around and marched into a room at the far end of the hall. Had the man nothing more to say to him? What kindness had his mother seen and talked about in this Gilbert of hers? Not a single word of condolence for his dead friend or enquiries about the grieving widow. It would be folly perhaps to reveal his economic situation to one so unfeeling.

The double curtains on the door fluttered to a hot breeze and for the second time that day, the land beneath him turned viscous. The house swayed slightly. A turbaned man standing in attendance at the door of his room anxiously stepped ahead with an extended hand to brace him and Richard refused with a quick shake of the head. No, he was fine, just fine, but his body was still at sea.

The man nodded and stepped back. The strange nostalgia for the boundless blue waters came flooding back to Richard's mind. All that he had hated about it now became endearing. He missed the incessant rocking, the wailing of the wind on choppy waves, even the gloomy nights in the captain's cabin where he had an open invitation to join for a glass of port that seldom came unaccompanied by sad stories of dead people and thwarted romances. This house, not a single sheet of glass in it and the barest of furniture, made him feel just as seasick as he had felt during the first week on the *Absalom*. He had appetite neither for the announced luncheon nor the prolonged company of the solemn man who was his only gateway into Fort St. George society. He sat on the edge of the cot, his head cradled in his hands, till something moved outside the curtains of his door. It was time to eat, the steward having been sent to cough a reminder.

The dining table was sturdy and plain, a perfect prop for Forbes who sat with a stern look that barely eased or changed contours when his guest reached the table with earnest apologies for causing the slight delay.

At a glance from his master, a waiting boy in a snug uniform he had outgrown stepped ahead to serve rice on their plates, bordering it with two curries of contrasting colours, one promised red meat and the other an assortment of vegetables. Richard felt the little appetite built by the morning exertions completely disappear. The steward carefully poured wine into their glasses. Forbes tossed the drink down. 'Madeira is the only wine that distinctly improves in Indian climate, Mr Dawson. I hope you remember to keep it close to your meals. It helps protect against nasty water diseases very common in our parts.'

It was clear that his host could talk and drink at the same time, and Richard spoke up only when he was asked something. Yes, his ship did stop at Madeira. No, he was not sure how many pipes had been loaded. Yes, it might have been a hundred.

Forbes smirked, his glass refilled with more wine and poised in mid-air to be emptied like the ones before. 'I was the same age as you when I first came to India. There was much on offer for a young man with enterprise. Plenty of money, very few laws apart from whatever suited us and no damn administrators sent fresh from Leadenhall Street to tell us how to eat our meat.'

Richard's head ached and the heat blunted by the tall roof continued to suffocate. He reluctantly pecked at a green lump from his plate.

Forbes was still talking. The times were grim indeed. There was a great deal that required his attention. The new Governor-General of India had arrived yesterday on HMS *Virginia*. A man to watch out for … Richard Wellesley, Earl of Mornington, on his way to Calcutta … Pitt's personal pony, another of those Eton boys, forceful ideas … There was a younger Wellesley in the army in India and another tagging along as private secretary, families grabbing titles and opportunities like frogs catching flies…

Richard opened his mouth to be excused from the meal. The oil from the lamb glazed over the cave of his mouth and the spices pricked his tongue till it curled. And then Forbes said something about Tipu Sultan. The new Governor-General had been sent to solve the problem for good and there were meetings Forbes had to attend in the fort.

'Tipu Sultan,' Richard promptly repeated.

'Ah yes! There isn't a single imbecile who hasn't heard of Tipu all the way from here to England. Too much talk and too little done about it. Lord Cornwallis, the old fool, spent a whole year and almost every single rupee of the Company coffers to bring the tyrant to his knees only to simply let him continue being the miserable beast that he is.'

Richard knew about the war. He started to say something but realized that his host did not notice or care if he contributed to the conversation. Forbes was busy speaking his mind on the business of losing the colonies in America and the rabble ruling Paris, cursing a whole lot of people and drinking even more. The servants were clearing the table and the steward continued to pour wine. Richard put his glass to his mouth and then set it down without taking a swig, nauseous from both the food and wine, but not daring to abandon the meal entirely. Forbes shook his head at the wine bottle in the steward's hands and it promptly disappeared. A plate of orange fruit cut open into slices was placed before them, filling the room with its sickly sweet smell.

'Mangoes,' introduced the host curtly.

Dear Lord, no! Richard held his breath to fight back the revulsion in his stomach.

'What is your line of expertise in the arts, Mr Dawson?'

'Portraits,' he said and then quickly added, 'I practise landscapes too. I was wondering if you…' Richard hesitated. Perhaps it was too early to state his monetary concerns. Instead he found himself saying, 'I saw some work by artists who were present during the Cornwallis campaign at the Academy exhibition in London. I was told one of them is still here and I am very eager to discuss my prospects with him.'

Forbes put his glass down with a sharp clink, and sharply turned his grey eyes on the young man. Surely he didn't mean Robert Havelock?

Richard nodded.

'A rogue!' Forbes was not shy of a tirade against his guest's profession. 'You would be wise to keep a distance from him, Mr Dawson. He is not fit for civilized society anymore and has probably even forgotten what his paintbrushes look like. These vain no-good artists...'

Richard pushed back in his chair. He now knew that there was no sympathy or support or patronage to be expected from Gilbert Forbes. His mind began to race, the options having drastically narrowed down. It was more important now to talk to Havelock who had spent over ten years travelling in India, even publishing his landscapes in a book called *The Select Views of Mysore Country*. Before his departure from London, Richard had spent months trying to locate another artist, Arthur William Devis, whose eleven years in India had garnered plenty of admiration and commissions, especially for his studies of Tipu Sultan's sons while in British captivity. And yet, when Richard met him, he had found the man entirely penniless and broken in spirit. From his many confused mutterings Richards was able to garner some leads: the South was a better option than Bengal where too many artists crowded for the same patronage and Robert Havelock was the man to consult in Madras.

Forbes tipped the empty glass into his mouth and smacked his lips. 'And if you must see Mr Havelock, you might have to rummage through the filth in Black Town. I strongly advise you against going, Mr Dawson. He has very few morals to speak of, this Havelock, spending all his time around a grimy little tavern, The Griffin, run by his Portuguese father-in-law and talking filth about all the respectable people in the fort...'

'Mr Havelock's morals don't concern me, sir. How far is Black Town from the Choultry Plains?'

The man grunted in disapproval and then turned to Ramaswamy. 'Has the driver come today? Ask him to prepare the carriage for Mr Dawson whenever he wishes to explore the seamier side of our good town.'

'I thank you very much for your kindness.'

'I trust your mother is in good health?' Forbes turned his steel gaze again on him.

It took him so long to remember, Richard thought, obviously she does not amount to much for him. And there was Mother. Mother, far across the seas, combing her hair and thinking not of his father, but this revolting man so full of himself.

'She is very well, sir,' he said with a more formal edge to his voice.

'A fine woman...' Forbes mused.

'She has sent a letter addressed to you and some new music she thought you might appreciate,' he said, thinking of his mother as a woman of little judgement. There was nothing to remotely suggest music or any finer sensibility in the house or the person of this man.

'Music!' Forbes rubbed his belly lightly with his fingertips. 'Oh! We should go to Dr Wheeler's house one of these evenings and I am sure his girls will be delighted to play it for us. James Wheeler is our esteemed surgeon, a good man with very lucky hands both for healing and the diamond business. As for his girls, I dare say there are very few young ladies as accomplished in the country, perfect wives for young men with aspirations.'

Richard pretended to miss the hint. The man was talking of wives when he barely knew what to do for his own existence. 'Mr Forbes,' he hesitated, 'there is a little matter that might be of some importance to the Company. Or perhaps it is common knowledge that is of no use. A little past the Mozambique Channel, we had the good fortune of the company of the East Indiaman *Dover.* The second mate happened to be a school friend of mine and was in possession of some pamphlets from the Isle of France. He was kind enough to spare me one. It is a proclamation made by Governor Malartic asking for volunteers in Port Louis for Tipu Sultan's army to fight the English in India.'

Even as he was speaking, Richard was aware of the transformation in the other man, now tense with attention and authority. The wine-loving nabob turning into an administrator who glued his ear to every closed door, a man who might even know that being the governor of the fort was not such an impossible dream for him. Here was information that could possibly change the course of his destiny and career in the civil service.

'We have heard something of it,' Forbes said cautiously. 'Does this paper have a date on it?'

'Thirtieth January of this year.'

'And you say you have the actual proclamation with you? Thank you, Dawson, very prudent of you to bring this to my notice. This is a sensitive matter and I urge you not to speak of this to anybody else. Please hand that pamphlet to Ramaswamy as soon as you retire to your room and he will bring it to me. I usually rest after luncheon but have just remembered some urgent business at the Government House.' He sprang up from his chair.

'The tavern you mentioned, sir ... The Griffin?'

Forbes stepped around and leaned over him, the light going out of his eyes and his voice hardening. 'Yes and that is what they'd call you and every other newcomer here – a griffin. Almost sounds like an insult, wouldn't you say? Now, you listen to me, lad. I care for nobody's skin but my own. So if you don't return from Black Town or any other place you might choose to venture to, I shall tell your mother that I never set eyes on you. And don't expect me to spend money on a gravestone either.'

Richard felt sick in the realization that if he were to disappear, with or without a gravestone, or if he were to survive and his mother had to listen to two stories, Gilbert Forbes would be the man she would believe, not her son.

Half Lion Half Eagle

The lion's body was slightly dwarfed, torso twisted to give an impression of being neither seated nor standing, but in the process of lazily rising. Its tail reached up to imitate a shepherd's crook, balancing the pair of outstretched eagle wings attached to its sides. The work of a painter, thought Richard, too busy to pay attention to details and smart enough to know drama mattered more than detail for someone paying for a tavern signboard in Black Town. THE GRIFFIN, said the bold letters suspended over the creature's head.

The rising curtain of Fort St. George made a formidable backdrop but nothing of its inner white splendour had survived beyond a mile to the north where clusters of grimy houses stood separated from the fort by fire lines to stem any outbreak of epidemics. Black Town was home to merchants from all over the world, where the weight of gold mattered far more than nationalities or religious affiliations, and empty pockets could easily roam and survive with a little ingenuity. Their colony was a delightful circus of vice where the high morals of the fort could be sneered at and they were proud of that.

A peculiar stench hung upon everything: smell of cooking meat, rotting meat, an intimacy of the senses that Richard had not known before, revulsion mixed with allure. Inside the tavern, the stench turned more intense, changed character. Now it smelt of tobacco and cheap whisky, of languor, wantonness and indulgence. For the first time in months, Richard felt at home.

A single room, broad and capacious, made up the entire tavern. It had neither segments nor partitions nor any kind of order. He made his way through the three billiards tables that stood at bold angles to each other, none being presently used for the purpose meant, instead serving as tables for some patrons and as chairs for others. Richard looked around for a face that might suggest itself as being the painter Havelock.

A burly man in a white sleeveless vest was walking straight to him. With his baldpate, scraggly beard and a fleshy lower lip that seemed to hang loose from his face, Pereira the innkeeper was a fearsome sight.

'You from the *Spencer*, eh?'

'No, the *Absalom*. I am looking—'

'For boarding? Sure, sure, for a pagoda a day, consider yourself king of all you can see here around you. Food and wine will cost extra of course.'

'That's very kind of you but ... no, not boarding. I am looking for someone. Perhaps you can help me. I am looking for Robert Havelock.'

The innkeeper stepped back, his demeanour changing in an instant, and looked his guest up and down. 'Let me guess,' he clicked his tongue against rotting teeth, 'oh yes, please do let me guess. Another artist! Both gifted and poor. Or am I wrong?'

Richard shrugged aside the sarcasm. He had to see Mr Havelock on a matter of importance…

'Do you owe him money?'

'No.'

'Does he owe you money?'

'No, but …'

'Fine! That is all I need to know. And I ask because my only child insists on wasting herself on him. I'll let the genius know you are looking for him. And meanwhile, if you can pay for it, I'll have a boy bring you a glass of our special punch. Made with the finest arrack in all of Coromandel!'

'I prefer claret,' Richard said, 'and will gladly pay for it.'

The innkeeper turned to greet a batch of soldiers who had sauntered in singing an old ditty in the most offbeat tune. Hardly had they grabbed glasses, one of them climbing on an overturned barrel to sing an encore, when another group of young men walked in through the door. Dressed smartly in high collars and bright cravats, they were talking all at once. Richard pulled a chair and turned it around to face the far end of the inn where between a few overturned chairs, a man played alone at a backgammon table. A high window was drawing in the golden light of a falling sun, making a faint halo in the man's tousled hair before sliding into a puddle at his feet. Richard stretched out in his chair. He loved watching moments like this, paintings that did not need painting, which would exist in perfection in life, flawless for a few brief moments and then lost. The man would stand or the light would change and the painting would forever be gone. But while it was there, he intended to watch it, and watch it with the eye of a connoisseur.

Never take light for granted, his teacher had said while they had pored over studies of the great masters. To the painter, light can be destructive, light can be benevolent, light alone can breathe permanence and brilliance into the canvas. It has to be craved for, worshipped and pursued with desperation. Only then can light become the timelessness of Vermeer, the transcendence of Raphael, the exactness of Rembrandt…

A chair dragged and a bottle of beer thumped down on the table beside his claret.

'Stale beer, sour claret, rotten ham, expensive services … Welcome to The Griffin!'

Richard turned to the man who now sat beside him. The stranger's long brown hair, neither powdered nor curled, hung limply around his sun-tinged face, falling just below his shoulders. He wore loose drawers and linen shirt spun on local looms, coarse as that of a workman, suggesting disdain for his countrymen whose clothes did not respect the local weather. Yet, his stature was aristocratic, and his impish eyes like polished green marble. He was now raising his voice, 'You'd be surprised to know the amount of money this dump churns out – three times the cost of everything!'

'None of which you pay for,' shouted a voice from across the room.

'Did I mention insolent landlords?' Havelock smiled.

Richard immediately took a liking to his companion and it made him bold enough to impulsively retort, 'And I trust his daughter is nothing like him?'

Robert Havelock laughed. 'Hey, you have some spirit in you! A refreshing change from the steady flow of conquerors coming from dear homeland on smelly ships.' They shook hands grinning at each other. Havelock took a long swig from his bottle. 'My Lily is nothing like that old goat you've just met. She takes after her mother, an Indian lady from a noble family, and you will do well to follow my example. The women here are divine ... bronze skin, deep curves, playful and docile ... nothing like the conniving stiff petticoats back home.'

Richard laughed in good humour. Pereira cursed loudly, but not at them. The soldiers had overturned a billiard table and the first signs of a fight began to show. The man at the backgammon game calmly got up, picked his hat and a small pile of parcels lying at his feet, and walked out. Away from the light, Richard saw the burden in his gait and the discolouration of his clothes.

'A clever move,' Havelock muttered to himself. 'The Jews always know the perfect time to leave. The Jews and the Armenians, which is why they survive the longest in Black Town. I suggest you hold on to your bottle, Dawson. They are the first casualties in a fight, but Pereira will have the place in control soon enough. I often suspect that he starts these fights so that he can get his own hands bloodied, just for a laugh.'

Havelock emptied his beer and then carefully pulled strands of hair away from his face with both hands. Long fine scars, like the teeth of a comb, ran down one side of his neck and into his shirt. Richard pushed his bottle of claret towards the other man and it was accepted without a fuss.

Richard cleared his throat and started hesitantly. 'I met Mr Arthur Devis in London before leaving and he was kind enough to tell me about you. I have seen and admired your work at the auction...'

'How is Devis? Poor devil!'

'In good health. But pressed for money, I believe...'

'I told him to stay on in India but he would not listen. We are just as pressed for commissions here, Dawson, but there is still a living to be made and the nabobs for all their silliness would not like a fellow countryman starving on foreign shores. The Company boys in particular have a weakness for owning their likeness captured on ivory. If you have any talent with that, I dare say you will be in business soon.'

Richard was relieved that the matter of money had been broached. He did not have any time to waste. Havelock wanted to know if Richard had a host in Fort St. George. Richard mentioned the temporary arrangement with an old family friend, but not that the friend was possibly the reason for his poverty, the reason for his mother hating the man she had wedded. Did Havelock know Gilbert Forbes?

'That's some friend for a family to have!' Havelock chortled wickedly. 'The man would sell his own grandmother if it helped keep the shiny stones rolling.' Diamonds, Havelock added an aside, was the best business, no papers and no records, but plenty of rewards. Forbes pocketed a salary from the Company as well and the pockets ran treacherously deep.

The words that followed were lost in the uproar. A soldier had broken a chair on the head of one of the more insolent clerks.

'Calm down, gentlemen!' Pereira shouted. 'Have you completely lost leave of your senses? Soldiers fighting writers! Pooh! I can't allow such an unfair massacre...'

The soldiers hooted and affronted Company clerks shouted back at them. Collars were grabbed and coats pulled off. Havelock talked calmly through the brawl. There was a demand for portraits in Fort St. George but only if the artist had the money to establish himself in the fort for a few months. Richard shook his head to say that he could not.

Havelock continued, 'Accommodation and living are expensive here. I could arrange something for you in Black Town but that would do you no good. Those vain powdered swans in the fort would think it beneath their station to be painted by someone living here. But if you choose to live among them, you will need plenty of money. So I suggest you travel. It is not entirely inexpensive but the rewards are there. In the Company Presidencies, the only Indians you will meet are servants, and I am sure you want to see more. I did that once, following Cornwallis and his army, sketching the forts of Mysore while they went after Tipu's army. I did not have to ship a single painting to London because they were all sold right here and handsomely too. The money may be in the portraits my friend, but the future is in the landscapes.'

Did Havelock still paint landscapes? Richard wanted to know.

'Now I only paint carriages and palanquins and an odd fence or two. Anything that keeps the small change rolling in the pockets…'

The brawl was now drowning out their words. The clerks had decided to retaliate. Under Pereira's screaming instructions, the waiters were gathering bottles, empty and full, from all the tables, and running out of a backdoor. The claret bottle stayed safely in Havelock's hands. 'How is work back in London?'

Richard had much to say on that. Reynolds and Gainsborough were dead but everyone still demanded to be painted by them. Dead men did better business than living starving artists. Or it had to be horses, like George Stubbs. Nobody cared for new ideas. A portrait surely ought to be more than style and likeness…

Robert Havelock yawned. 'When they pay you for a portrait here, Dawson, they expect likeness and a damned flattering one at that.

Sometimes I miss London and all their empty artistic chatter. They had irked me then, but might amuse me now.'

The leg of a chair flew past, narrowly missing their table. 'Could we meet tomorrow?' Richard was now anxious to leave the tavern.

'If I were you, Dawson, I would not waste my time with the likes of Forbes or me. I would head for Mysore country where there is a ripe harvest waiting to be gathered for any artist. Tipu Sultan may be crazy but he is the only one with the courage to fight us to the finish. You need do nothing but be there and wait for history to come looking for you.'

'Why don't ... why...' Richard fumbled, not sure if he should ask the obvious.

Havelock smirked. 'Why I won't go is because I don't much care for fortunes or painting anymore. A pity, you might say, and a waste of talent. Well, the talent is mine to waste, and I wish you luck, Mr Dawson.' He bowed a little, and before Richard could say anything, strolled away in perfect poise, the near-empty bottle dangling precariously from his fingers.

Seven miles in a rickety carriage, confined to the company of Gilbert Forbes who arranged and rearranged himself, was an ordeal. Richard had changed into his best clothes at the insistence of his host who was wearing a new pair of silk stockings which he looked down to admire every now and then. Richard's face was gloomily averted from Forbes and the smell of pomatum that hung around his powdered hair.

The sky was a magenta haze and the sea breeze tempered to a sultry simmer. The settlement of Fort St. George spilt out of the fort and spread out into weekend bungalows at St. Thomas Mount, popular with residents for the relative coolness of air and sport like hawking and fowling. They were headed to Doctor Wheeler's house, a fashionable address in the area. An Indian man in a long white dress and a turban of immense circumference stood on the bow of the carriage, a similar attired one at the rear and two more running on either side of the horses.

A week since his arrival, Richard had been cooped up in the bare white house, worrying about his future, while Forbes seemed preoccupied, meeting him only at the dinner table where he talked about his own political worries. Richard had expected to be grilled about his time in Black Town but the matter never came up.

The carriage tottered to one side and then straightened. Forbes put his head out and yelled in a strange language to the driver. It was the first time Richard had heard him speak in anything but English. Forbes settled back and angrily set about fashioning his dishevelled hair all over again.

Richard felt compelled to say something to break the awkwardness. 'I met Mr Cole earlier in the day and he sends you his regards.'

'Who the devil is Cole?' Forbes patted his snug waistcoat.

'Cole ... at the Customs House...' Richard was flustered at having started a conversation worse than the silence.

'India has become the perfect dumping ground for young men who are a nuisance back home, unable to secure steady jobs or lead responsible lives.'

Richard felt slighted at a barb he imagined was aimed at him. This man was the only one who knew the real story that had sunk his father's flourishing business, leaving him nothing to fall back on. In a burst of resentment, he snapped back, 'It could not have been so very different when you came to India, Mr Forbes.'

'I came here long ago, long enough to bury two wives and three children, long enough to survive two famines, three cyclones, French attacks, Mysore wars and more governors than you can count on your ten dainty fingers.'

Richard decided to shut up. The image of the churlish Gilbert Forbes as a family man, marrying, raising children and then burying his entire family came as a shock. What would his mother say, she who seemed unaware of the existence or death of wives and children during her many years of correspondence with a man who paid for her family's subsistence?

They were driving through the gates of an imposing house. Richard wished he had not come even though there was the faint possibility of this social encounter being good for business. He had hoped to stay on in Madras long enough to raise a subscription for some project or at least get a few commissions for portraits but the more he thought of depending on the hospitality of Forbes, who was yet to ask him of his plans, his resolve faltered.

'Now, remember we are going to be in very refined company,' Forbes was saying to him as the carriage came to a halt. 'Listen carefully to them and don't talk about yourself or about me or your life back home.'

Richard turned away angrily and jumped out of the carriage to avoid listening to more. The surgeon's house was palatial, a servant posted at every door and window, hundreds of candles ablaze inside. The nearest bungalow appeared to be miles away with a few twinkling lights of its own. Richard was beginning to understand his host's concerns with looking their best. This was clearly the setting of an important gathering.

Richard remembered Forbes insisting that Doctor Wheeler was a better diamond trader than man of medicine. 'If I were dying, I would send for the man who'd carve my gravestone, but if I had money to invest, I would call Wheeler.'

Now Richard could see why. They had stepped into a room enclosed by rich polished mahogany, lush Persian rugs and gold-framed mirrors flashing off white walls. At the far end a young lady played a catchy tune on a grand piano while two soldiers dressed in bright uniforms leaned towards her with open appreciation. They were men of the Royal Troops, professional men of war who had no hesitation in showing their disdain for the Company's officers or flaunt that they were in India on national duty and not chasing personal glory. They turned around, as did the other men and women in the room, when Doctor Wheeler introduced the new entrants.

The gathering's initial interest in Richard waned when they found he was neither pedigreed nor moneyed. They talked amongst themselves, and even when the conversation included him, he knew he was not expected to be anything more than a poor creature patronized by the powerful Gilbert Forbes. Only the doctor appeared to think of him of some consequence for he introduced his daughters to him, not once but twice. The elder daughter was a wiry young woman with lips pursed so tight that Richard feared to look in her eyes, but she had considerable influence on Forbes who stooped like a thirsty plant when she stood beside him. Anne was not only extremely strict about the calibre of her suitors but had, for some reason known only to herself, decided that Forbes in his grey years was worthy enough. When the doctor introduced his younger daughter for the third jovial time, the same one who was playing the music a while ago, Richard began to worry. He looked intently at the pale girl. Rose was both plain and shy, probably no older than fifteen, her only moments of comfort being at the piano stool; away from it she was a shadow to her sister, staying close to the walls and anxiously looking out for her father who would lunge for her arm and shepherd her around the room, her head bobbing to his robust laughter.

At the dinner table Richard found himself placed between Rose and a handsome young lady with a rising bosom, Mrs Oakley, dressed in flowing muslin that revealed more than it veiled. An army of servants was now moving food and plates around them. Richard realized the doctor was leaning over from the opposite side and saying something to him about the woman by his side, about Helena Oakley's aunt, a wonderful artist who had been asked to paint the ladies in the household of the Nawab of Arcot. Richard felt obliged to turn to his neighbour to say that she must be very proud of her dead aunt.

'Oh, don't listen to him.' The woman pouted at him before tossing down her wine. 'She was a dreadfully fretful woman and detested everything about India. As for her paintings, they were such a bother to dispose. Nobody wanted them.' With that, she turned away, as if the very mention of her dead aunt had made Richard odious beyond endurance.

'Catherine Read,' said a timid voice beside him. Rose's large watery eyes were shining on her narrow face. 'That was her name.'

Richard nodded and smiled at her for the thoughtful rescue. Rose hesitantly leaned towards him and whispered, 'It's all very scandalous how the poor old lady was treated. She was not just a chaperone but completely devoted to Helena who soon found a rich husband and turned her back on the aunt.'

'What happened to the old lady?' Richard whispered back.

'Oh, I do believe she was heartbroken. Father persuaded her to go to Cape Hope to regain her health but she died at sea.'

The sad story of the dead artist now out in the open, they both pulled apart solemnly and could not think of anything else to say.

'Gentlemen, please don't ignore the turkey. It has travelled all the way from Bengal to join us at this merry table.' The doctor guffawed at his own joke. Richard smiled politely.

'You are indeed a brave man, my dear Dawson. I hear you are heading for Mysore, straight into the cave of the beast,' the doctor winked. Richard opened and closed his mouth without saying anything. He had mentioned the possibility of Mysore in passing to Forbes. Why was his host discussing his plans? 'I am not acquainted with your work but you appear to be a young man of promise. If you could make me some paintings of the hill forts in Mysore … I am sure we could agree on a price that is satisfactory to you.'

Relief and gratitude sprang rapidly. His first commission! He wanted to reach over and pump the doctor's hand in agreement but they were distracted by an argument at the other end of the long table. The officers sitting on either side of Anne were loudly engaged in a debate with a red-faced Forbes who was saying, 'Oh, stop blaming the French for all our troubles! What about the bunch of imbeciles in London? They go about making and breaking laws, announcing wars and then signing treaties, and pick dunces among rotting aristocrats to speak for us.'

The officers exchanged incredulous glances. To laugh at the mistakes and unworthiness of France was the staple conversation of all the gatherings they had participated in. Even in times of forced peace, they all agreed that the pompous French were the real enemies, whether in Europe, America or Asia. To have their very fashionable views dismissed was an affront they did not know how to react to, particularly in the presence of a woman who seemed to want the other man to prevail.

Anne was now leaning ahead, her flat chest pressed against the table, making sure Forbes knew she was talking to him. 'I am a simple woman, Mr Forbes,' she said in a tone which implied precisely the opposite. 'All I understand is that my father's future and my own depends on the Company being wise enough to make the most of the uncertainty in this country. Who do we have to fear? The Indian princes hate each other. The Dutch and the Portuguese have low stakes. And the French have more troubles back home than they can manage – all that is left of them in India is a small tract of land here and there, a few thousand men each with the Marathas, the Nizam and Tipu. I am but a silly woman and yet even I can see that this is the perfect moment to send every single one of them back to their mothers in France.'

'Anne!' – the doctor choked on his drink and sprayed some of it – 'you … you speak much too strongly, my dear! This is a vast, generous land. There is enough here for them and us. If we can be neighbours in Europe, we can be neighbours here too.' He beamed at everyone, pleased with his own magnanimity.

Forbes, still irked with the doctor for making him sit near Mrs Steele, an elderly widow who believed herself a suitable bride for him, boomed back that the young woman spoke more sense than most men he had met at business. 'I have had the opportunity to dine with the Governor-General and his sentiments are much the same…'

Mrs Steel said something about the Governor-General having married a French woman but only after they had five children out of wedlock and Forbes snapped back that bedding French women had nothing to do with politics, which the gentleman sitting beside the doctor protested as highly unsuitable conversation for dinner tables and the company of ladies. The two men glowered at each other and turned to the voices of the young people. One of the officers, his arm draped behind Anne's chair, was saying to her, 'The French are never up to any good except sprouting fancy speeches and poetry and the only art they have truly mastered is chopping off heads.'

His colleague laughed in relief at getting back to the conversation they were most adept in, and said something about how there is needless fussing over that dwarf Bonaparte.

Forbes raised his voice. 'Who are we to blame others for our state of affairs? Aren't we the ones with an insane king? If Mad George did not think that taxing colonies was fashionable—'

'You go too far, sir! We cannot sit here and listen as you slur His Majesty's good name.' The officer pushed his chair back as if to shoot out of it.

'Gentlemen! Let us not compare kings now. The French have beheaded theirs quite efficiently' – Anne settled the matter – 'Mr Forbes has been kind enough to send us some new music that dear Rose has been practising all day. Let us now look forward to enjoy it as friends.'

Rose turned a deep red and Richard quickly rose to help her out of her seat. An overbearing sibling cannot be easy to bear, he thought.

He expected everyone to go the music room but instead they gathered in the verandah while the servants scampered around to line up hookahs. The conversation was soon drowned in the sound of gurgling water, the air thick with smoke from the pipes. Richard edged away from the strange sight, the overpowering odour of damp tobacco.

The farther he walked, away from them and towards the garden, the jarring sounds of the hookahs were replaced by the crackle of the leaves and the humming of insects. He walked aimlessly, thinking about his future. How worthless and adrift he felt! And how stupid it was of him not to show more enthusiasm for the doctor's offer. He remembered his mother, her many advice and warnings, and wondered how often she thought of him. The night continued to stew in its own bleakness as he walked further around the building.

A piano was playing, a melody of such power and resolve, the voice of a lonely star trying to brighten a blackened sky. He had been taught a little music but only enough to now enable him to recognize it came from the music sheets that had travelled with him as a gift from his mother for old crusty Forbes. It was Haydn, the Viennese who had charmed London. The tempo rose and drew him closer to the open windows. He stood on his toes to look in. Rose was sitting alone in the big empty room, with bent spine and hair in disarray, feverishly practising for a gathering that would forget to ask her to play.

Only a desperate man would travel westwards during these monsoon months, Forbes pointed out, as most roads would have collapsed into miles of slush and the rivers too turbulent to cross. It was impossible to find good servants willing to go on the journey. Unless they be desperate men too.

There seemed to be no dearth of desperation for his entourage was soon organized by Ramaswamy the steward who offered neither opinion nor advice but quietly took in Richard's explanation about limited resources and set about gathering the many servants that a white man would need as he journeyed through treacherous lands alone.

Forbes's impatience with his guest had begun to surface too often. Fort St. George had proved to be equally indifferent to Richard's talents and financial troubles. He escaped as often as he could to the wanton life of Black Town but there was not much to do there but drink. Sometimes he would go to Havelock's room above The Griffin where he could see studies of paintings his friend had made during the Cornwallis campaign. Soon Richard was convinced about making his own journey. Forbes called him a fool and refused to have anything to do with the Mysore project. If the young man wished to drown in the wretched rains or rot in one of those infernal dungeons of Tipu Sultan, he did not care one way or the other. He had nothing more to say on the matter.

Later at the tavern, Richard had plenty to say to Cole who appeared to have a life of pleasure away from the chaotic Customs House. Richard never knew what to make of Jonathan Cole, a man whose odd appearance, an egg-shaped head over a bony and diminutive body, made him impossible to miss. Cole's manner was earnest but his eyes were devious; he sat alone but keenly followed any exchange of words or money; he offered friendship to Richard but on his own terms. Some evenings when Richard longed for a drink he could not afford, and fear of the burly innkeeper did not allow him to ask for credit, he wished Cole would treat him to an occasional glass. But the man who listened to private conversations of strangers did not believe in buying intoxicants for anyone but himself.

Richard sat with a glass of cheap arrack that evening, sipping to make it last longer. The stench of damp clothes and muddy boots mixed with the burning of tobacco. Havelock was at the far end, standing atop a table and narrating what appeared to be a funny story, for the young soldiers around him slapped each other in raucous laughter. He was barefooted, bare-chested, clad only in white cotton drawers, his hair flying wildly across his face. A performing animal that likes to control his spectators, Richard thought and waved to the artist so caught up in his own pantomime. Havelock saw him and appeared to almost hop off his perch but did not. Richard's eyes darted with his to see the reason for the reluctance.

Cole was pushing his way through the crowd towards him. That is when Richard understood that his two friends did not like each other. He had never heard them talk ill of each other, but then he realized that he had never seen them together either.

'I cannot continue like this anymore. I need to find work,' he told Cole a minute later when they were squeezed next to each other at the table.

'I thought you had work. Aren't you doing a portrait for old Cunningham?'

Richard did not bother to ask how Cole knew of the only introduction that Forbes had grudgingly made for him. Cole always made it his business to be updated on all that happened around Fort St. George. 'Everybody has a hobby to amuse themselves in unpleasant climates. My hobby, dear Dawson, is to know what everybody else is amusing themselves with,' Cole would say with a laugh. His intimate knowledge of what transpired in Company offices was feared and respected but never questioned. It was not known how a man with clerical status came to have such long talons in the official machinery. All the young soldiers and tradesmen and writers did their best to soften Cole even when he was at his meanest; no assaults were made on his frail frame even when he taunted or manipulated them, for there were nothing but favours to be got out of such a resourceful man.

'Let us not talk of Mr Cunningham,' Richard moaned.

'Tell me. Perhaps I could help.' Cole's green eyes opened invitingly. 'Have you completed the portrait? Has he paid you your fifty mohurs?'

Again, Richard did not display surprise that his fee was known. He was glad to be able to vent his frustrations. 'Oh, there cannot be a more impossible man to paint! Constantly fidgeting and monitoring every stroke of my brush. Each coin he has to pay me has to be extracted with pleadings and tears. I cannot please him no matter what I say or do. First the whiskers needed to be more authoritative, then the eyebrows more kind, then the skin more eloquent ... I am beginning to think that this commission was more punishment than favour from my dear host who recommended me to him.'

Cole clucked his tongue in sympathy. 'Surely you see why Forbes and Cunningham are good friends. Rotten misers them both! The large store with Cunningham's name on the front did not sprout out of a pleasing personality. He has killed by the dozens to be as rich as he is today. No, no, don't ask me to say more on that. As for the painting, it is still a paying commission, even if it is an unhappy one. You are not the first painter to live with the agony of that.'

'If only it were that simple,' Richard replied silently, pressing his fingertips into his temples. He was not just a failing painter, he was a failing son. Unlike Forbes, his father had preferred dereliction to burrowing ahead in opportune lands. You'll end up like your father, Mother had warned. His father, the fatal dreamer, who had failed to provide for her or her children, who had grand plans that he could never execute well enough. His father, the perfect failure.

'I'd rather die,' Richard said aloud. 'I need to find a way to make paintings that sell before I completely run out of money. Havelock thinks I should go to Mysore. I can paint landscapes and hill forts and Havelock thinks—'

'Havelock wants you to die,' Cole interrupted calmly. 'I mean, he is a damn fool and does not care what happens to you. His woman feeds him and her father's liquor keeps him drunk enough to forget that there is a man inside of him. I would not advise you to go now, Dawson. Stay on in Fort St. George for a while. You would do much better to soften old Forbes. He has a fortune and no heirs.'

Richard put his glass down and looked at Cole with unmasked disgust.

Cole rolled his eyes and sighed. 'Morals! Fine, don't do that then. But you don't have to kill yourself either. There is going to be a war.'

Cole wiped his upper lip on his sleeve and smoothened his thin moustache with his nails. The Governor-General was baying for blood and he would settle for nothing less than Tipu Sultan's head. All his future titles and estates in Ireland and England depended on it. Colonel Kirkpatrick in Hyderabad had received orders to dismantle the Nizam's French troops and General Harris had begun to reorganize the army here.

Richard was not paying any attention. 'What do I care? If there is a war, what is it to me, a mere artist and chronicler? I would pick up my brush and record it for the likes of you to see later.'

Cole straightened and pulled back to look at his friend with raised eyebrows. 'Never knew you had this fatalistic side to you, Dawson. Go to Mysore if you must. You can always count on my humble assistance, if needed. Tipu Sultan hates all things English, but why would that bother you?'

It certainly bothered him. He needed travel papers. Where could he go, a stray Englishman? How could he get in touch with the Sultan? Was the Sultan really so vicious as to kill a poor artist just because he happens to be English? Won't he give talent a chance?

Cole bent his head and lowered his voice, 'Careful before you say anything that will put you in a locked cell in St. George instead of the Mysore countryside. No, you cannot contact the Sultan directly. But there is one way … one way … maybe…'

The idea was ludicrously simple. Havelock was planted at the heart of it. The hill fort of Nandidurga was in charge of a man called Jahangir Khan, whom the artist had a chance to meet after the Cornwallis victory. He was said to be a good and reasonable man enjoying the confidence of his master, Tipu Sultan. All hope depended on Richard safely making his way to this killedar or fort commander and Cole was to keep communication and supply channels open to send painting supplies from Madras.

A few days later, Richard received a rolled-up scroll from a messenger sent by Cole. It was an elaborate map of the route from Madras to Mysore drawn up for the Cornwallis campaign. A priceless document. Cole had either bribed heavily to have a copy pulled out of the Company archives or stolen it. Richard was far too grateful to grill for details. Havelock looked sceptical when told of his part but agreed. He would write an introduction to Jahangir Khan, vouching for the non-political nature of his artist friend Dawson and of his great talent that deserved the patronage of Tipu Sultan.

The plan went under way almost immediately, with only half payment from a disgruntled Cunningham who insisted that his hands looked more like claws in the painting and simply not good enough for the walls of his store. Richard gulped back the shame that he did not deserve to feel and put his hand out to point out the beautiful bust of Edmund Burke he had added to the background of the painting; the red velvet curtains that gave Cunningham's wigged head a royal halo; the character in his carefully crossed arms; the blue flowers sunk into the carpet weave to soften the leathery hide of the subject...

'Enough,' Cunningham had sighed and paid only half of what he owed the artist, 'the picture is not even good to be bequeathed to the servants.'

Shame burnt a crimson fire on Richard's face as he pulled himself up and walked out. His only commissioned work in months, his best abilities put in it and he had just been told he was worse than mediocre, he was a bad artist. But it can't be true, he gulped in the hurt, even if everyone said so, it can't be true. The force that guides my fingers tells me so. It quivers in my blood when I smell the paint. There is nothing between the canvas and me, nothing but the knowledge that the image is more real than the model. How can all of that be a lie?

'I understand. I do,' Cole purred, his sixth glass of port dribbling down his chin as he leaned his head into his hands.

No, you don't, thought Richard bitterly. He had given up too much for a profession that would not support him. Perhaps, he wondered, it would make more sense to take the next ship back to England. There were other things a man could do, to earn enough for wine and brothels, as did his friends at the painting studio back home. A blunt pain made its way through his body at the thought, stirred forgotten sensations. It had been so long since he had been with a woman. This forced chastity alone was enough to drive a man crazy. What was he doing in India? And what good was it to be talking to this drunk who cared little for him?

It was an unusual night at the inn. The place was desolate, with neither dwellers nor revellers. Or perhaps it was later than Cole's watch indicated. Innkeeper Pereira was not to be seen. Indisposed, said the gaunt assistant.

'Dying from an idle son-in-law is more the case,' slurred Cole.

'What do you have against Havelock?' Richard snapped.

'I keep discovering new facets to your charming personality, Dawson! I shall say no more to offend your loyalty to your friend.'

Cole started to sing, fingers drumming the table, 'O my love is like a red, red rose.'

'Ramaswamy helped me make a list,' Richard began.

'Show me.' Cole suddenly straightened, the crafty accountant surfacing above the inebriation. He pulled out his eyeglasses from a pocket and grabbed the narrow strip of paper Richard held.

1 attendant of mixed Indian and Portuguese blood
1 dubash
1 kitmatgar
1 chaukidar
2 kalassis tent pitchers
1 groom for the horse
6 bearers for the palanquin
2 bullock cart drivers
7 coolies to carry provisions and drawing table
1 cook
2 kitchen assistants
2 orderlies
1 grass cutter

'Very reasonable. I would take four more men if I were making the trip.' Cole handed the paper back to him and tried to revive his abandoned song.

'Reasonable? Twenty-eight men? For just one traveller? It is like leading an army!'

Cole reminded him he was in India. Everybody had a specific social and professional role. It would be unthinkable for the horse's groom to cut grass or for the cook to clean his dirty dishes. And on the road he would never be sorry for the extra hands. They were cheap anyway.

'Cheap? You have no idea. With a horse, a budgerow, the tents and bullocks, not to mention the provisions, painting supplies … I don't really have the money…'

Cole stood up shakily. 'Money is what you are going there to make, Dawson. Think of this as an investment. And keep sending me letters about your progress. I hope to see you return with an authentic princess, unlike Havelock there, or a diamond like Pitt.'

He looked around and fished up a packet. 'I found this lying around at the office. Unclaimed. Perhaps it is a bad book that simply cannot be endured. Or perhaps it is too good to bear. Since I don't care for men who waste their time writing poetry, it shall have the honour of becoming a parting gift for you, Dawson.'

Inside the stained crumpled brown wrapping were two sets of poems by the same man. William Blake. Uneasily wedged as he was, between the doors of innocence and experience, Richard felt overwhelmed by the appropriateness of the gifts, but Cole was already tottering out of the inn, indifferent to his gratitude, and the boy gathering the empty glasses from the counter looked at him with blank eyes.

Black Town had become a twisted mass of silhouettes. The flutter of men and women in the alleys, the snarls of street dogs, the pavement slightly damp from whimsical showers; it was a night well into its prime. Richard walked as fast as he could. The sea breeze wrapped itself around him like a lulling cocoon and if it were not for the screaming, the racing carriage would have mowed him down. He jumped aside, not a moment too soon. The wheels brushed past his coat ends and he could feel the lashing of the horse's tail on his face. Trembling with anger and shock, he waited for the carriage to stop while a woman inside continued to hoot in unearthly mirth. He saw her arms fluttering wildly, and then a shawl flung over the side of the carriage, deep voices of men trying to prevent her from stepping out. She swung out defiantly, grinned at him in friendly candour and called out an apology. It was Anne Wheeler, the doctor's daughter.

Richard politely walked towards her and then staggered backwards a bit, for holding her waist as she leaned out was Gilbert Forbes. The other man at the reins was one of the soldiers he had met at her father's house. Sitting in a corner of the carriage was Rose, holding her shawl tight at her chest, her eyes wishing she were elsewhere. She smiled at him timidly and then looked away.

'Oh dear, oh dear, did we kill you?' Anne giggled. Richard shook his head forgivingly. Her breath reeked of alcohol. He saw Forbes's eyes tighten into hard points, displeased to run into his guest in the very part of town he had derided so often.

'Miss Wheeler wanted some fresh air,' Forbes said curtly. Richard saw his fingers stretch up to settle under Anne's bosom asserting his ownership. She smiled seductively at Richard.

'So, artist! What lies beneath the skirt of Fort St. George? Show us where in Black Town I can lose this suffocating Miss Wheeler respectability?' She smacked her lips. Richard turned his head slightly to avoid the stale gusts of air she blew at him.

'She jokes!' guffawed the equally drunk soldier, his arms suspended to send the horses galloping again.

'She does not!' protested Anne.

'Anne, I am cold!' Rose cried out plaintively from inside the carriage.

'Good night, Dawson. I trust you will find your way home as you usually do.' Forbes firmly drew Anne closer to himself. The carriage rolled away as unceremoniously as it had appeared. And the shadows of Black Town returned to claim their space. Richard stood still, a vermin of the night, submerged in his own desolation and the vibrations of the disappearing carriage.

BOOK TWO

The River Island

They had been asked to send their best man. The Dewan of Mysore wanted a picture of his two boys for their mother who had caught the crazy fancy after one of her frequent visits to the palace harem. He grumbled that she had probably seen a portrait of the royal princes there and wagered with some eunuch about getting one done for her sons; or an evil spirit must have entered her while she combed her hair under the tamarind tree in the backyard; who knows why women behave the way they do? But when a wife goes into a fit and sets her mind to get something out of her husband, it does not matter that he is the most feared man in that kingdom or that he thinks artists are fools. She was adamant and the Dewan had dispatched his message: send your best man.

There were no volunteers for the job. If the picture was not satisfactory to the begum or her husband, the artist might never draw again. And if the job was found satisfactory, there was still no money to be made or praise to be earned. The bully and his brats had to be pleased and that was the only ordeal, the only reward on offer.

The Master Artist looked around the room at his many apprentices. They were all working more furiously today than usual, avoiding his eyes, diligently filling colours and adding outlines to his sketches, not wanting to be given the dreaded assignment.

The Master sighed. It was hard to spare anyone. The work was behind schedule and Tipu Sultan was not one to compromise on his book. It was to be a eulogy to the achievements of his brave father who turned a career as a lowly horseman into a sovereign of a vast fertile kingdom. He had called the Master into his chamber, rather than the Durbar where he usually gave audience. The gesture had overwhelmed the Master who walked with trembling feet, expecting the worst and silently praying for grace. Tipu had pulled out a book and laid it open for the Master to examine. It was a rare work from the court of Emperor Akbar. Every page was laden with inscriptions and illustrations in gold, silver, red, yellow, blue, green. The script was like a creeper filled with flowers, pleasing to the eyes and the heart. Every miniature was crammed with the most fastidious details. The Master bent lower and the richness of the page brought tears to his eyes. 'These are not illustrations by men,' he told the Sultan humbly, 'these were made by the gods and I have neither the training nor the talent to match them.'

Tipu Sultan had taken his gnarled hands gently into his own. 'I trust you to do the best you can,' he had said, 'and the world will see that the artists in my domain can match the Mughals in their integrity for I expect nothing more than that from you and your men. Paint my book with the eyes of your soul and it shall please me.'

The Master had no choice but to agree. Freshly written pages arrived at the artists' colony in Ganjam and illustrations were dispatched just as promptly but the Master was yet to hear any comments from the palace. It worried him more and more with every passing day. He lost appetite and sleep. The fatigue and stomach acidity made it impossible to sit still. He worked harder and stayed up all night trying to steady his twitching hand in the light of the oil lamp, hoping that when the other artists came to work in the morning, they would not notice the glaze of opium in his eyes. He sat at his seat and supervised their brushes, inspected the paints, wrote down the expenses and then dealt with his visitor. Mukunda, the

Brahmin boy, had been hanging around his colony for a long time, and after months of dissuasion had managed to earn an admission into the big workroom where a dozen craftsmen sat on bamboo mats and painted at low stools. At first the boy had stuck to his promise of watching silently. Soon he was waiting for the Master to look up in distraction so that a conversation could be launched. Added to the crushing silence of Tipu Sultan were now these persistent questions from the boy. The Master felt himself wearing out. He had never known anyone with as much curiosity. Then he found out quite by accident that there was something else unique about Mukunda. The boy could draw. Even when he made faithful copies, the lines emerged with fresh character. The Master had grown old believing that all talent came from practice or the inheritance of the blood in one's veins. Now in his fading years he had been chosen by providence to be a teacher to one whose gift could neither be attributed nor explained.

The enraged minister had sent word again. Why had no artist been sent to his house? Didn't they care for their lives anymore?

The Master grumbled under his breath. What is the world coming to? It was natural to paint the gods and goddesses or stories from the great epics and it was certainly prudent to paint stories of emperors when they so ordered. But to be painting brats of no consequence … ridiculous!

'I will go,' Mukunda offered and the Master ignored him. The project had to be kept a tight secret or they would all be punished equally.

'I would go myself if my health was not so shaky and the Sultan was not so particular about the weekly deadline.' The Master chewed on a lip. It was hard even to think of the young Brahmin as his student. He had merely watched them work and dabbled on his own accord. The Master did not wish to encourage waywardness or incur the wrath of the high castes. Why was the boy not among his own people learning the trade he was born into? The Master knew this rebellion would bring trouble to his doorstep and had done his best to project his lack of concern with what the boy chose to do with his time, even if it meant loitering on his premises.

'I will go. I have nothing to do here. Perhaps it will help you?'

The Master now began to ponder over the offer. The boy had a steady, faithful hand and a keen eye. With a little supervision … who was to say? Maybe it wasn't such a disastrous suggestion. Sometimes – he sighed deeply – one has to take a chance on somebody else's fate.

Mir Sadiq glared at the slender figure in front of him and snorted in disgust. So this is what the Master sends me, a lily plucked fresh out of the village pond!

Mukunda met his gaze, waiting for instructions, not permission.

Mir Sadiq paced angrily and in confusion, unaccustomed to such affront. What sort of an artist was this? Dreamy-eyed and with fingers as long as reeds; the miserable wretch could probably be knocked down by a good sneeze. How would he manage to get two restless boys to sit still and pose for him?

'Are you really any good? Why isn't the old fox here himself to give you a proper introduction?'

'The Master is in poor health and apologizes for not being here.'

'What did you say your name was? You don't look as if you belong to the artists' colony. Why … you look rather familiar…'

The curtains leading to the private quarters of the house parted a little and two nervous boys appeared, nudged through by a bangled hand. Pink from being freshly scrubbed, the boys rustled forward awkwardly in their new stiff clothes. They bowed a greeting to their father and eyed the stranger warily. Mir Sadiq readjusted the string of pearls around their necks, straightened embroidered collars and patted their oiled hair. They shrank from his touch and huddled close to each other.

The Master had warned Mukunda. Every bone in that man's body is cruel and manipulative. Show him your deference but not your fear.

Mir Sadiq was in favour with Tipu Sultan and made sure everyone was aware of that. The other ministers had tried their best to sidestep him and had nearly succeeded. Two years ago he had lost his office, his house had been raided and his wealth confiscated. Spies tagged his every step and the town's populace spat on his plight in glee. So he did what any bully would do; he lied, pretended to be remorseful, swore to reform, gave a written oath to Tipu Sultan – which was the greater challenge, for he could barely spell – and wept tears of gratitude on being made the prime minister. Since then he stood stoutly between a preoccupied ruler and the complaints of his subjects. An authority with no temperance. A nightmare.

And now, if it weren't for the presence behind the curtain, Mukunda was sure the boys would have bolted from their father and there would be no painting to discuss. Mukunda smiled at them reassuringly. He was raring to open the wooden box that the Master had lovingly placed in his hands.

Mir Sadiq growled at him, 'Well, you know what to do, I hope. Make them look exactly like themselves. In fact, make them look better than they are. That one's nose is too much like his crooked maternal uncle. Straighten it! They must look like princes! I want no trouble from you around here and not a single word of this must reach the Sultan or I will make you wish you had never been born.'

Mir Sadiq strode out and the room lightened with his exit. The boys stood undecidedly.

'Sit down, sit down,' the young artist said, dragging a stool, wondering how to place them. The curtain trembled slightly. Mukunda swirled around, inches away from the shifting figure as though he were not looking at cloth but straight into the woman's unseen face. He tilted his head very slowly and smiled in salutation. The figure on the other side stepped back a little in surprise. Mukunda dragged the stool beside the curtain, lifted the younger of the boys on it and bade the other stand right beside his brother. The boys slouched awkwardly.

Perfect! Mukunda settled on the floor mat beside his box. The woman had now boldly stepped ahead to have a better look at his setting, her bare feet visible below the curtain.

What is he doing? The younger boy slithered off his seat.

His brother whispered back something that made him break into a toothless grin. A hand quickly darted through the curtains and tapped the little boy sharply on his head. The boys giggled and obliged their chaperone by returning to their assigned positions.

'Oh, please let them be,' the artist called out to the woman behind the curtain who did not reply. 'I would be just as fidgety and distracted if I had to turn into a statue. Yes, yes, do let them be. This won't take any time at all.'

He smoothed the paper in front of him and began to hum softly. It was scarcely appropriate behaviour in his position but he imagined the tune made her feet happy and the day turned more resplendent than he ever thought possible.

At the same time, unknown to him, along a distant sunburnt coast in the east, under the watchful shadow of Fort St. George, a ship dropped anchor for a young artist in desperate search of both livelihood and reputation.

Deep in the heart of the plains, the river Kaveri loops to encase an island of luxuriant green, and a town germinates over hundreds of years. Whether the settlement grows around the temple or the temple is built to consecrate the island, it comes to be known as the town of Lord Sriranga. Srirangapatna. In a kingdom woven out of modest villages and even smaller communes, the bustling and thriving island is called Patna, simply 'the town'.

On the north west corner of the river island stands the fort, ripe with its own destiny. Fortified with brick and granite, skirting the vegetation of the riverbank, as homely as an old family dwelling, its bastions lazily jut out like pegs holding a tent together. Hardly the capital of a vast kingdom. Yet, under that deceptive placidity lies the story of years and years of martial history, of the rise and fall of dynasties, and the exploits of individual warriors as well as of influential kings.

They have borne patient witness, the townsfolk, and they like to talk about it. How like any other royal family, the Wodeyars of Mysore had their fair share of stalwarts as well as kings with plebeian spine. And how it was under the aegis of one such lackadaisical Wodeyar that the administrative power began slipping away, first into the hands of calculating ministers and then to the army commander, Haider Ali.

Back then, in 1757, a new order had reared its head above the tumult. The Mughal family that ruled over most of India had not fared any better than the Wodeyars in its production of kings. The vision of Babur, the imperial weight of Akbar and the enduring charm of Shah Jahan had turned into the malice of Aurangzeb and the wantonness of Shah Alam. Subordinates broke away into independent kingdoms and a little strip of land around Delhi was all that was left as legacy of a mighty empire. And then there were those traders from Europe who had begun to see that owning property and armies was very good for business. They were steadily making money and now it was time to make a tradition of it. The Battle of Plassey sealed matters. The British East Indian Company found a cushy home in Bengal and began casting an acquisitionist eye around.

That very year in Mysore, Haider Ali, resolute and fearless, saw the first contours of his own dynasty in his seven-year-old-son. So what if the boy looked more like a poet than a warrior, more like his mother than his father? He would just have to learn to be me, Haider had resolved.

Tipu Sultan is now almost fifty years old, trained and educated for his job from thc start. His illiterate father had made sure that knowledge of every nature, whether from book or sword was provided to the son, and with no recourse to either fear or failure. Ordered to lead unwieldy battalions while still a boy, Tipu had even been flogged in pubic for a stray act of disobedience. Haider had seen what weak links did to family chains and Tipu grew up knowing he had to take the brimming cup of authority from his father without spilling a single drop.

That cup was thrust into his hands when the father who set battlefields on fire was attacked by a virulent tumour and died without much fuss. From Haider's life Tipu learnt two lessons he could never allow himself to forget – kingship is ability, not lineage; and never trust the English.

This is the season of battles, of scarcity and endless months of seething uncertainty. Tipu Sultan, his subjects agree, can be temperamental, as cruel as he is kind, as ruthless as he is benevolent. Despite the initial doubts, he seems to be succeeding in keeping the precarious semblance of the old world while ushering in the new. He calls it the Khudadad Sarkar. Governance of God. But it is hard to completely trust a king who has powerful enemies and hardly any friends. Their fortunes dangle precariously alongside his. The Marathas, the Nizam of Hyderabad, the Malabar Nairs and the Nawab of Arcot – he has made sure all their neighbours hate them. Worse, the English have arrived at their doors, like locusts from distant lands. There are the French, of course, stationed in the same island, bonding with Tipu, but proving inadequate in the last battle.

Six years had passed since the last battle. The East India Company had taken away two of Tipu's sons as hostages till war fines were paid. The princes did eventually return, but half the kingdom remains lost and the score far from settled. The war has turned personal and the fort is its gaping wound.

'You are going to get both of us killed,' moaned the Master, holding his head in his hands. The workshop was empty. In the trembling flame of a single oil lamp, he was confronted by his pupil's work for the day. Feet! How could the boy get it so wrong? A woman's feet! And who is this woman? How did he get to see her? A woman from Mir Sadiq's household! Maybe his wife!

So, what did the Master think of his work? As a pupil, Mukunda was a slave, insecure and anxious. His teacher was noncommittal, demanding.

'He is going to slice you like chicken if he knew that you had dared glance at her feet, leave alone draw it when you have been ordered to prepare a portrait of his boys. A woman! I should have known not to trust you. Everyone calls you mad but I never paid it any attention. I should learn to listen better. You are completely out of your mind! Burn it immediately! Perhaps it is better if I go to Mir Sadiq tomorrow and do his work myself.'

The Master noticed but said nothing of the deviations in the drawing. There was none of those rounded broad outlines and the flat meticulous filling of space he had been teaching his students. Too much time had been spent on the jaggedness of the anklets, the thickness of the toe rings, even the chip in the nail of one little toe. It held the eye. Where had the boy learnt to do this? He could not question the grace of Goddess Nimishamba, but if Mir Sadiq were to find out that Mukunda was not one of his experienced workers…

But there was no going back now.

Mukunda was back at Mir Sadiq's house in the morning with his wooden box. The boys had been instructed to come in the same attire and they did so grumpily. Mukunda tried to talk to them but they only exchanged glances with each other and replied in monosyllables. Neither the Dewan nor the woman behind the curtain had turned up. The day was warm and the boys were sweaty in their voluminous clothes. Their tousled hair and grimy fingernails showed that the grooming had been neglected that day. Or perhaps the boys had decided to take matters in their own hands.

The artist was relieved to have no distractions. It was a good day for work; he could tell from the tingle in his hands, the perkiness of his spirit. He could feel it happening, the familiar sinking into a little cocoon of stillness, free from effort and thought, falling deeper and deeper into his core; the two bored boys standing by the curtains gradually slipping under the finished image in his mind; his fingers clearing through the debris of air and nothingness till there was one nucleus shared between him and his drawing. From a single stroke, the picture began to grow.

It was noon. A loud thud echoed through the house. Mukunda looked up and the stool was empty. Either on being prompted from behind the curtain or of their own accord, the boys had obviously wandered off. He began quickly to gather his things.

Mir Sadiq walked in, shouting for a missing servant. He glared at the artist. Yes, now he remembered why the boy looked so familiar. Wasn't he related to Purnaiah, that old Brahmin snake? A son?

'He is my mother's relative. Distant.'

'So what are you doing at the artists' colony? Does your family know about this? Is the Master trying to hoodwink me by sending a wily Brahmin?'

'I … I am merely helping out with the preliminary sketches. The Master will be here tomorrow to do the portrait himself.'

'I don't care. Tell the fool to finish it quickly and get the begum off my back. Wait! Where are you slinking off? How old are you?'

'Eighteen.'

'That is old enough to have some sense. My servant, that lazy bastard, has vanished, and so I need you to do something for me. Find your uncle and tell him that I have just received the messenger we were awaiting.'

Trouble had travelled from Mauritius. Last year a French seaman, Rimpaud, had landed in Tipu's court claiming that the French would do for Mysore what they had done for the American freedom fighters in the New World. Tipu, desperate for reinforcements, had sent his ambassadors with Rimpaud and asked them to come back with troops. And now the envoys had returned with bad news. Rimpaud had turned out to be nothing more than a privateer lying to save his skin and had absconded for good the moment the ship touched Port Louis. Worse, Governor Malartic of Mauritius had issued a proclamation that announced Tipu's plans to raise a foreign legion against the British in India. The enemy had been warned. Meanwhile, ninety-nine unskilled men, such as the ones on the returning ship, all promised atrociously high salaries, could have been easily gathered from the Mysore countryside. It was a message of betrayal.

Mukunda nodded, turned to go, but was stopped again by Mir Sadiq who demanded he repeat the message till it was accurate.

'Yes, yes, that will do. Let the Sultan hear about this from his trusty old servant, that wily uncle of yours. And if you forget even a word, I will personally flog you. Now, run!'

Another Man in My Skin

The Governor-General of the British East India Company stabbed the large ebony desk repeatedly with a paper knife, a copy of the *Bengal Gazette* spread out before him. Everyone in Calcutta would know by sundown that Tipu Sultan had sent for help from the French government in Mauritius, enlisting volunteers to fight a war against the British East India Company. Richard Wellesley twisted his knife deeper into a wooden scar. He had been sent to oversee a colony fraught with insecurities, Pitt's Act shackled around his ankles: no unprovoked war, no undue aggression, no more military expenses overshooting trading benefits that the directors in London would be forced to approve. Watch the French – he had been told – but don't fight them. Except. Except in dire circumstances.

Wellesley was an impatient man and he liked to think of it as a virtue. When impatience worked, it was called foresight; and for a man with foresight, there was no such thing as chance. The job came to him only because an aging Lord Cornwallis was reluctant to drag himself to India and preferred the charge of Ireland. And yet he had to encounter Cornwallis everywhere in India, in reputation, in the memories of people, even in his own office where a portrait of the portly General smiled down indulgently at him. Richard Wellesley, lean and brittle, his narrow face framed by a receding hairline, scowled back. The old man had lost the American colonies and tried to salvage his reputation by fighting Tipu Sultan, their country's most dreaded enemy. But that too had been nothing more than an unfinished job, the greatest political mistake. Wellesley both despised and thanked Cornwallis for it. It was almost as if that glory had been kept aside for him to claim. Every day he paced around the possibilities in his mind, studied the situation and waited for his opportunity.

A letter lay face up beside the newspaper. It had travelled from London with utmost haste and secrecy, its contents now known only to him. The information from the Secret Committee of the Court of Directors was incalculably more alarming than a bunch of island idiots landing on the shores of an unreasonable Indian prince. He looked over the few words again.

> *Possible plans of invasion by France. A very large armament of ships with troops and military stores was preparing to sail from Toulon under General Bonaparte. Destination unknown. Likely to come to India by way of Red Sea or way of Bussora.*

Wellesley put the paper knife aside and rubbed the face of the desk with his palms, before realizing the futility of undoing the damage and pulled the newspaper over the shallow grooves. He straightened himself and tugged the rope that rang a bell in the adjacent chamber. Henry Wellesley would be the first to hear of it, not as his brother, but as private secretary to the Governor-General. If Henry had any reactions of his own, he would prudently keep it unsaid. A message was dictated to be dispatched the very next day to Madras for General Harris, the acting governor of Fort St. George and Commander-in-Chief of the army on the Coromandel Coast.

> *It is my positive resolution to assemble the army upon the coast. I wish to receive from you by express a state of the force which you*

> *can put in motion immediately and within what time you can make any large additions to it...*

A second letter was addressed to James Kirkpatrick, the Resident at the Nizam's court in Hyderabad. The Nizam had a regiment of 14,000 French troops, much admired for its discipline and fighting abilities. They reported to the Nizam and not the French government, but if the call of the motherland were to come, Wellesley had no doubt about the outcome. He directed Kirkpatrick to open negotiations with the Nizam, proposing an addition to the British detachment in his capital and to dismantle the French corps under the promise of future protection from the British East India Company.

That only left the Marathas to worry about in the vicinity. The Nizam was a child and a simpleton compared to the fraction-ridden Marathas. The Marathas were a force needing to be watched warily rather than attempt to harness. Their participation in this confrontation was not crucial but their sympathies had to be bought at any cost.

The circumstances, Richard Wellesley decided, were dire enough.

Tipu Sultan dreams every night but on some mornings he wakes up and finds that the dream has not entirely evaporated from recollection but has left its residue, bright enough to be captured in words but also fading, fading so fast that he is anxious to relive it before it disappears. He closes the doors and windows of his room and pulls out his journal from its hiding place behind a loose brick in the wall. His journal of dreams. He writes in it slowly, dipping the silver quill in ink for every other word.

Ten thousand French soldiers have landed on his shores for the cause of the Khudadad Sarkar. He could see them so clearly, nearly count them, and definitely knew from the glint in their eyes that they were fired with both hunger of victory and deep loyalty to him.

A short fair man with a proud head is striding ahead of them as if he were the only one who mattered in a world he was born to rule.

The ways of Allah are unknown and wondrous. The French had made promises before that had not been honoured, as his ministers repeatedly reminded him. But the ship from Mauritius was a brief failure, and he saw hope, reinforcements from France would surely arrive in the coming months. There was the dream, wasn't there?

And then another dream had followed, less vivid but bearing the stamp of the same sleep. Three trays of dates placed before him – fresh, moist, juicy and grown in his garden. Yes, the messenger had worn new garbs but the message was unchanged.

He laughs gently with spreading pleasure. The three great shadows – British, Marathas, Nizam – all thorns in his side for so long, will soon be vanquished. He closes the journal and holds it tight against his chest. A man can be fooled by the whole world, his family or his courtiers, but his dreams are entirely his and entirely truthful.

The Master struggled for the right words to placate the young man who he wished had been born in his household. He could have handed his job over without any qualms and retired in joy, but now he had to ask Mukunda to stop these visits to their colony.

Why?

They may both live on the same island but they are not equals. The Master's ancestors – also painters and sculptors – came to Ganjam from Vijayanagara to work on the temples and have lived in the shade of the Srirangapatna fort since then. They considered themselves under the protection of Goddess Nimishamba, not the royal crown that gave them a livelihood.

The Master gently took away the paint box and Mukunda's sketch of the Dewan's boys. It was not right, he said. Mukunda was a Brahmin, born into a different vocation. Dabbling in all this for a boyish lark was fine, but this interest in drawing was starting to get a little obsessive and he wanted to have nothing more to do with it.

Go home, the old man advised. Go home and be a good son to your parents, a good husband to your wife, take up the family trade. There is no such thing in the adult world as living for oneself.

Mukunda tried to explain his malaise. Wouldn't he have done it if he could? His heart was not in his father's work. He wanted to do something else.

The Master was getting restless for his opium and wanted this conversation to end soon. They could hear children at play on the streets being called home by their mothers. It was time to light the evening lamps.

Mukunda wanted to say that he loved the Master's settlement more than his own home. The sloppy grass pathways from the fort into the rolling plains, the affectionate greetings of the villagers, the distant sizzle of the river currents as one walked deeper into the island, the rows of mud houses around the Master's workshop, the wind that whistled through the stone crevices of their temple, he loved it all but that seemed pointless now.

He took leave, trudged back towards the fort. In the violet light of early dusk it was a gigantic coiled serpent resting after a heavy meal. He thought of his father sitting on the stone verandah of their house, craning his neck so that he could tell yet again what a sorrow the boy was to his life. And if the words got too bitter, his mother would sniffle behind the kitchen door, wiping her tears on her sari. So little, they said, was being asked of their son – merely to assist his father in his job of reading horoscopes till he learned enough to let his father retire, and also to bring home his bride. Both thoughts filled him with fright. He had not seen his wife since their wedding day, both so young that he barely recalled her face. She was living with her parents as tradition demanded, enjoying the fast evaporating days of her girlhood. A few months back, her father had sent triumphant word – the girl has come of age, ready now to face her husband's world. His mother had beamed with pride. She was aching for someone to take over her domestic chores and fill the emptiness of living in a house with men who spoke only at nightfall. But there was still the cumbersome task of persuading Mukunda who keeps saying, no, not now, later.

He had always been the odd one among boys his age. Mercurial. Changing guises effortlessly, mimicking others so often that very few knew when he was being himself, he had wanted to try his hand at acting on a stage. The theatre group in the town avoided conversations about his lineage or intentions. They knew all they needed to know and did not wish to turn away cheap talent. He tried a few minor roles and then comfortably settled into playing the female lead in plays. Fair and slender, a sari draped perfectly around his waist. Fitted with a wig filled with jasmine flowers, his forehead shining with a circle of vermillion, he was transformed. He could be a goddess, a princess, a mythical damsel. People laughed when he smiled and wept torrents at his single tear. He was trapped between the bars of dialogue and action that made the prison of a play, and broke free when the applause crashed into his consciousness. Only when he stepped off the stage was he aware of being man again.

His parents moaned when they heard of the shame he was bringing to the family name in the playhouse. They never got to hear what the discerning patrons were saying about his voice, how it mesmerized them, awakened their forgotten passions. He could happily sing for hours. And if the tabla sounded upbeat, he could dance in its happiness too.

Why don't you do something about that son of yours? Relatives were coming home just to drink tea, just to say that.

'You shall get not a single coin from me till you come to your senses,' his father decreed. 'If it wasn't for your mother, I would turn you into the streets. Starving would cure you in an instant. But she has lost too many children and so long as she lives, you shall not be denied a meal in my house.'

But then Father is so gullible, Mukunda thought, not understanding that it does not take much to make enough money to survive, and that there is more to life than staring at horoscope charts. So long as Mukunda did not mention the family and caste he was born into, so long as the sacred thread marking his station of birth was slipped off his shoulders, a healthy boy with a sharp wit could never run out of ways to earn a few coins.

Mukunda dawdled on the stone bridge and looked down at the young cowherds in the slatey riverbed washing away the grime of the day. The mighty Kaveri reduced to a struggling stream would continue to shrink till the rains in June when she will overflow to wrap the fort in her fury. But he liked her better when she bared her heart like this. The pebbled bed bore countless signs of her true disposition. Such fathomless suffering. Deep furrows, trenches of mud, layers of silt from remote hills, he could study her forever, like his father did with the charts and palms of strangers.

'Tipu Sultan has less than a year to live and the Kaveri will be filled with blood!' his father had prophesied when all the doors and windows closed for the night, and his mother had muttered prayers for protection, not for the king, the fort, or the river, but her little family and hearth. The Sultan frequently consulted Mukunda's father on matters of importance and his father would then study the planets. Yet, this prediction had stayed trapped in his belly, not revealed to his client, and grown so large that he was compelled to blurt it out at home. The danger, he said, was incubating in the house of women. He then fell into a gloomy silence. The Wodeyars did not have to be named. Everyone knew how the throne had been taken from the ancient royal family, how all the kings had died, how all the queens had been locked away. What danger could they possibly pose?

From where Mukunda stood, he could see the roof of the house of women, a benign spot on the landscape. Did his father's predictions ever come true? Very often they did. But that he supposed was because his father was never dealing with great odds. Either people had children or they didn't, either the rains came on time or they didn't, either people lived or died. His father always had half a chance of being right and being an astute observer had taught him to lean towards the more probable option.

All my life, Mukunda thought, I have been told there are no secrets from the gods and the scriptures. Every truth having been explored and discovered before our times, all that is left to do is faithfully follow directions. Nobody could stir those lines of fate. However, I have a problem, one that I simply cannot resolve. My skin is my own but another man walks in it.

In the House of Women

How very afraid darkness is of us! It does not know what to do with our lamentations, those that brazenly claw at the walls in both resistance and protest, or the suffocating moans nobody hears outside of here. We are the unheard voices of the Wodeyar household, nine women, and no men, except for one little boy; sapling hidden by the overgrowth, a future king with neither kingdom nor wealth. In a house of women, lamps are never blown out all at once. The wicks burn out to replace one another, the oil drops into empty cavities of the lamps as do our tears, the light in one room is doused by one woman's fatigue and another lights hers with wakeful desire.

Where have all the men gone? Do we miss them at all? The ones that died we do not dare say much about. Some were great powerful kings wearing strings of pearls heavier than themselves. If they were wasteful and slothful, if they cast this wretched fate upon us, it is not for us to talk of it now. They will settle their dues in the merciless wheel of rebirth while this imprisonment here is our fate. What can we as women say? Sure, we did curse them. But we meant well. What can you do when someone steps on your feet and crushes the bones within? You cry out in pain. You wish the other dead. We might have done that as well.

In the house of women, there are no tools left to dig our way out of narrow walls, no maps to show the lay of the land beyond the yard, no keys for the locks on the doors. Like hens in a coop, we peck at each other's feathers and take joy in our pain. You would too, if you knew what we have endured.

No, it is not for us to speak of dead kings. Though an exception can be made for the one murdered. He had just turned from boy to man, wishing to do more than stamp seals when commanders thirsted for wars and booty. Or probably we are mistaken. There are many reasons why people die unexpectedly in the bath with marks of strangulation around their necks. Three decades of losing men have befuddled our brains. Three decades of kings changing like the seasons, dying, leaving behind sons with shorter lives or wives with hollow insides. Five of us were married to the same king and only one womb flowered. We love the little boy for bringing spring to a house of women ageing slowly, excruciatingly. We hate the little boy too – he makes us hope and go on living.

Lakshmi paced the room in five long strides, hit the wall with her fist and strode back to the wall opposite to it; five strides again, measured as carelessly but precisely. The boy watched her as he did the pendulum of the great clock pinned to the wall: back and forth, predictable and forceful, left and right. He looked down at his nails and thought they needed biting.

'No!' she snapped. 'Remember, you are a prince and soon, someday, you will be king.'

The boy morosely turned to the open window and stuck his nose as far out as he could between the wooden bars. She knew every thought that sneaked into his four-year-old head even before it was enacted. There was that onerous word again – 'king' – and he heard it most from her, his mother by politics, not blood, tightly reining in his childhood to make sure he kept the royal lineage alive. From his window he could see the house of the man who was the real master of Srirangapatna, who lived in the Lal

Mahal with its lofty roof, tall pillars of fluted wood and flowers painted on red walls; who had horses, elephants and thousands of attentive men at his bidding; Tipu Sultan ruled the land while she, Lakshmi Ammani, clinging to the moral authority given by her husband's name to call herself a queen, continued to pace and did not let him be a boy, only an imagined prince, one who could not go out to play with the other boys or bite his own nails when he so fancied.

An attendant, their only one now since Tipu Sultan had drastically reduced the monthly allowance for the royal family's subsistence, stood at the door.

'Is she here?' Lakshmi asked. 'Well, is she?'

A shadow shifted behind the attendant, making obvious a reluctance to be announced, seeking to step forward into the light. The Queen liked impatience, especially in women. It suggested a fine mettle. She waved an arm at the attendant who scuttled away with a glance of sympathy for the visitor. A queen fraught with passion and anger was not easy to serve.

The shadow glided into the room, turning into a young woman who bent down to touch the Queen's feet in respect and then straightened in attention. The boy being groomed to be king jumped up from his perch and dashed behind Lakshmi's sari that pampered his childish insecurities more than she did. He brushed his face against the soft fabric and peered shyly at the newcomer. The temple bells rang out for the main prayer and they listened in silent respect.

'An auspicious sign,' Lakshmi said gently as soon as the bells echoed out, then spoke to the boy without looking at him. 'It is time for your studies, Your Highness. We have work to do.' The royal title was a reminder that the moment was solemn and formal, that the visitor was a valued one. He aged in a twinkle, adding as many feigned years to himself as he could, nodded first to the Queen in obedience, then to the visitor in regal acknowledgement, and walked out with measured steps. As soon as he went around the door, they heard the sound of running feet, reckless, almost deliberately noisy, thumping through the dark corridor.

Lakshmi pulled close the wooden shutters of the window. 'You may think I don't trust my own people. I don't. I have lived long enough not to even trust myself entirely.' A lamp stirred sensuously, yellow flame slowly turning red, its shaky tip swaying between them. 'Suhasini, we are pleased you have come and consider it an honour to have the light of Kashi in our house, in our kingdom.'

Suhasini bent her head respectfully. 'The only light in Kashi belongs to Lord Vishwanath, Your Highness. I am merely an instrument, a student. My father said you needed me to do something for you. I am honoured you thought I could be of some use.'

'Humility is not always a virtue, my dear. Not when it comes from someone who has studied our ancient scriptures and debated with great scholars on the banks of Mother Ganga,' and then softening her voice, 'I hear it is hard on your father.'

'It is hard on him,' Suhasini repeated simply.

'And I hear your husband has refused his jewel of a bride. Men like intelligence in a woman that serves their pleasure and convenience. But intelligence in a woman that serves itself ... well, let's just say they would much rather she be a leper.'

Suhasini sat still, unresponsive to the bait.

'Yes,' Lakshmi nodded sympathetically at her silence, 'knowledge can be a marriage itself, demanding and fulfilling at the same time.'

'As perhaps is politics...' Suhasini softly suggested.

Lakshmi raised her eyebrows at the seeming affront. Her visitor was more outspoken than she had expected. She smiled to show her tolerance. Her being a blighted bride was part of national lore. The king of the land, having lost a wife, had decided to gain two new ones, both unlucky women, cursed with empty wombs. Two sons from the first marriage vouched for the king's potency, each getting to wear the crown after him in quick succession and with equally early deaths, till the house of the Wodeyars had no male child left to crown. An adoption was suggested, a teenager picked from the extended family for Lakshmi to groom into a king, but he did not live long either. The only survivor was his little son and Lakshmi's only passage back to political power. She had worked alone, isolated in the house of women for too long. Now she needed someone who could visit without drawing suspicion and leave with instructions to galvanize their freedom movement.

Suhasini had a worthy reputation but it had come into the room like a snail curled up under its shell, her dark calculating eyes giving little reassurance, revealing nothing. Sharp nose, high angular cheekbones, pointed chin, the young woman was like a shard of glass with many jagged edges. It made Lakshmi uneasy.

Some waters had to be dived into to truly know their depths. Lakshmi took a swift decision to be honest with Suhasini. She picked up a cushion from behind her, turned it around in her lap and tugged at the seams with her fingernails, pulling it open till her fingers could slip in and bring out a tightly folded wad of papers. She passed them on to Suhasini. They were letters received in the recent months from her ambassador in Tanjore and a few aging ones from the British governors in the past.

She talked while Suhasini read. For twenty-two years they were forced to live at the mercy of servants who had turned masters. At least Haider Ali had the decency to treat her son as the king, even if only in name, but Haider's son, this vulgar man who called himself an emperor, was bent on wiping out her family. She had not given up. Their ambassador, Thirumala Rao, had been trying to plead their cause with the English leaders who were more keen on signing useless treaties. Those men, it was too bad, were not tied to their thrones like her. And now…

Now the situation had changed. Suhasini thought the new English General had to be urged to act in haste. Or administrative routines might dull the blade of ambition before long.

'It takes a gambler to survive politics. And what a strange animal this politics is. I live with it but I don't belong to it. I have never been a very patient woman, Suhasini. And I wish I could live like other women, stirring the next meal and tending to the livestock and singing lullabies to the children. But if I turn away, this family and this kingdom are lost forever! And then neither the gods nor our mortal scribes of history will forgive me…' Lakshmi had seen her husband drinking away his responsibilities while ministers ate into the treasury like termites, and she had been reduced to a queen who counted oil drops that went into lamps, sometimes making a choice between food to eat and a lamp to light. 'I am a tired woman, an old woman, often wondering if a woman at all. Perhaps within a dark cell of solitary confinement, man and woman become the same kind of animals…'

Lakshmi pulled out a small sandalwood box, opened it, picked a needle and spool of thread. She wetted the end of the thread in her mouth and held it against the eye of the needle, narrowed her eyes and pushed it through, each time failing to make the narrow opening. She flicked the thread quickly through her lips again and squinted closer to the needle. Suhasini picked up the oil lamp and held it up between them. The long streaks of grey in Lakshmi's hair came alive. The thread struck through the metal slot. Lakshmi pulled it through and began to sew the letters back in the cushion as if she were alone in the room, talking quietly, while Suhasini listened.

Lakshmi did not care for her life, she was certain of that. She was nearly sixty and all those sixty years she would gladly shrug off, forgotten childhood, early widowhood, unborn children, public humiliations, and now this imprisonment and the life of a sentry; guarding a little boy with very little chances of survival. Everything he eats, even what his own mother feeds him, has to be fed to a dog first in her presence. How easy, how convenient, it would be for Tipu to kill him and let the Wodeyars vanish without a trace. Each day brought fresh petitions from her subjects smuggled in with the domestic help or wandering mendicants who came for alms. Her people looked to her for strength and direction while she was increasingly feeling depleted. This time it was a young Christian woman in Tipu Sultan's harem. Married only a week when her entire family was rounded up by soldiers and marched from the coast to the capital, her life saved by her beauty, she had ended up inside the walls of the harem. She had managed somehow to smuggle out a message to the Wodeyar queen, begging for help to find her husband who had made the arduous journey with her. But there was not much hope. The husband was most likely dead. If not, he would have been circumcised, turned into a Muslim and filed into Tipu's Ahmadi army. Forcible converts were like flies in the kingdom now, countless.

Suhasini would do what she could. She promised. But they were both aware of the odds. Thousands had paid dearly for siding with the British in defending Mangalore from Tipu Sultan, just like the hill people of Coorg and the Nairs further south, their rebellion ending in carnage, their settlements burnt to ash.

'I don't wish for you to be in any trouble on our account,' Lakshmi said, her voice tempered with concern. 'Are you sure you want to get involved? Fine, then I shall explain to your father and the women in this house that I need you to come and read the Bhagavad Gita to me every day, my eyesight being so poor and my soul seeking now to renounce all worldly matters…'

'I understand.'

Lakshmi reached over and patted Suhasini's left shoulder tenderly, slid fingers under the drapes of the sari and lovingly gathered it back towards her nape. She let the hands linger on, watching her bony pale fingers against the deep blue of the fabric and Suhasini's dark smooth skin that tensed at her touch. So inexperienced in the ways of the world, unlike herself who was raised in the bloodbath of politics, and yet the young woman's reserve of calm seemed deeper. Lakshmi whispered, 'For him who has conquered the mind, the mind is the best of friends; but for one who has failed to do so, his very mind will be the greatest enemy.'

The succeeding verse was on Suhasini's lips. 'For one who has conquered the mind, the soul is already reached, for he has attained tranquillity. To such a man, happiness and distress, heat and cold, honour and dishonour are all the same.'

Lakshmi smiled and stood up to pick a bulky object from the shelf, wrapped in faded silk of the finest quality. She handed it to Suhasini who opened it on her lap. They both knew it very well. Arjuna faltering in the face of battle against his kinsmen, kept from leaving the battlefield by the words of his charioteer. The soul is eternal and immortal. The war for righteousness has to be fought at all cost. Suhasini opened the first page and began to recite, her eyes not on the verses but the face of the older woman. Lakshmi walked over to the door and nudged it open. The melodious voice wafted through the tired walls of the house, and then was interrupted.

The women looked sharply at each other. That dull thud on the roof could be a falling coconut but it could also be a hovering threat. Suhasini moved closer to Lakshmi and continued to recite resolutely. Her warm body and sweet breath infused the older woman with desire; the years of fatigue and desperation now turned into quickening thoughts. There was much to be done. Freedom was at hand and inviting.

Darkness gathered in quick bursts over the river island. People closed doors and windows. Children cried restlessly and shuffled after adults who complained of the cold draughts in the house. Those who had stepped out, hurried back inside. Thunder clapped in the distance. A gale attacked all the lamps and lanterns in the fort at the same time. Very few of them survived. Voices and feet struggled to find their way across the darkness, flames coaxed back to life. Across the Kaveri, the dark hillock of Karibetta lit up from above for a brief moment. A sprawling branch of incandescent light struck the sky. Every speck of blue on the land turned into dazzling silver, a fine sprinkle of rain revealing itself, and then every object, lit and unlit, collapsed into a coarse black.

Beyond Is the Haze

Vendors had lined their straw mats on either side of the main streets of Srirangapatna, some spread out on bare earth and under an open sky, beside tall poles displaying sample wares for the weekly market. The potters scattered to avoid direct competition, making brown patterns of baked earth all around them. Bangle-sellers called out liltingly for the patronage of the women at the fair, only to be out-sung by weavers fluttering colourful fabric in the wind; sellers of vegetables and dairy products shouted out promises of reductions; livestock-dealers bragged about the health of even the frailest merchandise. Business had to be done and as quickly as possible, and nobody was above the age-old convenience of bartering even if they had enough coins. Instincts were pitted against instincts. Persuading, bargaining, cajoling, browbeating – a gigantic wheel of people and their possessions moved steadily in an arduous contest with the summer sun – smiling, sweating, mingling.

Mukunda made his way through the throng, passing by the large peepul tree where three of his old school friends huddled in the shade and laughed loudly, their heads close together. He did not mind being made fun of nor did he mind not being greeted. He walked on quickly, wanting to get as far away from his home as possible. The confusion and clamour of the market, the sight of strangers on familiar streets eased his anger.

It is time to bring Meenakshi home. His mother's eyes had pleaded with him. 'You don't have to concern yourself with it. This is a matter to be settled between us, the elders of the family.'

How could they possibly believe that the matter did not concern him? How could he possibly fight overriding adult decisions like this? A wife would come with her own ideas and notions, trained like all girls to respect convention and tame husbands. Being married had only been a label all these years, but now it would be a daily reality brandished in the face of his wanderings. And what if she turned out to be ugly, mean, more oppressive than life already seemed?

'She is your wife whether you like it or not,' they said as he was storming out of the house.

What purpose would all his protestations serve? Even if he postponed her arrival, he would not be able to renounce it.

His chest hurt. What was a boy's fault if he had outlived all his siblings? Why did it then enslave him to a mother's obsession? Why was he born in a fort with narrow streets and narrower minds? Why was he married to a little sleepy girl when he was only a little boy more intent in shredding the flowers in his garland than listening to the priest declaring him to be her protector? What did it matter that his bride had become a woman, when he was still not the man he wanted to be?

An acrobat flung his little brother in the air. The crowd held its breath. The boy cheerfully flapped his arms during the flight and made a perfect landing on the back of a bored donkey trotting slowly in a circle. Their sister ran around collecting coins. She did not get any from the young Brahmin who strode past without care for their act, a dark puff of smoke.

'I never knew it was possible for any man to experience such misery.' Andre Surcouf glanced up from his book, laughing.

Mukunda leaned against the wall of the Jacobin Club and moaned, 'I cannot go back home.' He had walked all the way to the French camp, a rocky outpost a few miles away from the fort where the

French contingent lived in tents and bided time till the next call to battle.

Mukunda had known the French camp ever since he had been a young boy and would come with his friends to explore the rocks. They had eagerly run errands for the French soldiers and hung around them till Mukunda could discern the contours of the language. Of late he had grown a puppy-like attachment to Surcouf, a soldier in times of war, but mostly a man of books. To the young artist's eye there was something mesmerizing about how the Frenchman moved the quill with quiet assurance at the writing table. Stories sprouted around Surcouf. They said he had come neither with the French troops nor the traders like the other Frenchmen but had turned up one day at the court of Tipu Sultan clutching a sealed letter, his skin clinging to his bones and covered by festering wounds. Some people said he told the Sultan the truth of his condition and others believed that he just made up a sorry yarn. Tipu never revealed the contents of the letter and ordered the French General to induct the officer in his army. The French camp speculated and argued about him. Surcouf, they whispered, was Robespierre's personal strategist on the run when the teeth of the revolution began biting the hands that reined it; he had been a spy, arsonist, assassin, fanatic, debauchee, manipulator; a man not to be judged, only feared. Surcouf himself never bothered to explain. India was as far as he wanted to get away and having done that, there was nothing for him to be nostalgic about. His intellect and composure kept hostile compatriots at bay. He was the only one apart from the head of the regiment to get summons for private audience at the royal palace where Tipu liked to discuss articles from Diderot's *Encyclopaedia*, comfortable with voicing his doubts and valuing Surcouf's honesty. Nobody wished to get on the wrong side of a man who had the ruler's ear, though that did not stop the rumours. And only Mukunda, apart from the Sultan, had managed to have Surcouf's unqualified attention whenever he needed it.

'I will never go home,' he repeated.

'If only someone gave me a gold coin every time I heard you say that. I would have enough wealth to buy this fort from the Sultan,' Surcouf muttered without putting his book down.

Mukunda knew the truth in that and also the futility of insisting that he meant it this time. No amount of raving ever helped him pack his bags. The thought of leaving home, though it promised escape, also flooded him with dread. Wasn't a familiar prison more comforting than vast untried liberty?

'It is too quiet here today.'

'Yes! So you do notice there is a world around you! Let me assure you, my dear friend, I intend to enjoy the peace to the hilt while it lasts. Monsieur Chapuis is having a drill for the newcomers and our boys have decided to attend out of solidarity.'

'You did not go?'

'No, I excused myself. You know about my dreadful arthritis … it has been acting up these days,' Surcouf said the words slowly, with a twinkle in his eyes, for it was his standard excuse for any official duties he wanted to avoid.

A year ago, when Rimpaud the conman had grandly paraded his lies in the fort and delivered a rousing speech about the ideals of the revolution, all the men in the French quarters had cheered in pride. A tree of liberty had been planted, a charter of rules drawn up and Tipu Sultan invited to be part of their celebrations as 'Citizen Tipu'. Surcouf had thought it ludicrous. He respected Tipu, but saw little sense in making a man who wished nothing more than building a dynasty of emperors to be the mascot of an event celebrating the right of citizens to govern their state. He had taken recourse to his imaginary arthritis and stayed away from the events.

The sounds of men walking towards them now wafted in little by little. Mukunda stood up. He was still uncomfortable with the newcomers from Mauritius who viewed the dark-skinned boy in their midst with disdain. Most of them did not look like soldiers nor did they qualify to be civilians with integrity. They drank and sang and gambled their time away. They spoke of valour and resolve but rarely cleaned their muskets unless senior officers demanded they do. For years they had lived on the little island in the Indian Ocean, forgotten if not disowned by the mother country, living off their own ingenuity and cunning. The trip to the kingdom of Mysore, despite all the talk of bloodshed with the British, was to them little more than a paid vacation. The more seasoned soldiers of the French regiment, who had been in India for many years, tried their best to pursue their routines with charitable tolerance of these unruly men who professed to be their fellow citizens. France was much too remote now, more idea than an ideal. It was Tipu Sultan who was the immediate owner of their fate, if not for life then at least for the next drink. The devout Muslim ruler had prohibited the sale of liquor in his kingdom but made an exception for the French contingent.

France and India are lovers who are afraid to make a commitment to each other, Surcouf said frequently, nervous about sharing destinies and responsibilities, while the gritty British made the most of the situation.

'What should I do? What should I do?' Mukunda moaned, having remembered his troubles afresh. 'Maybe I should just run away from home…'

'One can only run away from a place to which one belongs,' Surcouf jested, 'and if you did run away, you would probably find yourself back home with that wife of yours. Married life is not all that ruinous, I can assure you, or else so many of us men would not be repeating our father's mistakes. Perhaps you could give it a try and then you might find that you rather like it.'

Mukunda was unconvinced. Was Surcouf ever married?

'I have known women in a marriage sort of way. One does not need to go through the ordeal of a ceremony to get into a woman's bed – an important benefit of having a wife, wouldn't you say?'

Mukunda blushed. 'I am not even thinking of that…'

'Go home,' Surcouf said kindly. 'You'll know what to do when the time is right. Any advice from me in this matter is only bound to cause you more trouble. Go, go home.'

My father, the temple priest, has a daughter he is afraid of. Me. And he is not sure what he dreads more, the heat of scandal in the fort or the look of hurt in my eyes.

My name was given to me the day they first saw me, an orphaned baby who smiled like a garden in spring, Suhasini, and they did their best to dissuade any gossip about my adoption. When pressed, they said I was born to distant relatives, as purebred as their Brahmin forefathers, ignoring comments about my dark skin which someone unkindly said could only belong to a cobbler's wife. I grew up knowing I was not born to them but feeling like I was a daughter. The tongues in the Brahmin quarters of the fort haven't stopped wagging since we have come back. Father was once much envied, sent to Kashi by the Wodeyar himself, for the upkeep of their temple; a man with prospects and not much to worry about. And how proud he and mother had been of me, when they found me one morning in the prayer room, my doll forgotten behind the door, the Ramayana open before me. Father taught me to read and write, he taught me to think for myself, he taught me to question. He wished I could stay a little girl, never be a woman, because as a woman I would have to be just like everyone else. He called me his little quicksand, for devouring every piece of writing I came across. When scholars gathered at the temple, he let me listen to debates about scriptures and religious practices. Nothing was amiss. We were a happy family. Happy, till they thought of marriage. I had just turned fourteen, older than all my married friends. My parents had to do their duty.

The horoscopes were a perfect match, I was told. What I found out once the celebrations ebbed was that my husband was past his sixtieth year, more than a decade older than my father. That was not uncommon in our families, but my devotion to my studies was most certainly unacceptable in my new home. How could I give up my books? It was all I had there, to help me briefly escape that nauseating smell of marriage, the coarseness of that man's skin, his breath, the knots in his knees, the way he doused my spirit with the weight of his body. I fought to go home to my parents and then I fought when they suggested I return to the marital hearth. The husband never sent for me – I was too much trouble – and my parents could not persuade me to go.

They decided to return to their ancestral home, but that was not the solace they had hoped it would be. A married daughter at home was as good as unmarried. Everyone here felt sorry for my father. If only he had adopted a son, one who would have taken over his priestly duties in the temple by the holy Ganga. Father keeps his head low and nods with a sad smile when anyone speaks to him. He is grateful to have their pity – it protects him from their censure.

I chose to be deaf. Deaf to the world, but not to my queen. I listen to her very carefully and I work for her vision, for her freedom, for my own. The injustice never ends, in social obligations, in relationships, in public spheres. Tipu's shadow is swallowing us up. His ambitions, his vengeance, and all for a stolen crown and throne. I listen also to those who send out messages for our intervention. For what life is this that is guarded, stifled, demeaned, and all because it seeks dignity? It is not acceptable. Not to her, not to me.

My father, the temple priest, follows me this morning as I walk through the streets of the town. He trails at a distance, wanting to speak to me, yet does not. How can that which is unsaid inside the house get uttered under open skies? I made him a father but he did not make me. I came to his house a destitute and he was the one who led me through the words beneath the words I read, who spoke about the liberation that comes from thinking for oneself. Somehow he had started to think his daughter was a son. Now he is afraid to tell me to stop. Worse, he is afraid that if he tells me to stop, I will not.

I enter the prison for Wodeyar women as I do every day, to deal with the matters of the state, for it is still our state and it is our own people that need help. While we think of fighting the dictator, my father is only worried about his little domestic troubles, his little girl. I can hear him begging for an audience with the queen.

She thanks him profusely, not as a queen but as a sister, for sparing his only child to serve the widows of the royal family in their old age and social confinement. She hopes he does not grudge her this little solace in her days of distress. I listen through the doors. I don't watch his face for I know what it looks like. I watch hers, calmly claiming me from him.

He fumbles, he stammers, finally he stands up to leave. 'People talk and Suhasini is my only…'

'Lucky man! All the gods have smiled on you, for she is treasure, a light, a rare blessing. Your child is in my safekeeping. Go home and don't worry about it anymore.'

I knew he would not dare to say anymore. He will go home and write another letter to my husband pleading that I be admitted into the home I was married into. But my reputation always travels faster than his letters. A woman who thinks too much, reads too much and speaks her mind; she can manage books, not kitchens; she pushes ideas, not cradles. There will be no reply to his letter, as always.

My father slowly heads home, to more sorrowful resignation. I am the cause lost to him and that the queen has won. For that, I say a silent prayer of gratitude. There is much work to be done.

The young man pulled himself over the stone embankment and crawled into the shelter of the roadside choultry. He had been in such a hurry to get as far away from home as possible that it had taken him many hours to realize that he had not eaten anything or that his feet were bleeding or that his eyes were closing with sleep while he walked. He had no money, but kind strangers had ferried him across rivers and some had offered him rides on their bullock carts for short distances. He did not deny his name or his family – the astrologer's son from Srirangapatna. The rest was just spinning tales – there was a sudden death in the family, someone very close and dear to him. Much sympathy and little interrogation invariably followed that. He did offer some more truth though – he was headed for his uncle's house in Nandidurga.

I have often said I would do it, thought Mukunda, I have threatened it and I have wished for it. Now here I am, homeless and completely lost. How did this happen?

My nights at the theatre were a disappointment known but ignored by Father and Mother. They try not to imagine me, draped in a brocaded magenta sari, flowers in my hair and bangles on my wrists, singing songs of sweet secret longings to boisterous crowds. Who might wish that in a son? They pretend to be asleep when I sneak back home late in the night, smelling of the stage and intoxicated in the unconditional applause of my townsmen. In my sleep I continue to bear the weight of the little bells around my ankles as I submit to the rhythm of the story I narrate; I feel the tears of the characters I live; I toss in hope and turn in despair; lying in bed, my eyes closed, I am dancing like Lord Nataraja. All this they have learnt to accept as an aberration in their blood. Even the rumours and gossip that the callous women throw at my mother while she draws water at the well, that my father hears from his friends whose sons have the decency to live as they are told to, all that hurtful talk they have learnt to swallow and digest. But this is unthinkable. There I was, dressed as a woman, pouring my soul into the climax of the play, carrying the audience with me to heights of distress. I was Sita, suffering the worst ordeals a woman can, abducted and imprisoned by a demon, unable to enjoy the relief of rescue because the husband she loves now wishes her to prove her chastity.

How can the gods be so merciless?

I cry as a wronged Sita. An insensitive husband is asking me to walk through a raging fire so that I can return to my married life with him and I do it only to avoid shaming him before his army. I emerge unscathed from the fire but do not walk into his open arms. Instead, I shall cry out to my mother the earth to split open and swallow me up. So what if my husband is Lord Rama himself? A man is neither man nor god if he chooses to do this to a woman who loves him. Better death than this humiliation! He does not deserve me! And I cannot endure this unspeakable pain anymore! Here I go! Here I go!

The crowd stirred in empathy. I opened my tear-soaked eyes to glance in triumph as they give vent to emotions they are afraid to face in their own lives. And then I see the horrified expression on a face I haven't seen for a while – my wife's father. He is standing apart from everyone else, head bent in shame, and I know he is waiting to take me home. He must have come to town today to discuss his daughter's future. Perhaps my parents had sent for him and he must have wanted to see if the rumours about me were true. I panic. I jump off the stage. Everyone sees Sita descend into the netherworlds. They gasp in distress. I run out of the playhouse and into the unlit streets. I keep running, as fast as my feet can carry me, sweating my way through the starless night. I have finally become the runaway that I really am.

The Apprentice

The Englishman looked out from his tent flap, miserable. Richard had been warned over and over again about the merciless sun in India, the bloodthirsty insects, the sea breeze that made the heat stick to the body and then ooze from within; he had suffered it all and thought himself a better man for not having complained through the heartless summer he had been dumped in by the *Absalom*. He had consoled himself that the season was nearly over and would get progressively better, life and inspiration returning to his drained skin. Nobody had bothered to tell him about the Indian monsoons.

The party of artist and servants had set off bravely from Fort St. George into the westerly wind. On the second day they ran into the swollen clouds, and no matter how much they waited or moved, the rain drummed down with little mercy for their damp belongings or the collapsing mud roads. The wind howled with such ferocity that a man dared stand up only at the risk of being knocked down, while thunder and lightning kept them awake through the nights. On the third day of the journey their dubash vanished with whatever money had been handed over for buying provisions – fortunately, he had only been given what was needed for a few days – and with him absconded two of the servants. Richard scarcely knew what to do for there was no one to complain to and no hope of replacing the missing help. Francis, his half-Portuguese attendant (the other half was Tamil and quite unknown to Richard), offered to double up his duties without mentioning a corresponding hike in payment and somehow magically procured supplies from local markets. Richard welled with gratitude but kept the poise of a master. After dinner he slipped a glass of his precious stock of claret towards Francis and it was quickly swallowed.

At their first meeting, Richard could not believe that Francis was capable of anything but smiling sweetly. The sword in the delicate scabbard had been revealed on the very first day as they walked away from the sea and the Company flag. Francis quickly established his authority over the servants, talking to them sharply in Tamil while never out of earshot from the white horse that carried his master. Richard merely had to summon half a word on his lips and Francis would bound to his side like a tethered rabbit. Francis's father had been a sailor who loved his drink more than his family, but he was European, a social advantage that Francis had used to gain access to the confidence of the British in Fort St. George. It also allowed him to assert himself over the servants. He learnt the ways and languages of different people with dogged earnestness. He was shorter than all of them, his skin dark like his mother's, but his light brown eyes and his hair coloured like damp straw set him apart from the other men in Richard's employment. It was easy to forget how young he was, barely seventeen, as he efficiently organized the entourage and dealt with men double his age and size. If the pain of having to be a constant outsider, a foreigner to the Indians and a local to the white traders, was heavy on his heart, he never talked about it. It slowly became apparent that an identity devoid of any social standing was what made possible for Francis to be resourceful and adjusting even in the most demanding situations.

The Mysore frontiers opened up quietly and without any scare. There were no fences. There wasn't even a definite way of knowing where the borders began. They walked westwards, climbing over and then descending the rows of stumpy hills that would deliver them into the Deccan plateau. The villages they passed had witnessed Tipu's previous battle with the English, and the sight of a lone Englishman with a retinue of Indian servants was seen as an ominous sign, danger to be kept at a distance. Nobody greeted them, and sometimes people disappeared so rapidly, they were almost floating through a land of ghosts.

The first crisis they faced was not from the hostile weather but when three bottles of Madeira, a gift from Havelock who had swiped them from the inn, were smashed on the road. One of the servants had slipped while unloading the bullock cart. There were loud remonstrance and copious tears even before Richard could inquire into the matter. The guilty servant rolled on the ground in fear of being struck. Richard tried to placate and tell them that broken bottles were not of such great consequence. The more he smiled and talked politely, the contempt in their eyes became unmistakable. An air of disrespect hung about the travelling party for a few days till there was the matter of a box of paint supplies being left behind at a camp. Richard made it clear that here was finally a crime he simply couldn't forgive. He yelled his anger, while the servants watched with bent and wary eyes.

Francis pleaded on their behalf. It was just a box of odds and ends.

Richard flushed with rising rage. They were going back for that box and if even a single brush was found missing, they would all forgo a week's wages.

Francis grabbed the horse and trotted back on the road while they sat around silently underneath a twisted banyan tree till he returned with the missing item. The following day Richard noticed that his painting supplies were carefully placed in the centre and front of the cart. On catching his eye, the men tumbled over each other to shower some extra concern for those boxes. He was puzzled to find them more deferential, as he was to see Francis become friendlier towards him since then.

Richard tried to sketch the sights they passed. Confined to the palanquin by the constant drizzle and carried on the shoulders of men, was scarcely conducive to tame a pencil. The only other thing to do was to slump back, the hat covering his eyes, and pretend to sleep while his mind worried incessantly. He lay there, sedated by the bearers' monotonous grunting and chanting when they started fresh in the mornings. By evening, there was only the exhaustion of staggering feet. The progress in the rains was slow. Their spirits sagged in unison. On occasions, when the rains did stop briefly and Richard was able to get on his horse, he was startled to see the fertility and sensuality bursting forth all around them; layered curtains of green vines, clouds of moths with wings streaked with gold, wild jasmines sweetening the air with their fragrance, and peacocks with tails trembling like open fans of brocade silk. It was hard to rejoice in all that beauty for long as the menaces of the weather continued. Insects swarmed all over their bodies but those were welcome in comparison to snakes and scorpions that turned up in their bags and tents. Bloodsucking leeches burrowed into their flesh and had to be constantly pulled out. The agony turned worse at dusk when armies of mosquitoes descended for their share of blood. Richard had never seen anything as vicious and determined as these swift insects with strange coloured markings on their back, attacking all at once like little humming spears. His skin was covered with rashes and swellings. The gauze curtains he had been advised to carry offered little protection or sleep when hung above his bedding. He rolled himself up in them like an embalmed corpse and when that proved ineffective, he imitated Francis by dipping hands in the oil glasses of the lamps and rubbing the oil all over his body to deaden the intolerable itching.

As they trudged on, Richard clung to the map provided by Cole but often he did not even know where they were, and any questions addressed to Francis were answered with a shrug. His men, however, seemed to know where they were heading and so he returned to his sketchbook, drawing lines beside lines. The single confident stroke that the Greek painters competed to perfect – *nulla diem sine linea* – no day without a line. Every line had its own character and defied him as much as the weather. Once in a while the lines would curve and become a profile of Francis or the fallen bough of a mango tree.

Cunningham was right, Richard thought. He had the skill but not the vision. What made him any different from the hundreds of starving draughtsmen in the world who doodled recognizable objects when their pencil bored of the mechanical work? What set him apart from another who might draw a more alive-looking bird or could make light radiate from its feathers just by a different blend of colours? 'Just another painter,' as Forbes had said, as his mother's eyes had often doubted, and what was not good enough for her was never going to be good enough for anyone, not even himself. If only he could turn his men around just then, return to Fort St. George, take the ship back to London. But what was there at home except disappointment to embrace? His every possession, money and reputation, was invested in this India adventure.

'Francis!' Richard pushed his pencils aside as the boy walked in with a cup of steaming tea. 'What do you think?' He pulled up a sketch and held it under the candlelight. 'Francis?'

Francis hesitated. He had no way of knowing, nor did he care, how good an artist his paymaster was. The man was holding up a few lines that suggested a bloated cow and wanted to know if his teenage attendant liked it; a child seeking approval, so fragile, in anticipation, in hope.

'Nice, very nice,' muttered Francis and began to inch towards the tent flap. It was late in the evening and they had walked miles through slushy forest pathways. He still had to check on the provisions for the next day's cooking, make sure the servants were settled in without any brawls or mischief, and then eat his own solitary meal beside the dying embers of the stove that heated water for the master's wash.

And this? Richard felt encouraged to pull out an oil sketch he had made of one of the village children who had been brave enough to venture close to their camp the previous day, watching him work from behind the security of a rock. He felt particularly proud of the expression that had been captured in the young eyes, the curiosity and the impishness, and only by a few scratches in the iris...

'Also nice,' Francis assured him.

Richard gave up with a sigh. 'Is there any news?'

Francis shook his head. The letter had been sent and they were now waiting to hear from the killedar of Nandidurga, hoping that the man for whom the letter was addressed was still the one holding the fort. There was no way of knowing. Their safety depended on the wait being as short as possible. News would soon travel to Srirangapatna, detailing the audacity of a wandering party of men led by an Englishman. The open land on one side of their camp left them exposed to attacks and the dense forest on the other was infested with wild animals. Two men had to stay on guard all night and yet some bandits managed to sneak into the camp in the dark and make away with whatever livestock and copper pots they found. Richard worried less about bandits or animals than the dreaded dungeons of Srirangapatna that were more likely to be his immediate fate. If Cole's plan failed ... which Richard did not dare consider, for there was no returning now, nothing to do except move ahead. What would they do if Havelock's letter to the killedar was lost or not considered worthy of a reply?

Through the inertia of the morning sun, the heaviness of the steady downpours, the morbid aches of the afternoon, the sting of evenings, there was nothing else to do but wait.

When the rains briefly cleared, the Englishman's camp had a clear view of the landscape, a few scraggly hillocks scattered across flat land. Most of them were natural hill forts with hardly any water on them but making perfect stores for ammunition and supplies during war or natural duress. Nandidurga was the greener and more thriving fort with ample water supply. Tipu Sultan had built his summer palace at the very top where he could enjoy the coolness of the altitude and survey the open countryside he lorded over. It was like staring at a den bereft of the tiger, but no less terrifying.

It was then that Richard began thinking about the quality of waiting. The sketchbooks began to be filled with ideas that he scribbled with words rather than shapes. He began to think of a painting that would capture the pain and agony of waiting, the glimmer of hope as well, the possibility of the wait ripening into desired rewards. A great big canvas filled with an image that would literally lean out of the frame, heavy and ponderous, patiently waiting like nobody had ever waited in art before. A woman was emerging in the big vertical frame he was adjusting in his mind. Her hand stretched over something, pausing in the middle of labour. Her face filled with anxiety and uncertainty of the wait for her beloved who was far away, probably even dead. She had to wait to be sure of his fate, as also her own. And while she did, she would have to fight lust and avarice, the faces of greedy men peeking in through distant windows, wanting to convince her that she was a widow. A woman at the loom, patiently weaving despite the burden of love and waiting. She belonged to tradition as much as she belonged to Richard, and she was waiting. Penelope waiting.

'Mukunda, my boy, my dear boy,' my uncle said, trying to find the right words, stymied by his lack of experience in dealing with rebellious youngsters. 'It is not as though I do not understand. I do...'

My mother has often called her own brother a soft-spine dreamer but I thought he was doing better than my own father who had many more years to practise his parenting on me. I pretended not to pay attention and continued to sulk under the air of being misunderstood. I had not wanted to come here but after days of wandering with no plan and eating in temples, I had thought of the uncle in Nandidurga.

His wife banged pots in the kitchen. She had made it clear that if I was planning to outstay my unplanned visit longer, I was not bringing her any joy. Mother called her a witch and one who deserved to be barren. It is strange, I thought now, that she did not consider her brother being impotent. Or if she did, it would have been too much of a betrayal to say so. In her world, the women are always to blame.

Uncle paced around me, said his home was as much mine as his, that he has responsibilities as a brother, that my mother would be worried, that we would need to send word immediately about me being safe here with them.

'We need to send him back,' his wife shouted to correct his choice of words.

'You can throw me out if you wish,' I told him calmly, 'but I will never go home. There is nothing there for me.'

'I am waiting to serve dinner,' she called out, clearly making it out to be a distasteful task that she wanted done immediately. I don't like anything she makes, not even the water she boils.

'Let us eat, my boy,' my uncle said, putting a kindly hand on my shoulders, 'my boy, my boy' – still struggling for words – 'Let us eat and talk.'

Uncle glanced nervously between his wife and me, but neither of us indulged him. He made little sighing sounds every now and then, shuffling the rice around on the plantain leaf with his fingers and looked relieved when I did not ask for the second helping that had not been offered. I walked out to wash my hands in the yard. For the first time in days, there was no rain to avoid.

The night had grown large, ripened, turned fragrant. Little nameless flowers were blooming on the hillside. I washed my hands and wiped it on the length of white cloth wrapped around my waist. I looked up at the sky. Clouds swathed the stars but the moon shone without a care. I could not help leaning over the edge of the well and as expected it was brimming over with a silvery blue moonlight.

This was a yard and a well I had known from my boyhood. And I was there because it was the only other place I knew beside the river island, from the few occasions when my mother decided to visit her own aged mother and brother. I was then a little boy. Mother would tuck me under her left arm, propelling me forward, while carrying a bundle of our clothes under the other. She would bubble over with talk and laughter. She would point out little insects hidden in the grass as we walked and talk of the most wondrous artist of all, god. Back in her mother's house, she wanted so much to be proud of me, her only surviving child, but that was not easy around my aunt who had not managed to produce even one. Faults were picked in me, in the guise of good-humoured ribbing – my unruly hair, my uneven teeth, my dreamy gait. Worse of all, a tear in my new shirt I had made that very day, not giving Mother enough time to mend it. We would stay on and let ourselves be scrutinized for a few days even as I bounced around the hillside with neighbourhood boys my age. Very soon, Mother would have red eyes from crying about her hard-hearted relatives and would be ready to go back to where she was definitely needed. We would silently make our way across the plains to get back home, where she felt consoled that the kitchen fires would not burn without her, god and those wondrous creations not discussed anymore.

On rainy days, when father went away to discuss the affairs of the land with his old friends, mother and I, just the two of us, listened to the rain on the rooftop. 'You are my sun, you are my moon,' she would whisper. Her long fingers would dig into my hair, rub my scalp with warm sesame oil and she would sing of the gold trapped within a full-grown harvest. Sometimes I hummed along. Oh, how she must weep for me now!

'Let him sleep outside. He is a man now. Pity. Yes, I pity the poor girl who is stuck with someone like this for a husband.' My aunt slammed the door shut as soon as her husband stepped out to join me.

'My boy, I was young too once. I know life is not fair, not easy, and never sympathetic to the dreams of a young man.' He became more articulate with a full belly. I didn't want to listen to him but he wouldn't stop talking. 'Yes, I was young too. And I dreamt of running away. Your aunt is a good woman, but she never learnt how to let a man be, to let him simply lie in the starlight and listen to the crickets. One day, you would not believe this, she told me…'

'I am leaving tomorrow,' I announced, turning my back on his hurt face. I wished the old man would go back to the wife or, better still, finally bring himself to run away too.

'No, no, my boy, you misunderstand me. I was going to suggest that you should take up a job. I could use an assistant priest in the temple. It is not much of a living but people are generous with their offerings. I am sure your father has trained you well...'

'I cannot remember any prayers or chants. I like to paint.'

He was aghast. 'Painting? It is a messy and inferior work that any idiot can do. Suitable work for the lower castes, not you. How fortunate you are that you have been blessed with such opportunities to read all the knowledge given by Brahma himself!'

'I will leave as soon as it is morning,' I informed him and added with false bravado, 'I can even leave right now.'

'Will you go back home?'

No, I said, and that worried him very much. My mother was not one to be polite if she knew I had come to him and that he had let me wander off into the unknown. Uncle tried to placate me. 'I have heard of this white man, a painter, who is camping outside the fort. He wants to come up here and paint. The killedar is very worried and indeed he should be.'

White painter. Black night. I don't want to know. Leave me alone.

Mukunda peeked curiously into the tent. The wind slipped away from the clutches of the trees into his crumpled dhoti, caressed his sculpted thighs, created white flutters. Perhaps it was the wind that had willed him to leave the road that led to his uncle's house, to walk towards this cluster of tents, to find this white man submerged in a spread of dyes, oblivious to everything else.

Richard pounded at an intense red mixture, hesitantly added a few pellets of ochre, pounded some more, shook his head in dissatisfaction and worked the pestle harder. Still dissatisfied, he looked into his box of supplies with the brushes, the oils, the small boxes of colour – some finely powdered, some still clumpy inside their leather pouches – and began to pull everything out, scattering them around his feet. He looked up abruptly and frowned when he saw the young man staring at him from the flap of the tent. Richard straightened up and wiped his hands on a rag.

'Francis! Francis!'

Mukunda looked around to see what the yell produced. Francis sleepily emerged from behind him, tucking his shirt ends into his breeches. He stood between the two men, to be the bridge between languages.

'I am the astrologer's son. I would like to work for you.'

'I am sorry, but I have no work to give.'

Mukunda strode across the room, in his easy manner, the one that often earned him the Master's ire back at the artists' colony: Where is the humility, boy? Where is the surrender to god? What is a craftsman without divine benediction?

Richard and Francis looked at each other, puzzled. Francis said, breaking away from the shadow of Richard's voice, 'Hey you, what do you think you are doing?'

Mukunda did not respond. He sat down on the floor, crossed his leg decisively, pulled a sheet of paper from the folder that Richard had left lying, brought out a piece of charcoal from his pocket and began to calmly draw as if the audience had melted away. He started on what seemed the leg of a horse but soon became a restless snake and finally an abstract floral pattern. Lines became circles, waves, arrows, spirals. Everything then got encased in two square boxes. His fingers dashed around the page. Butterflies in the sun.

Richard knelt down to watch more closely, fascinated. The astrologer's son was an artist! A strange fellow with hands so certain of themselves…

The charcoal diminished into the growing blackness around Mukunda's fingers. Nearly done. The paper quivered.

'That's … that's wonderful! But I regret … I might have use for an assistant but only to help with odd jobs, maybe mix paints, maybe fill in some colour on the canvas (within lines I have drawn, nothing more, mind you, nothing of your own) … but maybe you should think it over … you might not want to waste your time or talent...'

'I do.'

'I cannot pay much…'

'I will take whatever you give me.'

'Don't hire him, sir.' Francis grabbed Richard's arm and pulled him aside. 'He is too proud.'

'I like him, Francis. He has reason to be proud. He has talent.'

'But he has come from nowhere, and we still don't know what the killedar is going to decide about us. How do we trust him? And he does not say much…'

'He showed me his work, the best recommendation he could bring, and good workers don't talk much,' Richard assured him. 'Tell him why we are here and what we plan to do. Tell him the situation is all uncertain and maybe even dangerous. But tell him also that I admire his work and hope I too can learn from him. Maybe we can mutually benefit from the association.'

Francis scowled but translated as he was told. Knowing the boy to be either desperate or worldly stupid, he fixed the working terms for food and board for three copper coins every month. Then he sauntered off to attend to his other managerial troubles. The poultry cage was in serious need of repairs and the cook claimed that another sack of onions was missing. His troubles were unending. If it were not for the wide blue eyes of the artist, completely trusting and depending on him, he too would have bolted like the dubash long ago, Francis told himself. Richard called out his gratitude behind Francis's back while Mukunda stepped in gingerly. He stopped at the bowls with the colours and bent over to inspect them.

'We need to find a way to communicate. You and me. How much English do you understand?'

Mukunda peered into the tall canister of oil. Smiled at his reflection. It was yellow. Then turned to his new employer curiously. What was he saying?

Richard was thinking aloud. Maybe Francis could give Mukunda a few lessons each day. Impatient and bossy, Francis was not the best of teachers, but he would oblige for a few extra coins.

Mukunda looked at him with happy uncomprehending eyes.

'Go away now,' Richard said, gesticulating impatiently. 'We will start tomorrow.' Mukunda stepped out into the sun.

His uncle, sapped from the heat, now sprang to life and bounded across the street to greet him. He felt fatherly, concerned and proud. What would his sister say, if she knew that he had found the boy a job with prospects? It was not work that their dead ancestors or gossipy relatives would heartily approve of, but he did not see how this wild spirited boy would sit in temples to read prayers, or pour over horoscopes like his father. It was much too bizarre even to imagine. The wife would be proud of him too, their uninvited visitor would be packing his few belongings and moving out today. Everything was working out just fine, just fine. He put his arm around his nephew and tried to match his long stride. It was not as hard as folks made it out to be, to bring up a boy in the world.

Francis hurried into the tent, short of breath – their messenger had returned from the fort! The killedar of Nandidurga had exchanged letters with Tipu Sultan and the intruders had been ordered to present themselves in the capital to make their intentions clear to the royal court without further delay.

Their belongings were tossed into bullock carts within the hour and set moving south. Mukunda, caught in the moving frenzy, was unable to break away and state his unwillingness to return home so soon after running away. His destiny, he thought, was against him, and not worth resisting. He was now in the Englishman's pay.

He tried to make himself useful but the other workers found out about his Brahmin identity and kept a deferential distance. Only Francis seemed to not care, even looked down on him, and Mukunda gratefully accepted his disdain.

The Englishman's party arrived at the outskirts of the Srirangapatna fort just as the sun dipped into the horizon and the landscape turned a dusty blur. The Kaveri was in spate from the rains and the choppy boat ride to the island had not gone down well with the travellers. Nausea battled with hunger and won. They collapsed sullenly in the abandoned stone granary they were shown to. Two tight-lipped sentries on the street kept a constant watch. Richard Dawson was now living just a few yards away from Tipu Sultan.

BOOK THREE

A Royal Audience

Lal Mahal was a double-storeyed red building that housed administrative offices and important state officials in its outer walls, and the royal living quarters and harem deep in its recess. A courtyard enclosed by pillared corridors functioned as a waiting room for petitioners, traders and officials from distant parts of the kingdom who sat against the edge of the raised floor of the corridors, speaking in stray whispers, battling terror more than boredom. For at the entrance of the room that led to the inner enclosure, where the Sultan gave audience, were three cheetahs on long iron chains. The creatures were tamed, it was whispered, and used by the Sultan during his hunting expeditions. They sprawled out for naps like house cats and stretched indolently when their caretakers were around, but were also known to make lightning swipes for no apparent reason.

For the Englishman, his new assistant and the translator, it was a wait more indefinite and fearsome than any other they had known before, and stretched to three days. Each dawn they returned to wait in the courtyard till they were turned out into the streets at dusk, no reason given. It was becoming impossible to enjoy a meal or sleep through the night. They were sick with worry. The faces waiting in the courtyard kept changing but the uneasiness around the cheetahs was still the same.

On the fourth day, Francis, who had fallen asleep against a pillar, found himself plodded awake by Richard. What was it? Had they been summoned?

'No, but shouldn't you go and find out? Why were we called here in such a hurry only to be ignored? I can't stand this waiting anymore. If he wants me dead or put behind bars or even fed to these beasts here, I would like to hear of it right now. Why must we wait entire days like this?'

'I don't know. I have made enquiries and they don't tell me anything.'

'Well, then ask them one more time.'

'I have asked and asked, and nobody really knows. Our cook who chanced to have a conversation with the royal barber says that there have been some important political developments that preoccupy the Sultan. Or maybe he is frolicking in the harem. Who is to say? None of the courtiers or administrative staff wants to be seen publicly speaking to us till the Sultan has announced his intentions. I am sorry, sir, but I don't think there is anything to do but wait.'

Behind them, Mukunda jumped up and ducked behind the pillar. Richard dropped his pencil. A spindly man with large intelligent eyes strode across them and headed towards the administrative wing. The petitioners bowed to him and he talked rapidly to a few among them and they responded by touching his feet. He looked directly at Richard, though only for an instant. Richard smiled tentatively but the man walked away with a deadpan expression.

Mukunda slowly emerged from behind the pillar. 'Purnaiah, an uncle,' he explained, 'very distant uncle.'

What is he doing here? Francis translated Mukunda's harried reply with his own asides. 'Purnaiah is the second-most important man in the government after the Dewan and heads the department of military accounts and supply. Both Haider and Tipu have trusted him unconditionally. Apparently a genius for making money as well as military strategies, and who happens to be an uncle of our friend here. And all this time you have been harassing *me* to gather information!'

Richard coaxed Mukunda. 'Why don't you ask him what the Sultan intends for us?'

Mukunda shook his head and sat apart from them, hugging his knees. Francis explained to Richard that Mukunda did not want his people to know he was at the palace.

'Well, how long does he think it will stay a secret on this pea-sized island? It would not hurt our cause if a bit of family connections came into play.'

Francis did not communicate this nor did he have his own speculations to add. He merely closed his eyes and pretended to go back to sleep. Richard pulled out his sketching pad and began to draw the cheetahs, first as little studies, a ear, a hind leg, an attentive tail, repeating them again and again till the lines began to pulsate and his hands ran through the entire length of a cheetah looking out of the page. He straightened himself and looked at the image. It did not seem quite right. He flicked it aside impatiently. Mukunda deftly caught the paper before it slid down to the floor. He went over to his little cloth bag kept behind the pillar and pulled out a piece of dry ochre pigment. Richard smiled indulgently as Mukunda filled in the ochre, rolling it with such deftness inside the creature's face that it seemed to twitch with life.

A curious courtier had bravely ventured closer to look at the sketch and make little appreciative chuckles.

'Francis, Francis,' Richard said in a soft voice, trying to mask the urgency, 'quick, talk to this man before he flees. Maybe the Sultan has not yet been informed that we are waiting here.'

The courtier merrily assured them that they did not have to worry about that. Oh no, the Sultan knows everything that happens in his palace, his court, his capital, his kingdom. He knows very well they were waiting. They wait because he wants it that way.

Mukunda thrust the sketch of the cheetah into the courtier's hands. Can this somehow be passed on to the Sultan? Richard tried to protest. 'No, not this rough sketch!' Francis looked at Mukunda with new respect, the boy had an idea that might work, and urged the courtier to take the paper. The courtier quickly grabbed it and disappeared inside the building.

Richard decided to write a letter and smoothed a fresh paper on his lap. Francis had recently managed to make contact with one of the Banjareys, the wandering tribe that carried on mercantile dealings between the kingdoms, often smuggling goods and organizing mobile markets for armies on the march. Sometimes, for a good price, they would also sneak letters to the enemy camp, even the English fort in Madras. If caught, execution was certain, but they were much too clever for that and found ingenious ways to hide the letters.

'Why do you have to write now? Don't you realize that every move of ours is being watched?' Francis was saying to him.

'This letter is for my friend Jonathan Cole who works at the Customs House in Fort St. George. It has been nearly two months since we left and nobody knows that we are alive and safe...'

'Alive ... for how much longer?' Francis muttered under his breath.

Just then the earth beneath their feet began to vibrate to rapidly approaching horse hooves. Everyone looked at each other nervously as the riding became more urgent and closer. The cheetahs sprang to their feet and paced around in circles. Through the big gates of the palace burst a man wrapped in layers of fabric from which a long scabbard jutted out, his face hidden by a turban tied low. He panted noisily as Purnaiah appeared in the centre of the courtyard. The rider quickly dropped a scroll into the minister's outstretched hands. The destiny of nations was curled up inside, signed by Napoleon Bonaparte; his army had just captured Malta and was headed for Alexandria; tracing the footsteps of his hero Alexander the Great, he wanted to conquer his way to India. Everyone watched in silence as Purnaiah held the scroll tightly and marched into the inner chambers of Tipu Sultan.

'Bow low, as low as your breeches allow, apply genuine deference but with character, then swoop up quickly, but not too quickly, keep your back straight, shoulders slightly hunched, let the gaze stay low but definitely attempt one memorable meeting of the eyes, no matter what is seen or heard, make sure that you neither flinch nor stare, speak up but not until he speaks to you first, wait, but do not fidget, breathe evenly for he has disdain for fear and he has scorn for arrogance in any man but himself, and yet he needs to know there is submission and acceptance of his greatness, even the pillars in his court shall judge and inspect, so whatever words come forth from your lips may they be the truth, hold on to your heart, hold on to your conscience, Tipu Sultan has decided to see you.'

Francis announced that he did not think he could go through the ordeal and slumped on the floor, breathless, eyes bulging as anxiety tightened his throat. Richard and Mukunda bent over him, each grabbing an arm. Francis felt his feet lift off the ground, thrash in the air, and buckle as it touched earth again.

'I cannot do it,' he whimpered, face turning sallow.

Richard looked at him in disbelief. He had grown used to Francis taking charge of their affairs and making them feel they would be utterly lost without him.

'You cannot leave me in the lurch now,' Richard whispered furiously to Francis as the guards waiting to escort them to court stepped closer, their mild amusement slowly turning into impatience. Tipu Sultan did not like to be made to wait.

The artist tried a different tone, more persuasive, gentle. 'He is a man, just like you and me, Francis, not a monster. Most of what we heard are rumours, fanciful stories. If he has to kill anyone, it will be me, the Englishman. You are my translator, mere hired help, every word from your lips are mine or they shall be his, not your own. Come, come, Francis, be professional.'

Francis turned to the wall and refused to move. Richard grabbed Mukunda's hand. 'We have to leave him here. You come with me. Surely the court has an English translator? We will manage. We have to.'

After avoiding his family and acquaintances assiduously since his return, Mukunda was now being asked to make a public appearance in the court. He hesitated briefly and then nodded. Perhaps this was the best way for everyone to find out how far he had wandered away from their notions of respectability, how much he was his own man. They let Francis sink back to the floor.

Mukunda thought of his father as he stepped across the threshold of the palace and silently followed the guards, almost feeling Richard's heart thumping in his palms. His own heart was calm. Father would be horrified to him see walk beside a white man into the royal presence. Almost from the moment of his birth, his father had wished to teach him the horoscope trade till he was good enough to be led into the imperial presence and be introduced as heir to the family's treasure of knowledge. Twice a month, at the change of the moon's cycle, the astrologers of the court gathered in the Sultan's presence, his father trying hard to blend in, hoping no question would be directly addressed to him, and that their many predictions pleased the Sultan into making generous endowments.

Mukunda walked now, not as that man's son, but as himself. He had a job that came from his abilities and not from his father's blood. The painter's apprentice.

They entered a hall with high painted ceilings and covered with thick Persian carpets. People stood on both sides of the hall, the more important officials seated around the raised platform at the far end, atop which sat the man they had waited to meet. Tipu Sultan was nothing like they had imagined from his reputation. He was rather comely looking, neither tall nor short, but middling. His skin, the colour of darkening wheat sheaves. Clean-shaven, with an aquiline nose, dreamy eyes and a thin moustache that curled up at the edges, he was dressed elegantly in a white muslin cloak, white drawers, wearing a string of white pearls around his neck and a white turban with a single white feather.

'And who is the boy?' Tipu Sultan's powerful eyes had hypnotically lingered on his face. His name was asked and then his father's, both echoed loudly in the royal audience hall.

The court interpreter explained. 'An artist, Your Highness, one who has flowered in your own backyard. The Englishman calls him a gifted assistant and bends low in gratitude for all that this beautiful land has to offer, especially your infinite generosity.'

Mukunda looked at the Sultan's face for recognition of his father's name but none was forthcoming. The Sultan had shifted his gaze to the Englishman. Mukunda felt sorry for his father, the old braggart, talking about his service to the great Tipu Sultan, flaunting his royal visits to all his relatives and neighbours, and trying the hardest to impress his son who now stood before the court to finally learn how undistinguished his father was.

Everyone in the hall was looking at them but Mukunda felt a different intensity from two pair of eyes. Purnaiah's revealed little, neither the ties of kinship nor the surprise at seeing the boy turn up in court under the present circumstances. Mir Sadiq, however, was biting his lips and scowling at him. It had taken him a little while to connect this face with that of the young artist who had come to draw his boys. So that inefficient imbecile had shifted from the artists' colony to the intruder's side! Mukunda glanced at both the ministers by turn, hoping fervently that neither would speak up in a situation already volatile and in which the Englishman's life hung by a thread. Perhaps his own as well.

The Sultan was having his doubts. 'Does the Englishman come with a message? Or does he dare think I can be hoodwinked into taking in a spy?'

'He has not been sent by anybody and he does not betray a house that shelters him. He comes on his own initiative. He seeks work. He desires your patronage. He pleads for your trust. He may be English but he thinks of himself only as an artist. A seeker of truth and beauty that is not limited by boundaries of countries, that resides in the hearts of all people.'

'Have the English gone so bankrupt that their painters have to crawl to enemy camp for alms?' Laughter echoed in the court. Tipu leaned forward, an elbow resting on a thigh and eyes narrowed at the visitors. The laughter abruptly died out.

'What do you think we should do with him?' Tipu Sultan asked his council of ministers and their leader Mir Sadiq did not hesitate with his answer. 'Death for unauthorized intrusion into the Mysore kingdom and for daring to think everyone here was stupid enough to believe that all this risk had been taken to make paintings. Was there nothing else left in the world to paint?'

Mukunda did not dare look up. He tucked his chin and hid his eyes behind the curls that tumbled down from his forehead. All he had to do now was to grab Richard's arm and dash out of there. They would probably not even make it to the gate, swords and spears of a dozen guards sticking into their flesh, but if they did, he would never make the mistake of walking back into this miserable island. He cursed himself for having been lured back by the watery noose of the river. And this Tipu Sultan was now going to pronounce their death sentence.

'And what does the French General think?' Tipu turned to the only other white men in the court, his French officers. Pierre Chapuis bowed and announced that the French troops believed that His Highness would take the best decision for all of them. Mukunda looked beyond Chapuis, to the kind face of his friend Andre Surcouf, who silently mouthed a message that the young man guessed at once. Go home. Mukunda looked away rebelliously.

Tipu Sultan was picking up a piece of paper from the little tray on his side, a mischievous smile on his face. Even from the distance, Richard could see the familiar lines of his own pencil.

'You chose the right messenger to send to me. This cheetah is dear to me and it now protects your life. I think lowly of your countrymen but since you have picked your identity so carefully and wisely, we shall look at your gifts for what they are. The Khudadad Sarkar,' he tapped his chest as if his entire kingdom were contained within him, 'understands that an empire needs its artists as much as it needs its farmers, its physicians or its administrators. We need to nourish beauty for men to believe in their souls, just as food nourishes their bodies. You can be our servant, paint at our bidding and for our pleasure, and we shall do you the honour of forgetting the taint of your contemptible homeland on your brow.'

'My home is where my feet are…'

'Do you think he cares? Do not interrupt!' the interpreter growled at Richard under his breath. 'Shut up and listen…'

Tipu Sultan looked at Mukunda. 'Take the Englishman to our Master Artist. Let him become familiar with our art, the extraordinary workmanship that we encourage and protect in our land. Take him also to our summer palace and show him the beautiful wall paintings our people have made. Keep a close eye on him. Teach him to live within the fence of our hospitality, in fear and gratitude.'

Mukunda bent in silent assent, his ears warm with self-importance, for the Sultan was now speaking to him. 'You work for the white painter, but remember that your life belongs to me. Is your master only good enough for copying chained animals or is his brush brave enough for some live action?'

Richard was told that he had been given the honour of making illustrations for the Sultan. The royal party on the cheetah hunt.

'I have never done anything like that before,' Richard whispered to the interpreter. 'I could try some sketches on the hunt and make the actual painting later, when we get back … but I have to admit that this is not what I do best. I am a portraitist.'

The court interpreter turned to him in exasperation and whispered, 'You do what you are told. I am now going to do you the biggest favour and save your skin by not repeating that.'

'Does the Englishman question our generosity?' Tipu's forehead folded.

'No, no, Your Highness, he feels extreme gratitude and enthusiasm at being allowed to capture the glorious hunting party and Your Highness's famed expertise as hunter in his drawings.'

The Sultan picked up a small cloth bag from the tray placed beside him. It jingled with coins. He held it out towards Richard who looked puzzled.

'I am a fair man and believe in paying my servants,' the Sultan said, narrowing his eyes.

Mukunda held his breath. The courtiers looked at each other smugly, always pleased to be present at a public humiliation that involved somebody else. Richard turned to the interpreter who was silent. What did the Sultan just say? The interpreter casually looked away as if his work were done. The bag of coins still dangled in the Sultan's hands. Richard stepped forward and took it from him, bowing as he did.

The audience was declared over by a wave of the Sultan's hand and Richard found them hustled towards the door. On their way out of the palace complex, they retrieved a dour Francis at the palace gates. He had been shocked by his own cowardice but pretended it was more a physical affliction, the nameless kind that descends in strange climates without warning.

They walked back to their stone dwelling in silence, both Francis and Mukunda worrying about how the recent turn of events would affect their lives. Richard could hardly believe that the meeting had taken place and with such wondrous outcome. It had almost been too good to believe, but there they were, in possession of both freedom and life, a little bag of coins nicely warming his pocket and spirits.

Between Shadows

'Life is terrifying. Death is terrifying. So long as death continues to be more terrifying of the two, I shall live...'

'It is not our decision to take. The gods...'

'The gods have all gone deaf and the prayers are drying up in my heart.'

Purnaiah stood in the outer chambers and readjusted his turban. He did not look directly at the drapes but was aware of the couch on its other side and the form sprawled on it. He had heard the Queen for years but had never known this tone of resignation before. He became impatient to finish his assignment and leave. 'The Sultan was concerned to receive your letter about the illness raging in the house. He sent me to make sure that you are well and that everything is taken care of. The royal physician has been put at your disposal and the guard posted at the door will fetch him any time you wish.'

'So he sent you to check if we will die from our misery and spare him the trouble of putting us to death...'

Purnaiah stepped closer to the drapes and tried to reason. 'Tipu Sultan has great respect for the Wodeyar family ... He is concerned...'

'Respect! Is that what they call imprisonment and untold humiliation these days in the royal court? But you are no stranger to my household, dear minister, do step in and take a seat and enjoy the little hospitality that we still dare offer here.'

Purnaiah shuffled impatiently. The old shrew, he thought peevishly, is getting exactly what she wants, a private interview with me with the official consent of the Sultan. Only, she is not going to talk illness or the life expectancy of the men in her family but something else. He was curious but not too eager to find out. There was bound to be trouble. He could hear the guards breathing outside the door and straining to catch every word being spoken. An impossible situation. He nodded at the woman attendant standing at a respectable distance, watching him with large frightened eyes. She came forward and parted the curtains. He stepped ahead while she quickly secured the doors behind him.

Purnaiah readjusted his turban. He had not made it that far up the administration without first learning to keep worry hidden under a veneer of inscrutability.

Lakshmi Ammani was not alone, as he had expected. There was a young woman standing in the shadows, her gold bangles flashing in the single droopy ray of light that had pushed through a crack in the closed window shutters. Purnaiah kept his eyes on the Queen who was covered in a quilt and propped up by many pillows, looking far from unwell. Yet they both knew the pretence had to be kept.

'I am sorry to hear Your Majesty is keeping poor health...'

'Well, at least you have the decency to still consider me a queen even though I have nothing to be a queen over, not even this prison of a house that your master has cunningly cornered us in. You have not forgotten that you were once on my husband's payroll, so what if you are now licking the shoes of an ingrate...'

'Your Majesty is angry...'

'Purnaiah, you would be angry too if your family was robbed of all respect, possession and freedom. I don't expect my people to die for me, but it hurts to see them frolic in the enemy camp ... I am disappointed in you.'

'I too have a family, Your Majesty, one that I have to feed and keep alive.'

The Queen rolled her eyes. 'Oh, don't expect me to sympathize! You are blessed with rare intelligence and the heart of a fox. You have no real masters or loyalties except your own skin and—'

'Your Majesty is wise,' Purnaiah interrupted her politely. 'I have done my duty in checking on your well-being. Can I meet the young prince? I would like to pay my respects and express our deep concerns for his health.'

'Purnaiah, do you honestly believe that Tipu Sultan will survive this rising storm? His foolish political alliances are leading to the most gruesome death a man can plan for himself. Your Sultan will fall, Purnaiah, and he will fall hard – that is certainly willed by the gods. You are a wise man and surely hear the approaching footsteps of his destiny. What will you do then? The people still love and respect my family as their rightful rulers. The young Wodeyar will ascend the throne and will require wise counsel from experienced statesmen, and I am sure he will think of you first for that honour, to be his reliable Regent…' She lowered her voice till it was barely audible. Purnaiah kept his eyes on the floor and bent forward to catch her words. The Queen paused dramatically and then laughed as if at a joke. 'But of course why would such a position interest you? You are already a wonderful servant to a powerful ruler … how silly of me to daydream like this…'

An uneasy coughing was heard outside the door where the guards began to show their resentment to it being closed. The Queen clapped her hands and the attendant appeared nervously at the door. She ordered that the poor guards standing out in the damp weather be offered some tea, with milk if there was any to spare, and a bit of jaggery perhaps, for the Wodeyars would rather starve themselves than treat their guests poorly.

Purnaiah was sitting back, deep in thought. His face was still reticent as when he had walked in but now many possibilities and calculations were gathering in his eyes. Lakshmi deeply inhaled her own satisfaction. She smiled at the person behind her and for the second time Purnaiah felt his eyes drawn to the watchful gold bangles there. Who was this other woman? Was she one of the other queens in the house? Since when did Lakshmi trust someone else with her machinations? There was no illness here and yet he had been summoned under the urgent pretext of one. Why?

'With the grace of Lord Sriranga the young prince will recover soon and have a long illustrious life. Maybe I should take your leave now.' Purnaiah stirred in his seat, not intending to go but trying to force the game out in the open.

'I heard there was an Englishman summoned to your master's court...'

Purnaiah now knew why. He nodded guardedly.

'What happened? Why is he here?'

The man's eyes darted to the hidden shape breathing softly in the corner. Lakshmi impatiently gathered her shawl and held out her hands to invite the other presence to sit beside her. 'Suhasini visits me and reads the scriptures to give me some peace during my troubled days of sickness. I trust her as if she were my own daughter. You can be reassured that she will not repeat anything that is said in here.'

Suhasini did not move but retreated further towards the wall where the minister could not even be sure if she was still in the room.

Purnaiah hesitated. The Queen was nodding her reassurance again. He decided there was no harm in telling her what every man in court knew. 'The Englishman is a painter. He is not an official emissary. He says he has come here on his own accord. The Sultan has decided to give him some work to do and see if he is any good.'

'It sounded improbable that a foreigner would wander into enemy territory on a whim or that Tipu would treat the matter so leniently.' Lakshmi did not like to be treated like a simpleton. Her anger began to fill in the silence between them. 'I would like to meet him myself and talk to him.'

It was an order. Purnaiah did not point out that she was trapped in her little house and he was an emissary from her jailor. He understood the pride of those born into power, born or married, just as he knew his own particular talent, to become indispensable to anyone in power.

'I don't think that is wise,' he cautioned. 'It is not easy to say what the Sultan is thinking and how long before the visitor is imprisoned. But if he is seen here, it is going to be death for everyone, for him as well as your whole family, including the young prince. It will be considered treason for you to meet anyone, let alone a suspicious Englishman.'

'The only treacherous one around here is that upstart.' Lakshmi's voice hardened with hatred. 'That son of a horseman calling himself an emperor.'

Son of a horseman, no doubt, thought the minister, but also a fine scholar, a man of science, an innovate administrator working long hours to revive local industries, promoting trade, building accountability in governance. A gifted man. A man of action with grand plans for his people that Purnaiah did not think the last Wodeyar king could have even imagined, leave alone attempted. But Tipu Sultan had his faults, grave ones, and could certainly not be called a hero in front of his victims. Lakshmi was in the right to curse him all she wanted.

Purnaiah heard the guards get restless again outside and thought of Tipu waiting for his report. What would he tell him? Naturally what he wanted to hear – there was an infectious illness in the Wodeyar household but it wasn't critical.

Purnaiah stood up to go. Suhasini leaned towards the Queen and said something to her very softly. Purnaiah stared hard at the sharp profile, the quick flash of thinking eyes and the natural poise. This was not just a casual visitor to the household and he made a mental note to investigate further. Lakshmi smiled and tilted her head, suggesting that the minister sit down again. She was consciously putting aside her regal demeanour for the more friendly approach. They were both in the same game now and he made his move with equal grace. If she could be humble enough, maybe his magnanimity would not be found wanting. He sat down.

'You know how we women love to gossip and I am sure you will indulge our idle minds. Someone in the harem was heard talking about Tipu Sultan receiving an important letter all the way from Afghanistan. Suhasini and I have been playing a little betting game between us trying to wonder what it might possibly say and of course only you can settle it for us. I hope I will win because I can scarcely afford to lose anymore of my little allowance to these smarter younger women. Well, so about the letter, I said to Suhasini here, "Zaman Shah is surely tired of being ruler of just Afghanistan and is going to look for territory in India. In return, Tipu gets an ally against the British." I would hate to be wrong…'

Purnaiah smiled back slyly. 'Your Majesty is going to be lucky this time with the bet. Zaman Shah is just about to march south of Afghanistan with his armies.'

'So I won!' Lakshmi arched her eyebrows at both of them and continued in the false jovial voice, 'I might just as well, since I lost my last bet about the great French General coming with his armies over the seas.'

'You accepted your defeat too soon then. The general or his army is not yet here…'

'You are right,' she lowered her voice, 'and I hear that a secret embassy from Tipu has set sail with Monsieur Duboc to make sure he does…'

Purnaiah rose slowly from his seat and adjusted his turban. He stared at the women, saying nothing, and they knew it to be an affirmation.

Lakshmi stood up as a sign of gratitude. 'Purnaiah, I know you are a good man and that you would have been true to my family if our men had not been spineless and let the kingdom slip through their fingers…'

'The Wodeyars have done right by our people for many hundreds of years, Your Majesty,' he said kindly.

'Then, you will organize an audience with the Englishman? It will be done very discreetly. Nobody needs to ever know your part in it. The life of a little boy, your true king, hangs in balance.'

Purnaiah wondered what the Queen might want with the stranger. He suddenly remembered the young man who had stood beside the Englishman in court, the only child of a cousin, a troublemaker who had strangely managed to turn up on the wrong side of the fence. He decided to arrange for the meeting, but in a way that could not be traced back to him. This was a favour he was doing for himself, just in case history decided that the young prince would someday be his king. He bowed low, his eyes staying on Lakshmi's face long enough for her to know that he would do her bidding, and was quickly gone from the room.

A Shade Yellow

Richard was reluctantly beginning to see that Francis had a point. The young Indian who had seduced him with the flair of his charcoal and his dark mysterious eyes was more trouble than help. They were still waiting to hear from the court about the hunting expedition when Richard decided to prepare himself for the assignment by making their living quarters an art studio as well. He tried to explain this to Mukunda while Francis sat grumpily in a corner chewing strong tobacco that made Richard's stomach turn. He had often forbidden Francis to come near him reeking of the stuff but did not wish to have another confrontation on his hands today. He tried to focus on the new apprentice.

'What do you mean no oil painting?'

Francis coolly chewed on. 'He says he has no idea about painting with oils. They just don't do them here. His master has done some great paintings on walls that he seems to be very proud of.'

'Murals?'

'And little illustrations for a book. With water he says, no oil.'

'Tempera. I have seen some samples in Havelock's studio. Indian miniature paintings are fascinating. Well, he can learn oil painting. He has steady hands and he is intelligent enough.'

Francis mumbled something about all this trouble for a wall painter's sidekick.

Richard pretended not to hear. 'I hope you remember our little agreement. Especially since you are getting paid for it. You need to be in the studio for a month, translating every word I say to him and every evening you are going to teach him English. And maybe you could teach me a bit of the local language as well.'

'There is so much to do. Who will go to the bazaars and shop for our food? Who will mind the servants?' Francis grumbled.

Richard rolled up his shirtsleeves and drew Mukunda over to the pestle. Francis could not help thinking how they looked like two unrelated trees with entangled roots; the pale and sturdy one fused with the lithe and dark one, and then admonished himself for beginning to think like the boss. Too much imagery was unhealthy. He dug out some more tobacco from the pouch at his waist.

Mukunda soon proved to be unpredictable. He started to appear and disappear at his own whim. Sometimes he went through his English lessons with Francis who had to admit that the boy was intelligent and quick at learning, soaking and repeating words with alarming rapidity. And when he did apply his mind to it, they were astonished to see him move like a wizard in the studio. The paints fell under his spell. Every shade that Richard worked on was duplicated in no time, with little to be faulted. Yet there were days when Mukunda simply folded his arms and moped in a corner, doodling on a corner of the wall that he had made his own. Sometimes he drew languid women sniffing flowers, and at other times unhappy horses marching to battle. On more overcast rainy days, Mukunda often drew faces darkened with zigzagged lines.

The young man is subject to melancholia, Richard surmised, persuading Francis to be more empathetic.

It was not till Richard suggested that they do a portrait of Francis that Mukunda perked up. Francis remonstrated but they did not care for his opinion. The artists now had a project.

As the portrait opened up, the disinterest and irreverence were slowly going out of Mukunda. He was alert and kept everything in the studio perfectly organized. On rainy evenings when Richard threw down his smock and pulled his chair to the threshold to enjoy his tea, Mukunda would retreat to his corner and scribble on the wall. An image of Francis slowly appeared on the wall just as Richard was framing him on the canvas, only more virile and agitated. The coarse lines hobbled over the texture of the wall. It was a crude copy of the painting that sat neatly on the easel and yet it was eloquent. Richard smiled to himself in satisfaction and in pride at his apprentice. Here was a natural portraitist!

The linen canvas had been carefully treated, coated eight times with a mixture of chalk and lead white. An initial drawing was laid in thin Indian ink. To Mukunda's shock, Francis was painted entirely in a translucent tan and orange. Richard explained that he wanted the skin to glow warmly from within and there would be many more colours to go over this one. The head was painted white again so that the last stroke could have some of the depth of the first and reflect more light through the layers of paint. The shadows were laid in first, in burnt sienna and Prussian blue. Then the middle tones in light ochre, and highlights laid in egg tempera. The mixing agent was carefully prepared and Mukunda told sternly never to tamper with the ratio. Richard had been experimenting with blends of some local oils which he hoped would not only make his ration of linseed oil last longer but might dry better in the local weather. He chose his pigments and waited for them to be ground each morning. He furiously mixed and dabbed, talking to himself and rejoicing in every little experimental shade that emerged. Richard had chosen verdigris for the backdrop, a fickle paint that required careful preparation and attentive layered application, then immediately varnished with the yolk of an egg, a sensual bluish-green that would over the course of a month change itself magically into a completely different shade of green, rich like the foliage in the rains. The artists no longer cared about time nor did they need Francis to be the communication between them. Both men worked in perfect unison, starting early at dawn and well into the thick of the night, while the green seeped deep into the canvas.

The portrait was slowly coming to life and Richard hovered around it all the time. But soon, from the furious scrapings of the palette knife and reworking, it was becoming evident to the watchful Mukunda that Francis's skin was not emerging in colour and texture as hoped. All of Richard's training and practice in portraits had been with European skin tones and they failed him here. Francis was neither light nor dark. His skin had become tough and tanned but still retained a certain gloss that Richard now tried hard to recreate. Where was he going to get that particular shade of fading walnut brown? For two days he toiled with bister, a dual tone colour that was mainly a watercolour pigment but was capable of moving between yellow and brown. When that did not produce results, he heated the Prussian blue till it turned into brown and then disappointedly put it aside for being much too heavy. For a day he remained with primitive red clay to see if that would help and then drank to a stupor when he saw it fail. He knew that manganese was the element that was going to make the brown possible but both the raw and burnt brown that he had brought with him were frustratingly off the mark. He could work with either of them with some trials but the very thought of compromise was revolting. Cassel brown. Gold ochre. Burnt sienna. His brushes crushed into them impatiently. Where was the right shade? Yellow orpiment or the glowing Naples yellow would darken to brown and Veronese red being half-yellow could be browned too. But not any old brown would work. The choice seemed to narrow down between making his subject look like the bark of a mouldy tree or a jaundiced turtle. It simply wouldn't do. For a painting going so well, he had to get the skin tone right. Not just right, but perfect.

Mukunda watched Richard struggle till he could stand it no more. He finally spoke up. For years and years, Indian painters had a luxury they were very proud of and could tweak to delightful ends. It could become anything from a sumptuous orange to a tranquil brown. Richard could barely contain his impatience.

'Where is this yellow?'

Mukunda ran to the artists' colony in the hope that the Master had some to spare and returned in a few hours with a box filled with a yellow pigment that turned transparent the moment it met a drop of oil. Here was the mysterious Indian yellow that Richard had heard about but never seen before, a yellow so elementary and brilliant that it would need thirteen opaque colours to replace it. He sat near the window, trying it out on a small piece of canvas, smeared on its own, mixed with gum arabic, churned into different consistencies with linseed oil and blended with his various reds.

Mukunda watched attentively as Richard worked through the night completely obsessed with this new pigment. Over all the layers of paint was emerging a beautiful shade of brown, and in the early light of the morning, they could see the painted skin breathe to life.

The artists finally put their brushes down to sip on sweet milky tea, listening to sparrows chirp, far too excited to go to bed, and decided to go for a walk instead. The fort was more compact than Richard had thought from its contours. The settlement inside the walls consisted of low-roofed modest houses closely packed together, crisscrossed by narrow lanes, a brisk walk of a few minutes in any direction offering a view of the fort embankments.

The river island was slowly opening up to the promise of light, to the sound of bangles and prayers as women swept their front doors, sprinkling water to settle the dust and drawing floral patterns on the ground with rice flour. After days of being shut inside the studio, the simple earthy beauty of the town and the melting tones of its greenery brewed their senses, as if the first flush of love. They had not gone far, or sunk deep enough in the newfound joy, when a hand suddenly appeared from around the corner of the street and grabbed Mukunda by the neck.

'Hey! Hey! Stop that! Let him go!' Richard reached over and tightly held Mukunda's hand as an older man continued to tug at him in the other direction. Strangely, Mukunda did not seem to fight the assault or look alarmed. Instead, he calmly disentangled Richard's grasp.

Richard let go and stepped back in dismay as the stranger burst forth a volley of exclamations. Richard could see it now. The distinct resemblance. Father and son. The father struck his son repeatedly across his shoulders and dragged him away, throwing a murderous glance at Richard. Mukunda neither protested nor tried to break away, simply cowered to protect his face from the blows. Richard watched helplessly. A small crowd had gathered to witness the skirmish and chime their approval of a wayward son getting a deserved punishment. Richard slumped under the shade of a tree, long after Mukunda had been taken away, long after the onlookers returned to their homes, and the streets turned empty again. He stayed there, clinging to his loneliness, till Francis came looking for him and silently led the way back to their stone dwelling.

French Rocks reverberated with the shouts and cheering of the men. Surcouf stood apart from the commotion and rubbed his palms together. He had heard the news much before the rest of them did, having been summoned to the palace by Tipu Sultan to make sure his understanding of the letter from Napoleon Bonaparte was accurate. Surcouf had recommended caution but Tipu was an optimist to the core and did not want to imagine failure. He declared celebrations to be in order in the French camp, expressing his desire to visit again as Citizen Tipu, to tap his feet to the '*La Marseillaise*', to listen yet again to old stories and new hopes from men about the renewed greatness of France, a place they had not seen in years and Tipu had only known from books.

The French soldiers were in their uniforms but in various stages of disarray, sleeves rolled, waistcoats flung on the grass and boots hanging from bushes. Some of the younger men of the regiment had ripped off their stockings and playfully grappled in the grass like the local wrestlers they often watched for entertainment. Senior officers passed around earthen cups that drizzled Madeira as the excitement jostled them together. The taste of baked earth seemed to induce an intoxication that the best champagne flutes in all of France could not. The true sign of freedom, they laughed, was when a man could get drunk with his colleagues in the middle of a working day. The light around them was diffused by layers of clouds and the sultry August wind played with the dust at their feet. They hooted and whistled. A few earthen cups tossed up in the air tried to defy the hypnotic pull of the earth and quickly shattered in dismay.

'Fools!' Surcouf sighed.

He turned around to enter his tent, walked straight to his table and placed his palms flat on the designs that lay scattered across it. The toy tiger lay dormant, waiting for him. He knew what he wanted the pieces of metal inside the wood casing to do for him. A childhood with a father who mended watches was his only apprenticeship but it was the ideal one. Once a mechanical device was taken apart, no matter how old or big or complicated, it was the same inside – helpless before the human mind that could put it back in order, that could coax it to work again.

And there it was, a six-foot effigy of an angry tiger pinning down an English soldier with its feet. The left flank was fitted with a flap that hid eighteen keys with musical pipes, a modest organ for those little floating notes, an instrument to cause delight as well as uneasiness. A crank on one side would cause the tiger to roar and the dying man to cry out. Macabre. Sir Henry Munro's son had been killed in the forests of Bengal by a tiger. Nothing had remained of him but his clothes. A grown son turned into a morsel, chewed away, spat out in bits. Tipu was fighting under the command of his father, Haider Ali, in 1781 when Munro had commanded a division on the English side. Tipu Sultan believed his favourite animal had been sent by god to punish the enemy with the loss of a child. Haider's son had lived to become an emperor. Munro's son, a tiger's meal. The Sultan had insisted: if that wasn't a message from above, what else could it possibly be? Surcouf had been too wise to argue. The Sultan now wanted to reward himself with a toy of hatred and the

Frenchman had been told to spare no expenses to make it deserving of such exactitude.

The toy tiger had roared only once and the sound had disturbed Surcouf so much, he had silenced it immediately. The roar was perfect but the casing had stood too still. Something was missing. He needed movement. Maybe the head of the tiger needed to be more expressive. Or maybe the arm of the soldier could move; the only part of him that was not pinned under the tiger's paws, for the animal stood entirely above him. Maybe the dying man ought to groan too. He pulled his chair closer to the table and began to scribble over the drawings quickly. Was it possible? Surely, it was. His father would have reminded him that sometimes an engineer can get too close to his machine – step back, and step back once more, step back as many times as it takes to look at the whole. Only then will the details offer their secrets. Details. Secrets.

He got up from his table and almost tumbled across the tent to the big crate. He fiddled impatiently with the lock and the hinges. The doors came apart to reveal his incomplete creation. From the left shoulder of the animal was a protruding crank handle that he caressed. Yes, the solider had to raise his left arm and cry out in pain to the tiger's roar. Every act of violence was styled with two faces. What would the victor be without the vanquished? Surcouf smiled at the tiger and lovingly caressed its neck. The darkening day was now in the tent and his eyes glowed in the dark with those of the beast and his prey.

There is a king who has learnt the art of reading the prophetic and mystical characters embedded in individual human skulls. One day he sees a fragment of a skull by the side of the road and picks it up to decipher its message. It says: this skull will cause the death of forty persons. To avert that disaster, he orders the fragment to be pounded into a fine powder which he then puts into a little box and deposits in a secret part of his cabinet to which nobody has access. His favourite wife observes him doing this and presumes because of his skill in pharmacy that it is some precious medicinal preparation. The king soon departs on a distant expedition that takes him away from the capital for several months. During this time, the queen who falls sick decides to try out the secret medicine. The king returns and is shocked to find her pregnant. She pleads her innocence but the enraged king orders all the harem eunuchs and guards to be killed. Finally, the queen confesses about having consumed the powder. The king then counts the number of people that he has ordered to be put to death so far and the number is an exact forty. The prophecy has been fulfilled!

This is the story that courtiers hear from Tipu Sultan today. He has dreamt it the previous night and believes Providence is sending him a message. If a filthy fragment of skull can kill forty people, the Sultan's misplaced trust in that no-good privateer from Mauritius will eventually clear out the British from India.

An army is coming from France, he is certain.

Hunting with the Cheetahs

Huddled against each other in a bullock cart with their basket of art supplies, Richard and Francis listened to the sound of twigs breaking beneath the feet of marching soldiers, the crunching of dried leaves, the twitter of foraging birds, the wooden carts groaning over gravely paths. They had been informed late in the night about Tipu Sultan's hunting plans and given orders to attach themselves to the hunting convoy before daybreak. Mukunda had not turned up for work, and two days had turned into two weeks. Richard's pleadings to Francis to send word for Mukunda had been argued against. It would be very wrong to interfere with the boy's family issues and if he wanted to come to work, he would. But Richard could not help worrying. What would they do without Mukunda? That had not bothered Francis who never quite understood what they needed the boy for in the first place.

The trees around them were becoming scarce and clearing out to open grasslands that rose and fell like drapes over squatty hillocks. Crouching behind a low mass of clouds, an orange sun was slowly lighting up the landscape.

Their cart came to a halt on the dome of a hillock and they were now in view of the royal convoy. Tents had been set up on the hillside a few yards away from them and all around the tents stood motionless men. A little apart from everyone, with his hands on his hips and looking down at the little valley, was the man Richard had seen briefly in court. Tipu Sultan was wearing the same white turban with its jaunty feather, his long white robe flapping like a flag in the wind. Richard could feel Francis tugging his hand. He turned around. The clouds sailed past the sun and the entire grasslands were infused with a golden tinge, revealing a herd of antelopes grazing peacefully in the far distance. The huntsmen had moved into their positions much like their cheetahs, swift and soundless.

Francis picked up the basket with their drawing implements and indicated to Richard to follow him. Nobody noticed them retreat to a cluster of rocks in the background. The five hooded cheetahs tugged at their leash as the wind carried the sweet smell of stirring earth mingled with the scent of prey. Sinews shifted beneath the thick dappled fur, tails poised in anticipation, faces taut, paws flexing.

All eyes were on the Sultan. Richard and Francis felt their hearts drop into their bellies and their palms sweat. They were the only ones there apart from the unsuspecting antelopes that did not know what to expect next. What were the cheetahs going to do when set loose? What if they decided to attack their keepers instead of the antelopes? How would they be captured again?

'Let us leave now. They will not notice that we are gone,' whispered Francis, white and fluttering like the paper in Richard's hands.

Richard shook his head, trying to steady his own nerves. 'Where will we go? Sit down here and don't move. I have to get some sketches done, anything at all.' He knew there was not much time and that whatever was going to happen would be so quick that a few blinks would lose it entirely. Nothing in his training or experience had prepared him for anything like this. He told himself to trust his mind's eyes to remember something of the quality of that air, that light and dust raised by the cheetahs as they were let loose. For indeed, just then he saw Tipu Sultan turn towards their party and raise his hand. He was holding up three fingers. Two of the five cheetah trainers pulled their animals back, disappointed. The hoods on the eyes of the other three cheetahs were taken off. The Sultan dropped his hand. The cheetahs were released.

The men stood very still, but their eyes glided with the racing cheetahs that stopped at the bottom of the slope and crouched into the grass, blending into the yellow, only the dark spots on their backs rippling with the wind. A couple of antelopes looked up sharply, their uneasiness spread to a few of their companions who stopped grazing. Richard turned to look at the Sultan and saw that he was staring at his prized predators, his body bent forward as if he were in the hunt, hiding in the grass with them, about to break into a desperate run.

For one moment that expanded indefinitely, there was absolute stillness, and then a big cloud of dust and pandemonium. The cheetahs leaped out of the earth, their limbs flaying powerfully with the wind, legs barely kissing the grass, darting ahead with a speed that Richard had never seen before, never even imagined possible. The antelopes had broken into a frenzied run for safety, most heading over the next hillock in a thundering mass. The cheetahs pursued them. The hunting party broke into a loud whoop now that the chase was on. The Sultan was slowly walking down the slope as if wanting a better look at the progress of his hunters. Not much was visible till the herd of antelopes had disappeared. The animal handlers ran into the valley. In the settling dust, they could see two of the cheetahs had been successful, holding their catch by the neck and waiting in the grass till the hoods were put back on their eyes. The necks of the antelopes were cut and then a couple of legs sawed off to be given to the victorious cheetahs as reward. The cheetah that had failed in the hunt prowled unhappily at a distance till his handler placed the hood over his eyes and led him back to the cart.

The hunting party was in a bustle now, everybody having some duty to perform. The kill would be skinned and cooked, and the Sultan would spend the rest of his day enjoying the feast, perhaps even go out with his gun to shoot a few wild animals himself. Richard turned to find Francis standing right behind him with wide-eyed awe. He was chattering excitedly with some of the huntsmen. Richard felt a sudden burst of relief that the hunt was over. His legs trembled as he walked back to his drawing materials.

'Come on, we have to go.' Francis was bouncing by his side. Richard rolled his eyes and began to explain all over again why they simply could not leave whenever Francis lost his nerve. Francis clicked his tongue impatiently to show that he had been misunderstood. 'No, that's not it. The Sultan has sent word for us. He wants to talk to you.'

Richard and Francis were gestured to step in as soon as they reached the large green tent. It was crowded inside, just as it had been in the audience hall of the palace. Officials stood close to each other, making concentric circles around the Sultan, some of them with quills poised over paper to take notes. The ministers sat on a crescent-shaped divan, Mir Sadiq towering over them with big gestures and rapid speech. The Sultan was nodding vigorously to whatever he was saying, his fingers fiddling with their many rings. The only notable difference from the previous audience was the absence of any of the French Generals in the tent. Some of the other courtiers were talking amongst themselves. Nobody paid any attention as the newcomers inched closer. Richard pulled at the end of Francis's shirt and got a shrug in reply. One of the ministers noticed the Englishman and went over to the Sultan who raised his hand. The chattering stopped immediately.

Tipu Sultan had received a letter. From Richard Wellesley, the Governor-General. Did they know anything about it?

Francis shook his head in sincere rebuttal and so did Richard as soon as the words were translated for him.

Tipu Sultan stared at both of them and then asked they be shown the letter. Mir Sadiq protested about showing crucial state correspondence to possible spies. The Sultan caustically reminded him that the suspect belonged to the very camp the letter had come from. 'Show it to him!'

Richard held the paper with trembling hands. The seal of the East India Company flashed at him. His throat tightened. There was no ambiguity in the few sentences. The Governor-General had knowledge of Tipu Sultan's dalliance with the French, the embassies he had sent to Paris and Mauritius requesting French troops, and suggested that their emissary Major Doveton be soon received to discuss the serious concerns that the Company had about their friendly ties with the Mysore kingdom.

'What makes the English think they can tell me who I can write letters to or make friends with?' Tipu Sultan growled.

'Tell him, Francis, that we are not politicians or even soldiers. Tell him I have not been in this country for more than these few months. I am an artist and I respect him. I don't know anything about these matters.'

Mir Sadiq declared he could not believe his ears that a man could utter falsehood so blatantly! A liar and a spy! It was a mistake to trust this Englishman, or any man from that infernal country.

Richard turned to look at Tipu, who calmly returned his gaze and took a long deep breath. Richard knew then that someone did believe his story and that he was safe.

'So what did you think of our hunt?' Tipu Sultan asked in a casual manner. 'I hope you are impressed by the genius of my people, that they can teach a wild animal to hunt for their entertainment. Or perhaps you have seen better displays in your country...'

'It was intense, unbelievable, masterful! I have never seen anything like it before. Words fail me...'

'But you don't need words, painter. I shall expect to see your compliment in paints.'

Unable to bear seeing the artist get away yet again without any punishment, Mir Sadiq angrily walked over to Richard and snatched Wellesley's letter from his hands. Another round of animated discussion followed among the ministers. Francis listened intently. The artist was not addressed again and the meeting continued till the Sultan suggested that they enjoy the cheetah's labour and taste the roasted antelope. Richard and Francis watched as the party dispersed, men gathering among their own friends and social equals to enjoy the feast. The Sultan continued his deliberations with the council of ministers over lunch. The artist and his interpreter were neither invited to eat nor enquired after.

Richard took Francis aside away from the hunting party, trying to gather more information of the discussion that had been taking place in the tent. What were they saying? What was it all about?

'Something about the Nizam of Hyderabad. Something about the Marathas.'

'Well, that makes no sense. Tell me what exactly is happening. Is it going to be war?'

'They kept talking about a war ... it was confusing ... something about a French contingent being dismantled and something about the Nizam being born with the head of an ass and a lot of terribly insulting things about the English that I don't wish to repeat and distress you.'

'Tell me, tell me.'

'Maybe I can be of some help?' A familiar figure was walking towards them.

Francis muttered under his breath, 'That's Purnaiah. Remember? The defence minister, the one we saw in the palace.' Then seeing Richard was still confused, he added, 'The distant uncle of our missing boy.'

Richard straightened. Yes, now he remembered. But what did the minister want from him? Was this about the letter? He did not know anything about it apart from what he had just read. The Governor-General was a very senior official in the Company. The one at the very top. Richard swung one hand as high above his head as he could and then took the other down to the earth to show his own position. And he was a nobody, just a penniless traveller. He didn't want any part of this politics.

Purnaiah spoke softly, slowly. 'Don't worry about the letter. We are used to these old games of diplomacy. A letter has gone out to Fort St. George from the Sultan saying that he is away on a hunting trip and other such pleasantries. We shall see the English ambassadors when we are ready to and not when we are ordered. You are however a different matter … and you make everybody nervous, whether the Frenchmen in our camp or the local officials, all but the Sultan who seems to believe that you are really as harmless as you claim to be. And that is extremely lucky for you, wouldn't you say?'

'I haven't done anything that I should not.'

'You did enter our territories without our permission.'

'I am guilty of that, yes, but my excuse is that I came here with the best of intentions. I am a professional who is looking for new challenging work. I was told so much about Mysore and…' And then it suddenly struck him. 'Why do the French object to my being here? I am clearly not a Company man.'

'The British fleet has been sighted off the Malabar coast with ships-of-line and frigates. Our informers tell us that a very large British army is being assembled at Vellore. Zaman Shah has set off from Afghanistan and the great French army is in Egypt on its way to our coast. What do you think?'

'Why are you telling us this?'

'Doesn't it seem a bit naïve that you are talking about paintings when we are all preparing for a bloodbath with your countrymen? However, you and me do have a common friend, don't we? I think it is time for me to pay a visit to my nephew as well.' Purnaiah was smiling coldly.

'Will you tell Mukunda to come and see me? I need his help with this painting that the Sultan wants of the hunt.'

Francis shook his head at that and turned back towards Richard angrily. He wasn't going to tell the minister that. Was the Englishman deaf or was Francis not translating right? A war, they were heading for a war, and the minister was telling them to pack their bags and get out of there as quickly as possible!

'Francis, I understand you are frightened. So am I. But that could be just the idea – to get us to panic and leave. The Sultan trusts me. I can sense it. But more than that, I can feel a certain ripening inside me. How can I explain it to you? As if this is my destiny, this is where

I will do my best work. I have nothing to go back to ... So, I would appreciate you keeping your opinions to yourself and just translate whatever I say to the Minister...'

'But he is gone,' Francis replied sullenly. Richard looked around. The minister had vanished and they were by themselves again.

The Griffin was falling upon lean times. War is terrible business, Pereira said, taking drinking customers to distant battlefields, depriving them of the essential joys that only a good old tavern can provide a young man. Cole laughed and reminded him that overworked officials of the administration in Madras, such as himself, were doing their very best to drink away their miseries in the evening and keep up the appearance of normalcy in the establishment.

Black Town was certainly changing in character and uncertain times could possibly take the blame. The loud jokes, street fights over trifles, and tuneless singing of old ditties were no longer as frequent as they used to be. People talked politics and the vagaries of life under a hot-headed Governor-General bent upon spilling blood to expand their territories.

Pereira announced he had no idea why Cole was looking for that wastrel again but he had chosen the right evening for it. Havelock had disappeared for a few days but had unfortunately turned up that morning with that same old insolent face. What can fathers do when daughters lose their heads over shameless men such as these?

'Oh, you should not praise me so much. It might go to my head! A little brandy on the other hand would be so much more encouraging.' Havelock sauntered in through the backdoor. Pereira cursed him and Cole quickly dropped two coins on the counter to conjure up that brandy and prevent more bickering. He did not have time for their domestic tussles. In his pocket was the letter he had received in the early hours, delivered by furtive strangers who had quietly taken the coin he held out to them and vanished in a blink. Cole waited till

Pereira disappeared into the kitchen to chase a thieving cat and told Havelock about it.

'A letter from Dawson? Why didn't you say so sooner? I have been feeling sick with guilt. It was a mistake, Cole, to send the poor boy to his death like that. We have been here longer and should have known better than to encourage such stupid notions of wandering into Tipu Sultan's kingdom.'

'But he did not die. He is in Srirangapatna and has got a commission from Tipu Sultan himself! Here, let me read it to you, he says…' Cole dug into his pocket.

Havelock snatched the letter from hands and skimmed over the words, slapping his sides with delight and hooting in disbelief. The nervous griffin had outdone all of them, been called into the audience of a man whose doors were guarded by cheetahs, only to walk away with a bag of coins, now living as a guest in the very fort that had witnessed the death of innumerable English soldiers. 'This is fantastic! Who would have ever thought it possible! Cole! This is…'

'Hush! Yes, it was not very wise of us to send him there but it will be much worse if it were known that he is living under the enemy's patronage and writing letters to us.'

'Why? In what land is that a crime for the gallows?'

'Are you blind and deaf, man? Can't you see our army is going to be in Mysore soon? I am leaving too, for Vellore. They have transferred me from the Customs House to the Military and Carriages department, a temporary deputation, but one I asked for. There is always money to be made during the war, all those tenders for equipment and supplies, and nobody with the time to look closely at the books…'

'Well, it's good to know you are not bashful about stealing.' Havelock grinned. 'May a bullet find its way to the counting house! I don't suppose it has occurred to you that a war is as much about death as profit…'

'I would suggest you come along too. When the palace of Tipu falls into our hands, there's going to be the prize money as well…'

'Oh you Company men, all the same! But look at our friend Dawson here. A true hero! I wonder if Tipu Sultan would sit for a portrait.'

'Let us hope he gets out of there alive.' Cole emptied his glass of brandy. 'I came to ask if you would be able to help with the painting supplies he says he needs.'

'I suppose I could spare some from my stock. I have hardly any use for them. Even the carriages in Fort St. George don't want to be painted by me anymore. But how do you know there is going to be a war? All this noise may just be a ploy by this Wellesley to intimidate the enemy.'

'No, he does not need to do that, not after what happened in Egypt.'

'And what happened in Egypt?'

Cole opened his mouth to burst into an emotional narration of the recent events in Egypt when he caught Havelock's teasing smile. Everyone knew what had happened in Egypt. After weeks of scouring the Mediterranean, the British fleet under the command of Rear Admiral Nelson had found the French fleet anchored in the Aboukir Bay and in a daring manoeuvre had sunk nearly the entire French fleet. With neither the men nor the ships to hold on to Egypt or to sail to India, Bonaparte was returning to France. The English were jubilant, and letters of gloating and cheers were carried all around the world by their ships.

Cole swallowed the brandy and stood up to go. 'I leave in the morning with the last battalion. And I think I shall be meeting our young painter friend in Mysore before long if the rumours of war are to be believed. If you wish to come…'

'Oh, run along, Cole. I shall leave the history-wooing to Dawson and the money-making to you. What would my poor father-in-law do if I were to become a martyr to the Company cause?'

Pereira shouted in Portuguese. Havelock waved at him cheerfully.

'Do you think it is time to let someone in the administration know that our man is out there in the enemy trenches?'

Havelock shrugged. Why? What would they do about it? If Forbes or any of his Company boys hadn't said a word so far, why should they? Egypt had gone to their heads and until that mist cleared, they would choose to see nothing else. No, they would keep their friend's impetuosity a secret. Sometimes the best thing to do is to do nothing.

'What is Tipu Sultan going to do?'

'There it had been, his one great hope, the French army backing him against the final reckoning with the English, and there it lay shattered with Bonaparte's changed fortunes.'

'What is the English General going to do?'

The conversation between the two courtiers stopped abruptly as a young man strode by them, slowing with every footstep, his back slumped in deep thought. The astrologer's son. They forgot about politics and moaned instead the grief that some children bring upon their hapless parents. The young man circled the old stone granary thrice, each time hesitating at the door, aware that the two men across the street were looking at him disapprovingly. He picked up a pebble and meditated over it.

'Mukunda!'

Mukunda reeled back and prepared to bolt, but was immediately enveloped in a tight embrace. The door had been flung wide on its weak hinges and Richard bounded out in his painter's smock, his wet palette now pressed unmindfully into Mukunda's back. Mukunda tried to pull away. Richard laughed and hauled him off the ground. It was strange to be hugged like this by a man who paid his wages. Completely inappropriate, confusing too. Francis understood that better, and having come out to investigate the noises, he quickly hustled the men indoors, away from prying eyes.

Something had happened to the boy. He had turned into a man. How could it have happened in a matter of days, just like that? Was it the squarer jaw? Was it the incline of the shoulders? Was it the way his eyes turned into needlepoints and his smile said more than it said? What makes a man? Whatever it was, they were in its presence.

Francis stepped between the two artists and harshly shook Mukunda by his shoulders. 'So what is your story, boy?'

'I have a wife,' Mukunda groaned and pushed Francis away.

'Ah! You disappear to get married and make merry and forget all about us!'

Mukunda protested. He had been married long back when a child and now she had come to stay with them for good. His parents wanted him to take up his responsibilities as a householder and he was nothing but a prisoner in that house. Richard saw the distress on Mukunda's face and hurried over to step between him and Francis who had stopped translating. He wanted to know what they were talking about and was still recovering from the surprise of realizing just how fond he had grown of his assistant.

'Leave him alone, Francis, leave him be,' Richard placated. 'Let me talk to him.'

Mukunda continued to gesticulate and talk rapidly. They had locked him up in his own house, something they had never managed before. He had been allowed to come now only because that sneaky uncle of his had sugar-talked his parents into sparing him for a favour...

'What is he saying?' Richard paced anxiously between them. Francis narrowed his eyes and said nothing. Mukunda continued to explain. Purnaiah wanted them to go to the Wodeyar house that night, in secret, but only for a few minutes, when the guards at their door changed duties. The Queen wanted to meet the Englishman herself.

'Francis! I want to know what Mukunda is saying!'

Francis was glowering at Mukunda. 'Why should we do it? We know what will happen when the Sultan finds out. We will be put to death. So why are you asking this man to do this?'

'Because I am miserable, because it is the only way they will let me come back to work,' Mukunda said tearfully. 'Or I shall continue to be locked up by my family and maybe never touch colours ever again in my life.' He wiped his eyes and turned to the door. 'I have to go now but I will be back after sundown. Francis, please do this for me…'

Richard was now red-faced with indignation and stepped menacingly towards Francis who sat down on the floor with a thud. He nodded wearily. Yes, he would explain every word of this blatant and atrocious arm-twisting. By now he knew Richard well enough to predict his reaction, a sentimentalist to the grain. They would go out to meet the queen but if it turned out to be a trap, they would have been inexcusably foolhardy. Well, this time Francis would make sure he was there to hear every word and do all he could to somehow get them out of there as quickly and safely as possible.

That night they walked in the shadows of trees and ancient walls, covered entirely in dark blankets. Mukunda had rubbed charcoal on Richard's face to mask his fair skin and Francis had wrapped his head in an old shawl. Richard did not understand how Mukunda had timed their arrival but when they had reached the little house by the temple, there were no guards, no nightly wanderers, not even street dogs. The December moon had dulled and not a leaf stirred. It felt unreal, so remote that they forgot to be afraid and made mock scary faces at each other.

The door gently swung open and Mukunda led the way in. He had been told that an owl would hoot when it was time for them to make a quick exit. The guards were having an unexpected inspection from the defence minister, highly irregular at that time of the night, but one that would evade suspicion if it stayed brief.

The room was barely lit. There were only two oil lamps and both the wicks had been pushed low into their slots. Three low stools had been set in a row. The men took off their blankets and settled down. A woman walked in stealthily, a lamp in her hand. She placed it in front of them and raised her eyes to look at each of them by turn and then broke into a smile. The men were taken aback to be stared at so boldly by a woman, and at such close quarters. They looked at each other and then realized that Richard's painted face had amused her.

'Your Majesty...' Francis began in supplication.

Suhasini shook her head at him and stepped back. The curtains opened and Lakshmi walked in and sat before them. 'You must excuse me for not offering any hospitality or pleasantries. Time is of the essence. I am sure you know me, the story of my life is familiar to all the stones in this fort, drenched as they are in the tears and blood of my family. I need to know where your loyalties lie. Is Tipu Sultan the master of your soul? Or perhaps you have come here with the same mission as mine, to work towards his destruction? If so, you can trust me ... the English Company has always been on the most sympathetic terms with the Wodeyar family.'

Richard repeated his lines about being just an artist, a lowly portrait painter. He had come to Mysore on his own initiative and expenses. He was not an employee of the Company or the British government. They did not even know he was there.

The Queen looked at Suhasini with a puzzled expression. They had not believed something so preposterous before and had no inclination to do so now. No one in his right mind would come all this way without support or protection. Suhasini bit her lip, suddenly conscious that Mukunda was staring at her, his brow wrinkled, as if he were trying to recognize someone he knew well once and had since forgotten. She had never seen him before, and considering how all their lives hung in balance, she did not think she was in any danger of being given away. An irksome man, she thought, impolite, and clearly not bright either. She looked away dismissively.

Lakshmi was saying, 'We have heard rumours of war preparations on your front. We have our agents communicating with the Company officials in Madras. If there is to be a confrontation, we want you to know that we support your side. We hope that you will trust us and keep us informed.'

'We are related!' Mukunda slapped his hand on his thigh in gleeful recognition. 'You're Venkatashastri's daughter and you have just moved from Kashi, haven't you? My father is your mother's sister's—'

Lakshmi intervened. 'This is not the time or place, young man, for filial bonding. Though that does make it easier for us to stay in touch. I trust Suhasini as if she were my own daughter. If you, Englishman, decide that you can do better in this war than paint pictures, and will play your part in giving my family long-awaited justice, we shall be obliged, and you shall be well rewarded when my son is king again.'

'The owl is hooting! The owl is hooting!' Francis stood up in a terror. It was their signal to leave.

The Queen quickly blew out the lamp by her side and left the room without a word or a backward glance. Richard stood up to bend low even though she was gone, and then turned to Suhasini, bowing again with a flourish. She nodded stiffly and crossed her hands across her chest. Francis was already on his way out. He stumbled on the threshold and ran ahead in panic till he was hidden from the moonlight by an overgrown hedge. Mukunda walked out next in long purposeful strides. Richard hesitated as he looked over at Suhasini again. He thought he had never seen such an eloquent face. A lot could be drawn out of those eyes and they were definitely worth a little more study. The hoot was heard again, this time long and menacing.

Richard joined Mukunda and Francis as they made their way back along the shadows of the town; inside the comforting privacy of their blankets, each man tangled in his own thoughts.

The fort of St. George was finding itself in curious circumstances: nearly drained of its young men, and having two masters to entertain and pay respects. There was a new governor, Lord Richard Clive, the son of the great strategist, Robert Clive, a man of refined manners but lacking his father's political instincts. Fort St. George showed its pleasure at his arrival with parties and speeches, but with soldiers gone to prepare for war there could be no parade. Clive reassured them that he did not care that much for saluting uniforms. It was

Richard Wellesley who was a worry – an unpredictable man, quick to take slight and quicker to insult. He had sent them a letter announcing his decision to relocate from Calcutta to Madras, setting up the Governor-General's office in Fort St. George. Too much time was being wasted in the movement of important correspondence with Tipu Sultan when he was in Bengal and now that he had made up his mind to resolve this deadlock while the current military season lasted, Wellesley wanted to be close to the action. If war was declared, he wanted a resolute victory that left nothing to chance. However, he assured in his letter to Lord Clive, he expected not to be fussed over and would expect the Company business to carry on as normal under the governor's able leadership.

Quite by chance, a secret messenger sent by Tipu was intercepted making his way to the Dutch port of Tranquebar on the east coast. It was addressed to a Monsieur Duboc and was to be delivered with a bag of gold coins. The letter, written in French, confirmed that Tipu was preparing for an embassy led by a French officer to go to Paris and present his case to the Directory for urgent military assistance. Wellesley thought it time to send another 'letter of friendship' to Mysore. He did not wish to settle for anything less than unconditional surrender to terms that ensured Tipu would cease to be a constant threat to the Company's interests. Only five months stood between them and the oncoming monsoons when the season for military offences would have to be put on hold, and Tipu Sultan was trying to buy time till it would be too late for them to lay siege on Mysore. All of the British East India Company's resources would now be directed towards not letting that happen.

As much as Clive tried to understand the hive of activity he had been sent to supervise, it became more convenient to stay in his large office to attend to the little details of a new administration while Wellesley took blame or glory. The ship bringing the zealous Governor-General from Calcutta would land in Madras on the last day of the year. Meanwhile, formalities or not, Fort St George was lighting up its parlours and stocking its kitchens, trying to forget the war, at least till Christmas had been duly celebrated.

For Stolen Promises

The artists emerged into the nippy morning, paint scrubbed off from all but their fingernails, wearing spotless white clothes and beaming happiness. In front of them, through an open arch, the summer palace sat in the middle of a neatly laid out garden, shining indolently in the sunlight. A white rectangular structure, with many delicate doors and windows hanging by arches, a dreamy lantern porous to wind and light. They watched it claim its name effortlessly, Dariya Daulat, the river's treasure.

Mukunda took in the awestruck looks on his companions and puffed with pride. Tipu Sultan did not live there anymore, he explained, because the English army had captured it in the last war and turned it into a garrison. Tipu refused to sleep in the same place as the English General.

Francis thought such pride ridiculous and said so. Why would any man turn away from such comfort?

The sentries at the gate examined the letter that carried the court seal and then clicked their tongues in sympathy, their eyes rolling towards Richard. He is not going to live very long, is he? Every Englishman captured in wars with Tipu had ended up in dungeons or graves.

'Who? The Englishman? But the Sultan likes this one!' Mukunda laughed. 'Why else would we be here?'

They looked unconvinced and more so when Richard joined his palms and bobbed his head. 'Namaskara.'

Francis rolled his eyes. 'This won't help our situation, you know,' he told Richard, 'being foreigners that everybody thinks will die soon, and then also bowing before every beggar we meet.'

Richard laughed, leaned over to put his arms around Francis and playfully squeezed him closer. Startled at the sudden intimacy, Francis staggered ahead and then kept on with his indignant march.

'Francis!' Mukunda called out.

Francis stopped and turned snootily. 'Now what is it?'

Mukunda reeled out a string of words that did not make any sense. Richard hooted and clutched his stomach in laughter. Mukunda was mimicking Francis admonishing Richard in English.

Francis huffed and walked on, swinging his arms angrily. 'Worse than spoilt children!' he said loudly, once in English and then in Kannada. They howled back in mirth.

Francis thought of how easy it was to forget that he was the youngest of the three when they cared so little for caution. His was the ear on the ground, and they could not possibly put two things together at the house without him. How insufferable these painter buddies were becoming ever since that meeting with the strange queen in the middle of the night! Mukunda was coming to work regularly, going back to his own home in the nights, while Richard continued to work till the early hours in a feverish pitch, putting his brushes down for a little rest only when Mukunda returned with the sun. They worked sporadically on the painting of Tipu's cheetah hunt, but they were clearly more excited about the nearly complete portrait of Francis. Richard would give crisp instructions to his apprentice, now trusting him with the brush as well for filling in colour or varnish in certain portions. Mukunda absorbed every move of the painter around the canvas and tried to copy it when Richard stepped away to lie down. They were now communicating with very little help from Francis, often without a single word being uttered. Their fingers touched the same canvas, the same brushes and colours. To work intensely was now the same as the rapture of being able to share it with each other, to sometimes play with the canvas, and often to wrestle with it till it began to yield to their ideas.

'It is shocking,' Mukunda would declare to acquaintances on the street, 'how much Francis's portrait looks like Francis. Just like him!'

Everything Mukunda was learning about paints from Richard was confusing and magical at the same time. That colours could layer, rise, create texture was a revelation; and that lines could move around to capture resemblances, that each canvas was a cosmos of which the artist could be the Creator. It went against everything Mukunda had seen in the Master's workshop. 'You are an artist,' Richard would tell him often, and he felt the weight of the words, but never quite knew what it implied for his life there in the fort.

'Look at all those painters!' Richard pointed out as they walked down the long garden path, flanked by fountains and flowering bushes. Against the side of the palace wall sat a row of artists, some mixing colours, few standing on scaffolds facing the wall.

'My friends, the artists of Srirangapatna,' Mukunda said proudly, 'and there, that old man you see sitting by the pillar, he is the Master, my teacher, the one the Sultan wanted you to meet.'

The Master slowly lifted his hand to shade his eyes and squinted at the approaching figures. His men had stopped work to exchange comments. The Master cleared his throat and the men immediately fell back to work but kept their attention on the three men now standing among them.

'Mukunda! My son!' The Master's eyes filled with tears as soon as the boy went down on his knees and respectfully touched his head to his teacher's feet. 'No, no, don't do that, this is not my workshop and you are a Brahmin boy. What will people say?' The Master pulled up the end of his waistcloth to wipe the tears that ran freely down his cheeks. 'Where have you been? One has been hearing so many rumours, even that you have, god forbid, jumped into the river! And what are you doing with these white men? Are these your friends from the French camp?'

'No, no, this is the Englishman I work for...'

The Master gasped. The English! Richard joined his palms to repeat his greeting. Mukunda drew closer to the Master to reassure. There was nothing to fear. The Sultan had ordered him to bring the Englishman to meet the Master, to see their work.

The clouds cleared from the Master's brow and he opened his arms. 'Yes, yes, of course, please sit down. Can I offer you some beetle leaves? No? Please look at our work as much as you want to, and perhaps we shall be fortunate enough to see your painting too. We are an ancient people, doing nothing new now, just the same old thing our forefathers did, ancient art, ancient minds...'

Richard was not listening. His attention drifted from them as he began walking slowly along the pillared verandah that went all around the palace. Entire walls covered from roof to floor by painted figures, a large mural made up of smaller compositions, each a complete painting, sometimes in conversation with others. The wall around the bend was filled with portraits, small boxes lined up one next to another within horizontal bands – men of the nobility, women of the harem, soldiers and men of business, birds and animals, trees and flowers. Windows of stories leading to other untold stories. The war paintings held his eye the longest, for they were chronicles of Tipu and his father Haider's encounters with the English soldiers in the last three Mysore wars. It showed the enemy lost, scattered, cowardly, in captive, or miserably routed. There was Colonel Baillie sitting in a palanquin in the midst of the Polillur battlefield, biting his fingernails. Around the fallen Englishmen, the valiant-looking Mysore troops held aloft their bows, spears and swords.

There was even a painting of a royal hunt, but nothing like the one he was making. None of that fuss about dimensionality or dynamism. Both prey and hunter were laid out flat, both given to that moment, the colouring more important than the posture or emotion. Richard's painting of Tipu's cheetah hunt would look very different and he worried about it now. Landscapes bring out my worst insecurities, he thought. I know the music of paints, but I sing it better in painting faces than I do in grasslands. And I feel as sorry for the cheetah as I do for the antelope. He is not going to like what I have to offer him.

'Look here, here, here.' Mukunda was eager for him to walk ahead, to see the rest of the mural as it wrapped around the corner and continued on another wall.

Even at a glance, Richard could tell that the paintings were not all done at the same time. Some of them showed their age beneath fading gold paint, other fragments so fresh that the colours shone like stained glass. Upon a bamboo scaffold at the far end of the wall were a group of men scraping away at the wall. Mukunda had told them earlier about this. Tipu Sultan had wanted the Nizam of Hyderabad to be painted in 'proper light' in the war scenes – a rose-sniffing ruler followed by a regiment of elephants carrying empty howdahs, and a black boar to make the humiliation unambiguous. A fellow Muslim and a neighbouring ruler, the Nizam had not only signed up with the English, but a possible marriage alliance that Tipu Sultan had repeatedly suggested between his son and the Nizam's daughter, in the interests of the uniting the two Islamic powers of the region, had been spat upon and rejected by the Nizam's wives. The artists of the Ganjam colony were charged with the duty of now telling the world what Tipu Sultan thought of the Nizam. Words uttered in court or behind harem veils evaporate, but here, on the murals of his palace walls, the truth would be painted for people to know for years hence.

Richard turned around and met the Master's anxious gaze. 'Wonderful!'

The Master did not need any translation of the delight in Richard's eyes. He broke into a toothless grin and folded his palms in acknowledgement. 'What are we men capable of? Nothing. It is as the gods desire. Sage Narayana drew Urvashi on his thigh, and Vishwakarma, the celestial architect, learnt it from him to pass it down to us. We are their humble servants, carrying on the age-old tradition of our forefathers ... and then it is our good fortune that there is a patron like the Sultan who appreciates our work and provides a roof over our heads...'

Richard had always wondered and here was a wise man with some answers. Why does everyone look alike in Indian paintings? Men whether nobles or soldiers, women whether maids or princesses, why do they have the same face, the same eyes? Why are they all typical, even the trees and the birds? Real life is not like that, is it? Each person is different and that is the true challenge of painting faces, or so he thought.

The Master listened to Francis repeat the questions and laughed. 'Real? What is real? Everything in the world is an illusion. All Maya.'

Mukunda blurted out, 'Master, you should see how the Englishman draws. Very different from us. He likes to copy things exactly as the eye sees it.'

The old man patted him indulgently. 'A real artist does not know what he likes, my dear boy, but likes what he knows.'

Richard sat down in front of the Master. Between them was the low stand on which the Master had been trying out some colours on a slab of dried plaster. Richard pulled out a sheet of paper from his pocket and from the Master's side picked up a piece of neem twig that had been roasted to work like a charcoal stick. All the other workers gathered around to watch, captivated. The Master's wrinkled face was beginning to crudely emerge in the hurried strokes. The audience made appreciating noises.

The Master looked at his own face on the paper for what seemed an eternity and then spoke slowly. 'My wise father used to say that a picture reflects the merits of the artist. Now I see why Mukunda is the perfect assistant for you. This boy too tries to see the real in everything. It is the blessings of the gods that he also sees beauty in everything. But you, learned sir, you try to see the sorrows too, and if you are not careful, that can only bring sorrows for you.'

Father announces that we are returning to Kashi. It is not in him to go against the royal family that has patronized his family for centuries. The Queen can claim all she wanted of his daughter and it is his lot to endure it. It is also beyond him to keep politics out of our house – it enters through the kitchen door. Spaces he cannot fence. Women meet in backyards, at wells and rivers, in temples, at ceremonial gatherings. The network runs wide, seeps deep, news travels in the blink of an eye. That the Queen, even though locked up, would remain deeply submerged in political jugglery was expected, but the surprise was her new conduit with the world. Me.

Send her to her husband's home, whether she likes it or not, she belongs there, send her. The aunts in the house buzz around my father like pesky bees. A man like my father with a detached wife and an adopted daughter is never short of sympathy and pampering from older women.

Mother says less and less with each passing day. The physicians say that there is nothing wrong with her, and yet she is ill. We can all see the life slowly ebb out of her. Maybe she is like those monks, who can die peacefully at will. As if in preparation for it, she has withdrawn to a little alcove in her mind where it is possible to be passive and disinterested at nearly all times. Has it been a happy transition for her, a welcome evolution in her self-awareness? Or have we failed her collectively, me particularly? Sometimes I think we are very alike, even if our bond is of adoption and not blood, and that while she chose to gently sink to the bottom of an unfriendly river, I thrash to stay afloat.

Father is adamant. We are leaving by the end of the month, back north to the banks of the Ganga, to the little Bhairava temple where he conducted prayers for years. Not far from there is my husband's home. Reasons are not given, just that we must pack our belongings. Say nothing to the Queen, he warns me.

I try to stall, ask for more time, suggest that we wait till the next festival, but I am silenced by angry words and helpless looks.

A turn in events is needed. Something to shift the balance of force. Some unexpected element, fresh impetus, a new player. A catalyst could help hasten and bring plans to fruition. Father's mind could change too with that.

The English are our last hope, but our greatest fear as well. Have we been inviting rats home to get rid of the tiger? Are the foreigners to be trusted or will they use our desperation to grab and deprive us of the little dignity left?

It is getting more and more difficult for any correspondence to be smuggled between our island and the English fort in Madras. If even a single letter is intercepted, the house of Wodeyar women would be razed to the ground, their lives with it. The royalists had been roused once, a coup attempted from within the fort. But the plot was thwarted, the leader shut in a big iron cage like a bird and put on display. As a woman, my fate would be worst.

From my window I see the temple tower. An orange dusk scatters clouds over the walls of the ancient temple complex. A group of women carrying plates of offerings for the evening aarthi talk all at once as their children play hide and seek around their saris. Deep inside the temple hall, past the stone pillars, rooms leading to smaller rooms till the one at the very centre, swathed in darkness with only the door for an opening, is the god in whom we have reposed our trust. Vishnu reclining, the curled serpent his bed, his hand propping his head, his feet pressed by his consort, all in the blackest granite. The temple bells peal again, announcing the start of the prayers and the children run past the women, through the temple gateway.

There is Tipu Sultan, preparing for his final battle, and I am preparing for mine. He thinks he is fighting the British. The other war is unseen to him. A woman against an emperor. Pawn against king. I am the only one who can see the entire game board. It is now my move.

The painting was gone. Every corner of the sparsely furnished room was scoured and every employee lined for questioning, but the portrait of Francis had vanished from its perch. With neither clues nor witnesses to chase, the men settled into a glum evening. Mukunda dragged himself homewards when the last light of the day had turned into an uneasy purple. Francis, aware of Richard's despondency, now bustled around to make sure that extra attention was being paid towards dinner. The men in the workers' quarters had been told to stay quiet and out of sight. For the first time, Francis was nervous around the painter he had taken delight in treating like an incompetent child. Richard sat where the painting had been, as though to take its place, his head in his hands, refusing to say anything. When dinner was served, he ate quietly and then returned to his painting corner to clean all his paintbrushes, vigorously and repeatedly. It worried Francis to see him so withdrawn.

'It is only a painting,' he said, not able to hold himself back anymore, 'and we just have to write our losses off. Such things happen…'

'If only I had a chance to finish it first.'

Francis went around putting out all the lamps. 'Go to bed now,' he said kindly. 'There is nothing a good night's sleep cannot ease.'

'Leave them on,' Richard ordered. 'I need light to work, don't I?'

Francis opened his mouth to point that there was no canvas to work on, but held himself back, and sat down to go over the accounts book for one more time that day.

The knock on the door was sharp. Richard jumped up. Maybe it was back!

Paintings didn't go wandering off and then walk themselves back home, Francis muttered as Richard bounded to the door, flung it open. 'Who are you? What do you want?'

Francis heard him and grabbed the dagger from under his pillow and rushed to the door.

A cloaked figure stepped in and closed the door behind itself.

'What is the meaning of this?' Francis's voice was shrill. 'I am warning you we are armed and can defend ourselves very well.' His knees were folding.

'Stop shouting, you fool!' The shawl fell back to reveal Suhasini, her eyes flashing anger. 'You are going to get all of us into trouble.'

Francis was equally angry. 'Me? You think I am going to get us into trouble? And exactly what do you think you are doing here? What business could you possibly have with us? Go away, right this moment.'

'I am not here to talk to you. So stop barking at me like a street dog. I am here to talk to him…'

Richard was delighted. It was the woman he had met at the Queen's house the other night! He bowed at the slender arms pointed out towards him. He was listening with pleasure to the sounds that her words made as they rolled together. He liked watching Francis being cut down to size.

'This man?' Francis growled back, trying to keep his voice low. 'He told your precious Queen the truth. He truly does not know anything and can be of no help to you, unless you wish to buy a painting.'

Richard smiled at Suhasini and indicated a chair, wiping his hands on his smock while shaking it off. Francis stood back against the wall, knowing that his presence there now was only as a passage between two languages. A fly on the wall. They did not look or talk to him again.

'I am sorry. We were not expecting guests,' Richard said.

'You are the guest here in this fort, not me, and it would be to your benefit to keep that in mind.' She waved the chair away and continued to stand. She did not want the white man's kindness and she did not like how he looked at her, smiling vacantly, probing with his blue eyes. She was there as an emissary of her Queen, and to be appraised as if she were a statue was irksome.

'Yes, you are right. We are your guests and we hope we haven't done anything to offend Her Majesty,' Richard said, in an effort to pacify her. He did not miss how she kept away from the light and preferred the shadows. It could not have been easy or advisable for her to visit strangers in the middle of the night. For such high risks, there were surely expectations just as high. Yet her face gave nothing away. Her face. It was dark as the shadows. Her hair, pulled back tightly from her face, darker still. The lone diamond on her nose shining like the North Star in an overcast night sky. In the sudden silence between them, he could see her eyes thinking, the rest of her taut body thinking too. He was now grateful for the dark spots in the room, for what he was able to sense was more valuable than what he could not see. And he sensed a warm pillar of energy and courage. It comforted him, and in its presence he felt chastised for the desire that ached within, just as it had at their first meeting, then too in the tight folds of a night.

'I have something with me that might be of interest to you.'

From beneath Suhasini's shawl, a package revealed itself. Richard peered over and saw his name on it, written neatly in English. Was this the package that he hoped Cole would send for him through the gypsies?

Suhasini pulled the package back to herself. 'Yes, it is what you are thinking. Your friend in Madras has received your letter. He sends you some news about your people and some of the paints you wanted.'

'You opened a parcel that was mine ... my letters!'

'The gypsies are reliable messengers, but it is not true that they have no loyalties except money. They respect the ancient royal family, and rightly so. We have the right to monitor suspicious foreigners and their activities on our soil.'

Richard's face turned red from anger and the heat of the mockery in her eyes. The attraction turned bitter and crushing. What could he say to her, a woman he wished to impress, who taunted him so? He held his hands out. Could he have his property back now?

'Yes, but on promise of a returned favour.' She drew the shawl over her hands and the parcel.

'And why do you think we won't just grab it from you, something that has our name on it?' Francis spoke up, unable to hold back his thoughts.

'Because we don't think you are barbarians who pounce on political ambassadors. Or perhaps you wish to prove me wrong. Bargains have to be made in politics and we are not unreasonable. Her Highness wishes that you report a certain matter to us. A letter has arrived from the English Governor. Our spies in the palace say that Tipu Sultan is enraged, venting more than his usual tantrums. He is going to call you to the palace in the morning. If you get to see the contents of the letter, and mind you, we will know if you do, we want to know exactly what is in it. Write down everything you can remember soon after and the paper will be collected from you by one of our people. We trust you to be truthful to us.'

'Trust?' Richard exclaimed. 'How am I to trust people who steal and read my letters? If Tipu Sultan were to find out about these midnight dalliances, I shall have to pay for it with my life. I don't want to get involved in your dirty politics. And I don't want my parcel. You can keep it if it is of any use to you.'

'But you will help us. I can tell you want to do that. You are probably a good man and will understand that our battle is for righteousness, for getting rid of an oppressor, for returning our land and freedom to us. Or perhaps you wish to save the life of a little prince.'

She was now walking towards the door, but her eyes lingered persuasively on his face. The light from the fickle lamp now lit her in a ghoulish way. Both Richard and Francis understood why she had the upper hand. They were racked with uneasiness, standing on the fringes of this game, while she had staked all.

'Why do you hate him so? Tipu Sultan cannot be that bad,' Richard said.

What if Richard's house was burnt, his people slaughtered, his wife raped? What if he was then dragged miles away from his home, forcibly circumcised, converted into a Muslim and turned into a foot soldier? How would he feel about Tipu then?

'I don't believe he would do that.'

'But he has, to thousands and thousands. Many of your own countrymen have languished in his prisons and been killed like worms. You are a fool if you fall in love with a whirlpool for its patterns, and a greater fool if you think he needs your admiration. He admires himself enough. I shall be back…'

Richard walked towards her, confused, dreading the moment of parting that was near, yet fearing worse if she were to stay. A strong draught hit his face. The door crashed back noisily. It felt as though the rectangle of black that opened to the outside was now poised on a precipice at the very end of the world, one step outside being a plunge to death. And into that void she vanished.

The sun was high in the sky and beating down on Richard's face as he struggled to wake. A goat stuck its hairy chin through the open window beside his bed and morosely chewed an orange peel forgotten on the sill. Mukunda was shaking Richard by the leg and Francis by the arm.

'Stop dreaming!' Francis was saying. 'You have been muttering all night, but you simply have to get up now. We have just received summons to be at the palace. Tipu Sultan wants to see you. Shoo … shoo…'

The goat reluctantly withdrew. Richard pulled the sheet over his head, and tried to retrieve his dream and her face in there somewhere, but Francis would not stop. Suhasini had known they would be summoned to the palace today. How? She must be a witch.

Richard sat up quickly. This was surely about the Governor-General's latest letter. She knew more than she had told them, and he needed to get that package sent by Cole.

Naturally, they waited to hear any mention of the letter, right from the doorkeeper who suspiciously admitted them into the inner chambers of the palace to the minister in charge of the fort who asked some questions about their recent movements around the island; and then when Tipu Sultan walked into the Durbar Hall, they thought they knew what would emerge next – the letter that had come from Madras.

However, not only was there no mention of any letter, they might just as well been visiting a friendly neighbour. Tipu Sultan merely nodded at them and talked to his ministers about certain petitions. Refreshments arrived on silver salvers, cool sherbets in silver goblets and an array of sweets, with friendly persuasions to taste them all.

Tipu Sultan stood up and everybody else with him. He turned to go but stopped, as if remembering something. The painter.

'It is the opinion of this court to employ you to make a portrait fitting for the grand occasion of our seventeenth year as Padshah of Mysore. The treasurer will take care of the expenses. You can come during the hour we hold public audience and make your sketches.'

Richard bowed low in agreement, his head reeling with pride and delight. 'A royal portrait!' he whispered to Francis. But what about the painting of the cheetah hunt? Should he complete it first?

Francis had barely translated Richard's query when one of the courtiers snapped, 'What cheetah painting? Is the painter hard of hearing or just plain insolent? The Sultan said he wants a portrait and he wants it soon.'

'Francis, ask him for private sittings. I would need his attention if the portrait is to be any good.'

Francis thought it wise not to say anything after that admonishment. 'Why not just do as he wants? Maybe if he is pleased with the work, he will agree for private sittings later…'

'Well, what do you know about painting?' Richard was irked. What was he supposed to do about the incomplete painting of the hunt? And what if Tipu changed his mind about the portrait as well? Was there going to be any money in it? Oh, if only he could retire to some tavern and drown in some wine.

Francis could not help him with that either and said so. Their stocks had been used up. The only people in the kingdom allowed to drink alcohol were the French but they did not want to have anything to do with the Englishman till the Sultan approved. Richard would just have to do without his drink.

They emerged from the audience hall to see Mukunda scurrying down a corridor of the administrative offices. He grabbed Richard's hand, agitated, but would not say why, and dragged him into one of the rooms. It was filled with clerks sitting on mats at low wooden tables and making careful copies of the royal correspondence in different languages. Behind the clerks, at the far corner of the room, was propped a large canvas, its identity unmistakable even with face turned towards the wall. The men could not believe their eyes. Their missing portrait was right there, innocuously sitting in Tipu's palace. Richard started to make his way towards the canvas, every eye in the room now lifted from poised quills to his face.

'There it is! Look, Francis, my painting!'

Suddenly a couple of soldiers stepped into the room, demanding to know what the racket was about. One of the clerks had raised an alarm. The soldiers asked Francis if his white man wanted a taste of their local whip and stepped ahead menacingly.

'Don't say anything or do anything. Let's leave … let's leave now. Now…' Francis hissed between his teeth, and strode away. Richard and Mukunda glanced at each other and then followed Francis meekly.

'Well, that painting is mine!' Richard burst out as soon they were away from the palace and walking down the sandy pathway along the river. 'How can they just take it away like that and leave it lying around? I have a right to have it back.'

Mukunda said something to Francis. Richard demanded to know what he was saying.

'For once, the boy is talking good sense. He says only the Sultan could have ordered the painting to be taken from our house to the palace. It might be best to just forget about it for now…'

Richard picked a handful of pebbles and flung them violently towards the river. The pebbles clattered down together, a little short of the water. Then he dug his boot into the sand and kicked angrily.

Francis took Mukunda's hand and walked ahead pretending Richard's outburst was none of their business. When they finally gave in to the temptation to look over their shoulders at a sharp bend in the river, Richard was walking slowly, his hands in his pockets, chin hovering over his chest, still kicking objects, most of them imaginary, from his path.

More surprises awaited them back in the stone room. A brown package tied up with a piece of string had been placed on Richard's bed. Next to it was a small cane basket filled with guavas and pomegranates.

'Now what is the meaning of this? After all the threat and melodrama of last night, your parcel is returned with gifts.' Francis raised his arms in bewilderment.

'They know … they know that the Sultan did not talk to me about the Governor-General's letter. No, that's not it. They already know what they wanted me to find out,' Richard said quietly and picked up a fruit from the basket. Were they from her garden, picked by her own hands, sent as an apology, or maybe … dare he hope … a sign of affection? Or was there another message or threat in it? He polished the fruit off his waistcoat and bit into it thoughtfully.

Francis was impatient for him to open the brown package. Apart from the pouches of paint and a scrawl from Cole cheering his bravado, it contained a letter from London. His mother's familiar handwriting, painfully small and written with a backward slant, tumbled out. Holding it was like holding her perpetually cold hands and the memory made him shiver. The letter spoke of troubles, his sister's poor choice in marrying an impoverished man for love, the predictions of a brutal winter, the younger children taking turns with a fever, unexpected expenses, and the suggestion that he convince their benefactor to increase their allowance. Forbes's business was once theirs too, she reminded her son, as if he could possibly forget it. She did not make any demands from him. There was only the unmentioned expectation, almost against her judgement, that he would not fail her.

In an uncharacteristic burst of impulse, Richard ripped the letter and tossed the bits across the yard where he hoped the goat would make a feast of it. He rolled his sleeves and began walking towards one of the winding alleys in their vicinity, the first time he had ventured out without plan or escort. There was a pounding between his ears and weightlessness in his feet.

He hadn't been paying attention, he chided himself. He came to India and became a caricature Englishman. Art, career, livelihood, that's all he had been thinking about. That's all others saw in him. To every single one of them, Forbes, Cole, Havelock, Francis, Mukunda, Tipu, this woman who threatened one night and sent fruit the next day, even Mother, particularly Mother, and anyone who may chance upon his story, he had become his work, for all he did was go on and on about art. What else was there to think about? Well, why not this deliciously long pause of leisure? Why not the scent of ripe jackfruits on this street? Why not the musical laughter of the village children running around him right then? He could starve, he could die, he could be forgotten, but he refused anymore to be someone to whom things happened all the time, moving from one point on the map to another, rolling from one event to another, just a spoke in the wheel of a tale and no more.

'Wait! Wait for me! Wait!'

Richard did not know that he was grinning broadly when he turned around or that his hands had tousled his hair into abandon. Running to catch up with him, Mukunda easily forgot the man was his paymaster and a foreigner. Richard's skin had tanned under the Indian sun and brown hair darkened so much that he blended among the fort inhabitants. Only his eyes seemed to be capable of every shade of blue, like the paints he pounded, sometimes the regality of a lapis lazuli, or the flippancy of an azurite, or the mischief of a turquoise. And now like a cloudless lush sky, they welcomed Mukunda.

'Let me show you something.' Mukunda pointed to the east. He would take Richard to the murals that Tipu Sultan had ordered to be painted on the outside of ordinary homes. Mud walls with eloquent lampoons of white men in India. The two-dimensional figures, men with their faces pressed to their left or right wore European clothes, some explicitly soldiers of the British Company, all looking alike. Here was one whose hands were tied, his face half-blacked, sitting on an ass, face to tail. The Englishman in the next wall had a worse fate assigned to him; a tiger calmly tore him apart while he plaintively looked on a friend being crushed by an elephant. Strange must be the people, Richard thought, who lived in houses that constantly depicted a bloodbath, gory tales that never reached completion; the tiger would eat but never finish his meal and the bubbles from the blood would never burst nor the spectacle of death be muted. The fort inhabitants had no choice before their Sultan's whims, but that did not occur to him then. He grinned at the absurdity of these drawings, at his own abandon, and then hurried to keep up with Mukunda. Dante being led by Virgil, he thought. On the next wall four British soldiers being executed at the point of smoking rifles; the next promised revelry – seven men in top hats with tippling glasses by mouths open with silent laughter, and then he saw that they were surrounded by pigs wallowing in muck.

Mukunda kicked a pebble high into the air and whistled an odd tune. Richard caught up with him, tried to whistle the same tune and sounded terrible. They laughed again. How could a boy who had grown up seeing these paintings be so indifferent to Richard being an Englishman? It warmed Richard's heart. Suddenly, for all the differences, they seemed two of a kind, two outliers. He was himself again.

All of us on the island know about it. One day to reply. One day to avoid war.

We are there when the messenger rides into town at berserk speed, bringing Tipu Sultan a letter from his enemy. We are there when the pages are read aloud in court. Pages and pages, every bit of transgression against the Company administration numbered, underlined, repeated. An ultimatum that pretends to negotiate.

But just one day to respond? That was a stroke of genius by the English; do the right thing but do it quickly, so that the other side is at a loss. The French General had to turn back from Egypt and now the Afghan emperor has also returned to fix some trouble in his own land.

Tomorrow is the tenth day of 1799. We know it will come and go. There are no surprises, no rescues, no twists. This story has been around longer than us. War is a beast that obeys no masters and together we are counting down the days.

Beneath the Embers

'Mukunda...'

There is my father again, trying to claim me with my name. The astrologers have never had it better and he too has to be present at the Durbar every day. Tipu Sultan wants the movements of planets in his natal chart to be closely monitored. The threat to his life will pass when the rains arrive in June and make war impossible. But between February and June are five long months, perfect conditions for an assault on Mysore and not a single ally for the home army to turn to for reinforcements.

People come to our house in the guise of wanting to know what the planets have decided for their crops this year, but ask about the fortunes of Tipu Sultan instead.

'Not good, not good at all. His Saturn is on a rampage.' My father mysteriously refuses to say more.

Tipu Sultan has heard that too and does not wish to take any chances with appropriating Saturn. Every Saturday he unfailingly makes an offering to the seven planets, seven different kinds of grain, his reflection in an iron pan filled with sesame oil, a blue cap and coat, one black sheep and donations to needy Brahmins. On the fingers of his right hand he wears a ring, with diamonds or rubies or emeralds, but only after making sure the stone would appease the planet of the day.

'Mukunda...'

Not again! If times are bad, business is good for my father. I have to stay home in the mornings now to help him with his work. He patiently explains the rules all over again, the calculations from the almanac to figure out the placement of heavenly bodies in the sky at the exact moment of birth. I am supposed to remember and know this as well as him, so often has it been repeated to me, but he ignores that my heart is not in his work. And when I start to bungle the calculations, my father smacks his head with his palm, curses his fate for making his only child such a wastrel, and puts me to work on his accounts.

I fare a little better being his accountant than an astrologer. If I hold my peace, I can leave by noon for the work I do care for, there in the old stone granary. The Englishman works on the new portrait now, studying his daily sketches of Tipu Sultan made in the Durbar, while I work silently at coating the large canvas cloth he has measured out. He frets more this time about layering the grounding; he wants the image to have a distinct quality he says, a grey dignity, a brown intelligence, a yellow courage, a blue ruthlessness. He wants a mirror, every painting to look just like the person he draws on it.

The Master would say that a mirror is a mirror and a painting is a painting.

I think of the Englishman, sitting with the windows thrown open to let the flies float in with the sunlight, despairing over an empty canvas as I have seen him do before. No, my father will have to do without me this morning.

I decide to sneak out through the door that opens to our backyard, and walk towards the kitchen where I know my kind mother will pretend she did not see me. As will my wife. How strange that word sounds, still a word and not a person. Wife. Meenakshi and I have learnt to live together beneath a veil of shyness. Only in the nights are we alone, when she finishes her housework for the day, walks into our room and shuts the door softly after her. She lies down in bed, waiting for me to speak to her. I try but never more than a handful of words. The smell of jasmine flowers from her thick hair intoxicates me, the curve of her breasts shifting under her sari are all I see. Her eyes are downcast as I touch her; if she feels pleasure, the only signs are soft shudders of the skin, tremors that might also be fear, or pain, or repulsion. I am not man enough to ask or find out. I don't know how. The surge of blood in my body hides all but the pressing need to touch her, hurry past the layers of her sari, press and thrust till I find my way into multiplying delights and then explode into a cloud of power. Hardly does my heavy breathing even out, my back touches the mattress again, and sweet satisfying sleep takes over. In the morning she is gone, attending to the housework, same as every other day. Who is she inside that warm body lying beneath mine? She must not think much of me, coming to her only in lust, with muffled screams of pleasure. I know so little of her, my wife, and it feels safe to keep it that way, neither to know nor be known. But perhaps I shall meet her eye this morning, and perhaps I will smile at her, and perhaps her eyes will talk back to me. What does one feel about him who is a husband only inside a dark closed room?

There are visitors in our kitchen!

They are as shocked to see me, an intruder into their world. Four women huddled around the stove's fire and drinking tea together from brass tumblers that shine beside their faces, laughing together at something just shared. Meenakshi too, and a laughter of abandon I have never known before. I stare at her in shock. She knows I am there before the others do. Her body familiar with the breathing of my skin responds instinctively. There is dismay and confusion in her eyes, the laughter contracts from her lips. She pulls her sari tighter around her shoulders and nudges my mother. I cringe to see that her body has different memories of our nights. I stand there in the middle of the kitchen, awkward and undecided. Perhaps I should have darted straight for the backdoor and disappeared before the women broke their intimacy for an outsider. But I stand there because my eyes had moved from Meenakshi to another face.

Suhasini.

Richard was allowed to walk into the Durbar, his drawing board tucked under his armpits, but Francis was held back. Richard raised his voice, hoping to intimidate the guards, and the complaint passed from one officer to another, before finally reaching Mir Sadiq's ears. It was too small a matter to trouble the Dewan, but the Englishman was becoming a nuisance, pleading to take his shifty-eyed assistant with him everywhere.

Mir Sadiq snarled at all of them and settled the matter in an instant. No. Tipu Sultan does not want his paid servant, this artist, this despicable foreigner to understand the proceedings of the court. And so he is to come alone, and only bring whatever implements he needs for his drawing work. He will be searched each time he enters and exits the court, and he is to speak to nobody at all. Is that understood?

'A private audience, I need sittings for the portrait.' Richard pushed a cringing Francis into asking.

'No! Do whatever you have to do during the Durbar time. There are more important matters of state requiring the Padshah's attention. I still fail to understand what he sees in you, when all you deserve is to be squashed by a heavy shoe, vermin that you are.'

So Richard sat through the proceedings alone, on a cushioned chair that one of the guards pointed out to him. He had to admit that the view was not bad. It would mean painting the Sultan in profile, looking at some point out of the canvas, but not at the viewer. Richard consoled himself that it was better that way. He would need to know his subject, really know him, to hold his gaze in a portrait. Not Tipu Sultan as the ruler of Mysore, but as the person beneath the crown. Behind the seat Tipu took each day was a magnificent gold throne studded with precious jewels. It was said that Tipu had sworn not to ascend the throne till the British had been uprooted. Richard did not know what to do with a monarch who kept a throne waiting and it showed in his sketches. He tried to concentrate, shut out the voices of the supplicants who appeared in court and the ministers who read out reports, to listen only to Tipu's voice whenever he spoke, to notice every move of his body, the stillness too.

A week into his sketches, Richard received another delivery through the gypsies, a letter from Cole, bursting with news as usual, announcing his new position in the army as part of the support staff. What did he mean by saying that they might be meeting soon? The letter did not mention the word 'war' but the implication was there between every second word, written carefully to avoid anything political that might cause him trouble. Folded behind Cole's letter was a newspaper clipping from the *Madras Gazette* that announced the engagement of Gilbert Forbes with Anne Wheeler, the nineteen-year-old daughter of the surgeon at Fort St. George. Cole had not been able to resist cutting out the whole column to include the rest of the local gossip as well, none of which interested Richard.

All he saw were waves towering over a narrow boat, a piano carried across the heated sand, a plate of cut mangoes, and then a blur, a room of glass, a woman laughing, and that horrible old man laughing, and then another blur.

Francis stepped into the room just then and quickly retreated at the sight of the artist ripping the newspaper clipping into small pieces and scattering it to the winds.

'I remember playing with you when we were kids,' Suhasini arched her eyebrows at Mukunda, 'and you haven't changed much at all.'

The women laughed.

His mother flapped around him. 'Oh, he does not know that he is no more a child. Look at him, tall as a coconut tree and a wife at home, but simply cannot manage without me.'

Mukunda blushed. They did not know he had met Suhasini not so long ago, when he had recognized her in those few stolen moments at the Queen's house. She was here with her mother, to visit his family, and this meeting between them was supposed to be accidental, but she did not care to wear surprise on her face, or even the slightest hint of embarrassment. She locked eyes instead, silently mocking his confusion and enjoying her performance. He waited for her to look away demurely from the gaze of a man not closely related to her, like all the women he had ever known. Wasn't she afraid of what people might say of such brashness? He turned to his mother for reassurance. If the other women did not notice her expression – he seemed to be the only one who seemed to think the whole situation amiss – it was surely because they were in the kitchen. Their domain. He was the outsider, the boy who refused to grow old enough for his mother to call him a man, with a reputation of being a vagabond that had spread beyond the confines of their little river island. Why should they care what he thinks? He watched his wife from the corner of his eyes. Meenakshi seemed bolder in the company of the women, laughing with them as his face continued to redden.

'I … I have to go. I am late.' He tried to skirt around them, reaching desperately for the door.

'We have frightened you away from your own house.' Suhasini smiled mockingly and pulled her braid playfully over her shoulders. A few jasmine flowers from the long strands woven in her hair came loose and tumbled to the floor. Mukunda was looking at Meenakshi, now standing directly behind Suhasini. Fair Meenakshi, her cream complexion the great acquisition of his mother's life, much admired among her friends, a daughter-in-law so gentle and submissive, trained from the youngest age at every skill a good housekeeper needs. His wife, bending her head now, trying not to show her delight at the harmless ribbing that her husband was getting from someone who was not expected to revere him, unlike her.

'Would you do mind doing a favour? Actually, it is for Her Majesty,' Suhasini was saying. 'She needs some medicines and I was just taking the note over to the old physician Sheshappa who lives by the temple pond. You know him, don't you?'

She was holding out something to him, but it blurred as he focused on her face instead. Suhasini, her skin brown like earth soaked in rain, eyes piercing into his thoughts, chin pointing haughtily to the paper in her hands. Detached, crammed with mysteries, she was what he could never be.

He grabbed the paper from her hands, mumbled something indistinct to his mother and dashed out of the door. As he negotiated his way through the streets, walking in the opposite direction from where he had to go, he did not wonder why he was running the errand when he was late for work. Nor did he question why a simple list of medicines had run into sheaves carefully sealed with the royal insignia. He jumped across a ditch and ran along the fort ramparts, lifting his face to a passing breeze to douse his agitation, ears smarting with words and images playing over and over again in his mind. Suhasini tilting her head questioningly, his mother's proud eyes, Meenakshi's laughter, the bangles on their hands, toe-rings sparkling against the red kitchen floor, wood cracking in the stove, the feel of the paper, the paper that had turned in her hands now pressing against his clammy palms. It was a letter addressed to the British Governor-General with updates of all the military preparations in Mysore kingdom and a pledge of support from the Wodeyars for any action taken against Tipu, but Mukunda would never know that. He felt his heart tug away from him and float gently over the river – happy, ashamed, confused, victorious – now on its own for the first time, away from his fears and habits, away from the constraints of their little understandings.

Lines and colours did not make a portrait, but personality did, and his conviction about that was being tried in a peculiar way. Richard sat just a few feet from Tipu Sultan but it felt like a view across a yawning chasm. The courtiers did not meet his eyes and took their Padshah's cue by ignoring him completely. Richard was like one of the shiny wooden pillars, neither understanding nor able to communicate, but watching intently as Tipu presided over court. How could this man be messiah to some and monster to others? And so he searched every morning, through the distracting Durbar proceedings, to catch a glimpse of a despicable cruel man slipping from behind the veneer of the sovereign. Instead, he had to admit that Tipu Sultan listened to his people with attention, gave orders with careful enunciation and was the very soul of punctuality and concentration. Sheaves of correspondence would be read aloud by scribes who also took dictations in various languages. All the military men and ministers stood to the right of the throne, each giving a report when called out to, followed by a discussion with the Fort Commander on special reinforcements being constructed by French engineers at certain sections of the fort that Tipu Sultan had identified as being vulnerable to attacks.

What am I to make of a man such as this? Richard would debate aloud in front of his canvas back in the stone room.

Francis told him not to overthink it. Richard just had to draw Tipu like he did everyone else. It was just another job.

'No, it wasn't.' Richard's fingers curled above the paints in apprehension and doubt. It wasn't easy to see evil in a man who constantly walked in the colour of conciliation. White robes with white diamond buttons, white drawers, white feather in a white turban, white pearls around a white waistcoat – reflecting and defying light all at once. He found himself thinking about white itself, began to notice it more acutely around him. He placed one white object against another, adding more white around, staring at them for long, the paler shades, the deeper ones, every visible distinction that could possibly spring from white. Tightly sealed pigskin pouches of poisonous white lead lay punctured and squeezed to the last drop.

Mukunda had powdered conch shells as the local painters did for the murals. Surrounded by all that white, Richard's drawings began to improve. He was drawn deeper into Tipu's large expressive eyes, he imagined they radiated acquired royalty and plebeian ancestry all at once. The personality was beginning to emerge, not too strong, but just with enough clarity for the portrait to start its journey on the freshly prepared canvas.

February sneaks up on the island. The winter obligingly slips away with warm winds that tickle branches into new bloom. It will soon be time for singing with the sleepy river, for listening to koels ache for their first spring, and forgetting our mundane worries. But something is different this year.

This year, February has tied itself into big knots that hang heavy in our chests. The earth tilts nervously as if hundreds of horsemen are charging towards us. We sit around and talk in whispers. Men who have been to battle before remember the smell of fresh blood softening the soil, curses of the dying, reproach of the dead. The English army is waiting for orders at Vellore to march towards us. If the Marathas were to press in from the north while the English and the Nizam charge from the east, even as our neighbours in the south pull out their arms to settle old scores, where does it leave us? To the west is the salty sea and it is to the west that Tipu Sultan fixes his gaze every day. Three emissaries had left with his plea for military reinforcements, one to Paris, another to Constantinople, and a third to Kabul.

We fear the help will never come, or if it does, it will be too late and our little island will be flooded, not by the river Kaveri, but by our blood. We pray to the gods every hour and the prayers rise with as much fervour from the Sriranga temple as it does from Ali Masjid. We are willing to pray to the enemy's god too. Somebody needs to reveal the truth to us, if it is a good truth, or else to tell a harmless lie that will give us faint succour.

BOOK FOUR

Enter the English

The two village boys on top of the hill, sprawled out beside their grazing goats, were not sure what they were looking at. The joys of munching on stolen sugarcane faded. They squinted in disbelief and ran to the edge of the rock to have a better look. The goats shifted around them and continued to chew grass indifferently.

From the east, which the sun had skimmed not so long ago, a large cloud of dust was moving steadily. Stretching across folds of hills, covering every inch of earth for miles, the dark specks on the green land emerged from behind the horizon and crawled ahead ominously. The ground vibrated and twittering birds vanished to make way for a hollow hum as if by invading locusts. The boys looked at each other in terror. A monstrous civilization seemed to have awakened in the netherworlds and was coming out angrily to meet them. They screamed and ran towards the village to warn the others.

'The English are here!'

Not much later, a band of villagers clutching children and livestock, their meagre belongings hastily thrown into cloth bundles, gathered on the same rock to watch the giant cloud of dust move, come closer, closer still, then slowly inch past their deserted village. They looked out anxiously but the strangers did not break ranks to plunder their homes as had been feared. They huddled closer, in relief, muttering prayers, consoling each other. They lived on the green fringes between kingdoms. Depending on the political season and the aggressiveness of the rulers on either side, they were marked on maps as belonging to this kingdom or the other. Their land so minuscule, it did not merit footnotes in war treaties, just an emptiness fending for itself. They eked out such measly living from the forest that even the tax collectors did not bother with them anymore. The village elders were their rulers, and the scrawny children running around the village, their future.

As the infantry forming the main column of the army came into view, soldiers sullenly marching to the beat of the army band, followed by benign bullock carts groaning on with their load of cannons and gunpowder, it occurred to the villagers that the bloodshed would occur somewhere far away from them. Men killing each other till one side gave up. Leaders would meet, papers would be signed and maps redrawn, their little village somewhere along a fence again, life continuing as before. The villagers squatted on the rock and made themselves comfortable to watch the show. Little boys and girls clapped their hands at the most spectacular sight they would see in their lifetimes – the entire world moving across their eyes! Women chucked at babies under chins and pointed out great shiny metal guns being pulled on carriages drawn by bullocks, one followed by another, a caravan without end.

The British army had launched from Vellore two days before Tipu's reply to Richard Wellesley had reached Madras and all negotiations were now going to be on military and not political terms. Large sums of money had been raised at Fort St. George for the war, collected by bankers and commercial agents and civil servants in the name of public service, not all of which entered the books. But nothing was to be held back in the supply of equipment or supplies or livestock to the marching army. Every able person, soldier or administrator in the East India Company was called to stand on alert for any contingency, to be part of this fight to the finish.

Spirits were high in the invading army. It moved in large lumbering columns, men of all sizes, shades, girth, faces blurred by the rising dust, feet moving along like clogs. Progress had been exasperatingly slow, barely five miles each day, the route through the hills exhausting and not easy for the broad train of carriages that moved in the centre like a spine, heaving the ammunition along at an agonizingly slow pace. Frequent repairs and rest were unavoidable, the struggle to live as a milling mobile camp and adjusting to the naked sun. The Nizam's army led by Colonel Arthur Wellesley had joined the main stream of General Harris's army long before the borders of Mysore kingdom had been violated. The air was charged with a palpable tension at the knowledge that they had turned from men on a vigorous march in their own territory into invaders and aggressors.

To every fighting man there were many more men enlisted to meet their needs, every horse and bullock similarly accompanied. Alongside weapons and equipment, entire homes were carried, tent and provisions, servants and attendants. Every single need of this vast army had to be met by its own resources with very little sustenance from the enemy countryside, the only exception being acres of fresh grass cut each day for fodder. A community of gypsies travelled with this moving multitude. Each day when the army pitched camp, they set up a market that catered to every possible need of the soldiers. Fresh food came from villages, sometimes pillaged, sometimes paid a pittance, and the less perishable supplies, whether grains or goats and chickens, were carefully hoarded. The gypsies took no sides in a war. It was just another day of business, and some of them waved to the crowd watching them from the hilltop.

More than a million horses and bullocks moved before the amazed eyes of the villagers and six times as many men, soldiers and servants, all pushing in the same direction as the setting sun. Closely packed muddy boots and hooves, wooden cartwheels and metal pikes carrying flags, crushed the soil and trampled past without hesitation or mercy. Trees lost branches, hedges fell apart, small bushes flattened lower than the grass, to make way for the procession of colours. Red. Blue. White. Green. A giant flag of people had been laid out across the earth, from one end to the other.

'No, no paintbrushes today. No, no pencils either, no charcoal, no drawing paper.'

'Well, that is just ridiculous! I am sick of being bullied by both of you.'

The last traces of reluctance in Richard faded as soon as they stepped out into the sun and it did not seem so ridiculous any longer. This had been Mukunda's plan, to get away from their work, quickly endorsed by Francis. They had been there on the beautiful island for months, Francis had complained, and done nothing but hang around their smelly dump where one inhaled more paint fumes than fresh air and their only outings were to the miserable palace when summoned like slaves.

Any suffering, physical or moral, to come from the English army entering Mysore territory, they had tacitly decided not to speak about. And everybody in the fort seemed to have agreed to the same pretence. They believed that Tipu Sultan would take care of the matter immediately and long before the enemy reached the river island. Reassuringly enough, Tipu Sultan had left the fort a few days ago, heading a contingent armed to the hilt. Everyone left behind waited to hear the happy news of the invaders put to rout while carrying on with their daily routine.

A picnic in wartime. It was decadent. Too tempting to put off, and the very thought of a change of scenery made their feet restless, but the palace had issued strict orders forbidding the Englishman's group from leaving the island. Francis did not want to risk frightening the guards or themselves. So Mukunda had a suggestion. Why not get away as far as we are allowed to? To the very edge of the island? If this end is the fort, where the river splits to create their piece of elevated earth, at the other end is Sangam, where the two arms of the river join again. Let's go there!

A selection of men from their group gathered in the yard under Francis's orders. The cook was among them, gleeful to get a chance to prepare food in the open and demonstrate his skills to the townsfolk. Utensils and cutlery were carefully packed and loaded on a bullock cart that Francis hired for the day. They did not have far to go considering the island was barely five kilometres in length and the men decided to walk while the provisions left in advance for the riverside.

'This has always been my favourite place in the island, even as a little boy when I came here with my friends,' Mukunda chattered along the way, letting every curious passer-by know where they were going, 'I am taking the Englishman to Sangam!'

'Well, at least the whole world knows where to toss out nets if we drown,' Francis teased. He was dressed in his Indian clothes for a change, his Portuguese father now only in his grey guarded eyes, while his mother's spirit was impishly emerging from the rest. He stretched out on his back in the grass, merely a carefree teenager under a flawless sky. It was a transformation that both shocked and cheered the artists. They took turns to ruffle his hair, tickle his neck with reeds, throw little frogs down his open collar and then flee in mock fear when he danced to extract them. Even their attendants forget the habitual servility and joined in the fun. It was a day for ignoring rules, for being grateful that the same burst of life that raced through the green cover of sugarcane fields and coconut groves was in their veins too.

The men had reached the small stretch of land that jutted out from the island, where the waters flowing on both sides merged into one river again, grassy green and restless with crosscurrents, its gurgle refreshingly different from the stoicism of the fort.

Village boys splashing in the waters howled and waved at the new arrivals. Richard took off his hat and waved back at them. Encouraged, they began to clamour for the white man to join them.

Richard calmly walked down the stone steps laid out on the edge of the bank and continued straight into the water. The river wrapped around his knees and swirled in delicate patterns. The water was cool, even though the sunlight it reflected stung his eyes. Slippery stones beneath his toes released a slimy layer of moss and it ran up against his skin, awakening new sensations, drawing his body away from him. He slapped the water with his hands and laughed loudly.

Suddenly Richard found himself pulled into the river. One of the younger boys had boldly and playfully reached out for him. Taken unawares, Richard floundered, gasped for breath, and flopped around. The children were delighted and he joined in their laughter as an image of himself formed in his head: fully dressed in his European clothes and surrounded by a group of naked Indian boys in the middle of a river. His hat had floated away with the currents and was being given chase by one of the boys.

So long, Richard thought, it had been so long since he had known such happiness. And for a little while he forgot all about his work, the rare occasion when it was possible for the artist to be parted from the art.

Tipu Sultan refusing to give private sittings for the portrait had meant unhappy adjustments. Richard's sketches in the Durbar helped create the face but he had struggled without the live model to do the rest. After looking at a constant stream of visitors gathered by Francis for the purpose, he had chosen two different models, one to pose as Tipu Sultan's torso and the other for his hands, much to the amusement of the townsfolk who gathered in hordes around his room to watch him work. It was unavoidable. He had needed both the fresh air and light from the open doors and windows and soon grew used to working while changing groups of people whispered and pointed fingers at his canvas.

Richard bobbed up and down on his back, almost empty, letting the waves splash over him. Circles of colour converged and split behind his closed eyelids. His thoughts sank gently into the shallow depths of the river. He did not bother to retrieve them. The swimming boys had tired of Richard's passive sport and paddled away to climb onto mango tree branches that bent low over the river. Richard was hardly aware of them anymore, or of his own heartbeat. He was listening to the river and it was droning a song just for him.

A boy again, back in England, on a lazy Sunday afternoon of summertime, another river had sung the same song to him. No gravity, no tether, no awareness of time lived, no worries about the years ahead. Just expanding wonder in his core. One moment he had been a speck on the river, the next a man of worries staking his future on a paintbrush. Everything in between vanished, forgotten. Where did all lost time go?

He felt the gaze, somehow, past ears blocked with water and eyes closed to the sun, even past the river's song. He struggled to get a foothold on the rocks, dunked under the water, spluttered his way out and turned towards the bank. He saw Francis and Mukunda but they were not looking at him. He followed their line of vision. And there she stood with a large brass plate of prayer offerings in her hand, wearing an aquamarine sari as though she had emerged from the waters herself. She was with a group of people, most of them talking to her, and she was turning to leave, but her eyes stayed on him. Only him.

The guards waited in the courtyard respectfully as Lakshmi stepped into the inner sanctorum of the temple. Suhasini walked behind her with the prayer offerings; jasmine buds strung with fragrant leaves, two shorn coconuts, silver bowls of vermillion and turmeric, camphor, long sticks of incense, and freshly harvested bananas. Devotees in the temple rushed ahead to touch the Queen's feet, bowed in homage, and sat back to watch as the head priest came forward to greet them. Lakshmi spoke to him in a soft whisper and he accepted the plate from Suhasini's hand and placed it at the feet of the silk-and-gold-draped deity. The women joined their hands and listened to the chanting of the priests, offering prayers for the safety of the people of Mysore kingdom, seeking protection against any evil befalling them from enemies far and near.

Nadeem Khan, the killedar of the Srirangapatna fort, had agreed to let Lakshmi pray at the temple at Sangam after multiple and frequent requisitions. With all the commanders and ministers away with the army, he was in charge of the island and did not think it would hurt to have some prayers for their cause. He had stipulated that she never step out of sight of the accompanying guards, but the guards being old-time employees of the Wodeyar king were willing to do anything Lakshmi requested, treating the women not like prisoners but sacred royalty. They kept a respectful distance and watched while the women walked from one shrine to another, conversing in low voices.

'Have we received any news? Anything at all?' Lakshmi drew Suhasini beside her on a low stone plinth shaded by palm leaves. They were still within the temple precinct, but at a deserted end of the compound, just beside the dark navagraha idols that stood together with their backs to each other, where whispers could be mistaken for the play of wind. It was their first meeting outside the house of women, that familiar cage where lines between domestic and national intrigues had long blurred, and an old affinity was tinged by new awkwardness. But the ticking of the political clock was hard to ignore, now that the enemy army was bearing down on them from two fronts – General Harris leading from the north-east accompanied by the Nizam's contingent and General Stuart with the Bombay army from the south-west. Tipu Sultan had dispatched some infantry under the command of his senior generals towards Harris to give the impression of being readied for battle while he had led the main wing of the army to take Stuart's 6,000 men by surprise in the thickly wooded mountains of Coorg. Nothing had gone as Tipu had planned.

'Are you sure about it? How reliable is the information?' Lakshmi was not convinced.

Suhasini was careful not to name Tipu even though they could be quite sure of not being overheard. The woman who brought the message came early in the morning while Suhasini was drawing water at the well and was quite confident. The encounter took place at Siddeshwar. He had an early advantage but the opposition was strong on the first day and then moved positions the next day. There was no victory. He had also lost Benky Nawab, his most fierce and reliable general, and was on his way back to the capital to refit before the next assault.

Lakshmi hoped this meant the English got their message. If only they had managed to kill Tipu and end the agony. How much longer did this agony have to be endured, to watch her subjects being taken to their death?

Tipu Sultan's secret battle plans had not been secret enough. Within the hour of his battle plans being drawn up, one of the Hindu women in the harem had sewed a note in the hem of her blouse and sent it over to Suhasini's house asking if she could kindly find someone to embroider it with lotus flowers. Lakshmi had parted with one of her gold bangles to pay for the secret to reach Coorg ahead of Tipu.

'This time we managed to send the message in time and it seemed to have done some good,' Lakshmi said. 'But what about the next time? What about tomorrow and the day after? We don't have the people or the resources that these men have to fight this battle with. And I might not live long enough to fight another one.'

'We will win this one. We just need a reliable way to stay in touch with the English generals. And I have a plan that might just work, even though I am afraid to even think of it,' Suhasini whispered.

Lakshmi put her hands on the younger woman's shoulder for support as she slowly got back on her feet. 'This knee is much older than the rest of me. We should not give these poor guards reasons to worry. God will take care of us. It is time to go back to our prison now.'

Suhasini was taken aback. Didn't the Queen want to know what she had in mind?

Lakshmi smiled gently. 'Yes, I want to know, but only when the plan is successful, as I have no doubt it will be. I trust you. How wonderful it is to be out in the sun and feeling the breeze glide off the river … how wonderful it is to be free…'

Cajoled back home by the dusk, they tumbled into the room, limbs dangling with fatigue, jaws aching with laughter. Richard headed straight for the portrait of Tipu Sultan, nearly complete, and pulled off the cover from the easel.

'Look, a miracle!' he announced. 'Not stolen!'

Francis and Mukunda laughed as did the men carrying in their luggage from the cart, glad to be part of a rare happiness, the sort that springs from no reason, except perhaps to forget all the worries prowling on the fringes of their lives. Francis gave loud directions to the men as they unpacked and began to set the room in order. Richard joined palms in exaggerated supplication at Francis to let the men go to bed and leave the tidying for daylight. Francis ignored him and continued with his supervisions.

Richard sprawled out on the cot and put his hand behind his head and watched the bustle around the room. His heart swelled with affection for his little company of men and he had to sit up again to breathe easily. Suddenly the cold stone granary had turned into a home, a space to call his own, where he was cared for and his art had found a foothold. Today he did not mind the cockroaches that scampered around the room, or the howling of jackals in the fields or the sting of his sunburnt skin. He could not remember just then what his life had been months ago in the country of his birth. Could there possibly have been another reality just as solid as this? If so, it surely belonged to a different self he was willing to forget.

Francis was looming over him with a look that Richard had learnt not to dismiss. 'Well, what is it? What did I do now?'

'Not you. Him!' Francis pointed out to Mukunda. 'Tell him to stop scribbling on the walls and go home.'

Richard sat up with a smile that vanished as soon as he saw the wall opposite him. The feeble light of the lamp lit up Mukunda's bare arm as it swayed with the shadows, clutching charcoal, lost in the vision that seared inside him.

Despite the distance, despite the inadequate light, Richard knew what was emerging on the wall. Suhasini's face. He had not been the only one to spot her by the river. He stared at the wall with such ferocity that Francis sullenly slunk away. 'You are both equally mad,' he grumbled and lay in his bed, his face turned away from them.

With no model or illumination to inspire his fingers, Mukunda continued to draw with a blind fury. He had seen her so closely, so briefly, flooded in a blue light, and he wished to see her again. His fingers were clearly racing ahead of his mind. The lines did not capture her likeness. And yet, there she was. Unmistakably. Richard saw the sculpted nose, the diamond stud on one side of it, the high cheekbones that dipped into soft dimples. He got out of bed and pulled out his drawing pad and tossed it at Francis's bed with a jealous fury. 'Tell him that if he must draw, he had better start using paper. Tell him…' and then he raised his voice, 'Tell him to leave the wall alone!'

As if conjured up by the churning in their hearts, she returned that night. Richard dragged Francis out of bed and Francis was vocal about his resentment. What did she want this time? Suhasini stood in the middle of the room, her shawl no longer shrouding her, looking around confidently, while they moved like blind kittens in her presence. Mukunda was acknowledged with a sweep of her head but that she was there to talk to Richard was obvious. As for Francis, she would not even look at him and he scowled to show the derision was mutual. The welcome that shone from the artists was embarrassing, Francis thought, but he would play his part. He repeated the question. So, what could they do for her this time?

Suhasini was too far away to notice Mukunda's drawing, her eyes now on the easel where Tipu's portrait created an eerie counterbalance to her presence. 'Not bad,' she mused. 'You actually do see him as a rather upright decent man, don't you?'

Richard straightened his shirt and stepped in front of the easel purposefully, blocking her view. Don't lose your mind, not now, he told himself. An incomplete canvas is like fragile glassware just emerging from the blowpipe. Unprepared for a critic. Don't be baited into defending or explaining the work. She had guessed a lot by a glance, but how?

She looked straight into his eyes. 'Here we believe art is a reflection not merely of what has been seen, but what has been lived. Surely your friend has already explained it to you.'

Mukunda flinched when she arched her eyebrows towards him. An unknown sensation rippled through him. He pressed his back against the outline he had just been drawing, feeling the rock reach out to his bones, wanting to keep her from looking at him again. He did not know about her earlier visit and it shocked him to see her talking to Richard with such assurance and familiarity. The woman standing there was not the one he had seen in his mother's kitchen, or the one walking under the temple trees earlier that day, or even the face on the wall he was shielding. He did not want to know this woman talking in measured words or bear the pain of discovering that the two women were the same; the product of his imagination more real than the face he was seeing, or the voice he was hearing.

Suhasini and Richard were conversing rapidly now.

'What do you want from me this time?' Francis repeated Richard's words faithfully but the tone was his own, loud and aggressive. Suhasini smiled deliberately at Francis and he blushed at breaching the ethics of translation. He had been shown his place and he did not speak out as himself again.

She abruptly sat down in the lone chair in the room, Richard's chair. The circle of light from the lamp fell on her lap, on the dark green pleats of the sari flowing from her hips to the floor. Back erect, held tilted up, she met their collective gaze with poise. 'The same as before. Friendship and help.'

'I cannot help you. You found that out last time as well. I am an employee of Tipu Sultan, not his confidant, not even a man seen important enough to be the enemy. I am nothing.'

Suhasini folded her hands across her chest. Calm. She would explain if he wanted her to, if he was willing to listen. Richard nodded and sat down on the edge of his cot.

'You will offer yourself as a spy to Tipu, volunteer to go to the invading army, to give false leads to the English officers and to bring back inside information. He will agree ... well, for many reasons, this naïve painting, for instance, and because he has no other surprises to throw at the enemy. Also because someone he trusts in the Council of Ministers, one of our supporters, will convince him to trust you.'

Richard shook his head with a dry laugh. 'You are forgetting something, aren't you? I am not a spy and I don't want to be one.'

'Please let me finish,' Suhasini taunted him with a tone of false patience. 'You will go as a spy but you won't be working in Tipu's interests. You will serve your own people, help the English win the war, and in the process help free my people from this tyranny. Surely, there is a patriot inside you somewhere, a man who believes in freedom.'

'No,' Richard said and then thought about it a little, speaking out louder this time. 'No.'

Francis did not have to repeat that. Suhasini pushed her chair back and the circle of light jumped from her lap into the cracks in the floor. A silence spread out in which they could almost see through each other, irritation in Mukunda, nervousness from Francis, and Richard's impatience, while she watched them grow uncomfortable with themselves.

Richard wanted so much to get closer to this woman, to be liked by her. He wanted to reach over and hold her hand, draw in the warmth of her body, envelop the fire that must make her talk like this, of matters that did not matter at all. He took deep breaths, the intoxication of jasmine, the tingle of clove, the dense blend of skin and earth, the smell of a woman's sweat. The hunger for neglected pleasures was growing and distracting him.

'Let us try this again,' she spoke up and the men shifted with the relief of being released from the weight of the silence. 'What will it take to convince you to do this … this assignment?'

Richard looked at Francis whose head moved slightly sideways as if to say: Don't fall for the oldest trick in negotiations; there is to be no deal here.

'So, don't you care that I am going to be dead very soon? Or that Tipu Sultan has decided all nine women of the Wodeyar family and their little prince are to be secretly executed? Isn't there any humanity in you that I can appeal to? You, and you alone, could save their lives.'

She is lying, said Francis's eyes, and manipulating you. Richard turned to Mukunda who was nearly invisible now, pressed against the wall, hardly breathing, eyes shifting between Suhasini and the Englishman. Richard knew then that Mukunda and he were both caught in the same snare and that he had to move first, move decisively. He would do anything she wanted, but only if…

Her guard dropped. She pushed her chair back and stood up angrily. He wanted her to pose for a painting. Did he have any idea how this would ruin her? Her family, her reputation, if anyone were to find out, she would be ostracized.

If she had managed to come to their house in the night, not once but twice, she could do this too, he was sure. She would never be alone, Richard reminded her, for her cousin would be there too. Surely she trusted her own blood?

'Nobody knows about my blood,' she snapped back. 'And it is a good thing too. I don't mind shedding it for a good cause, unlike you who can only think of something as selfish as a painting when people are dying.'

Richard did not want to see it that way. Why should he? This woman knew what she was asking of him. Didn't his life and desires mean anything at all? What could she possibly know of the horror of failure, of constantly falling short of promises made to others and to himself?

'I came for a livelihood, not martyrdom,' he mumbled to himself and held up a hand to Francis to prevent the translation. He needed to think this over. The appeal to chivalry was harder to ignore. If he could prevent any harm coming to these women and the little prince ... Suddenly he saw that he had been trusted with the embers of another war, one that had been kept alive beneath the clash of great armies that everybody else was fussing about. He was this other war.

Yes, he would do anything to help her. Richard made Francis repeat that twice.

Suhasini's eyes softened with gratitude. Richard knew then that she would fulfil his condition in return.

Her instructions were specific. First to convince Tipu that the artist wanted to show his appreciation for the royal hospitality and generosity. Richard would have to insist on going to the English camp without an escort and after getting there would reveal that he was representing the Wodeyar interests. He had to persuade the British to stay away from Bangalore where Tipu had military reinforcements. It was more important for them to get to the capital directly and to do so by taking the circuitous southern road. Then he would have to come back to the Sultan and tell him exactly the opposite: that the English were planning to first conquer Bangalore fort before marching down the central road to Srirangapatna.

Francis and Richard repeated the information back and forth, asking questions and directions. She waited till they looked back at her with some semblance of comprehension and then reached for the door. Mukunda stepped away from the wall as soon as she was gone. They did not know what to say to each other, not even Francis, drained from the effort of juggling words. They had started the day as merry picnickers, men of equal merit, and now they were wedged apart by a fault line of history. Mukunda strode to a corner of the room where his old mattress had been rolled and stacked on top of some earthen pots. He picked it up purposefully and unfurled it on the floor beside Francis's cot. The thought of going away to his parents and wife was unthinkable. This was his home now.

Crossing Sides

The earth beneath his feet moved of its own accord. He had just stood there, quivering with the words he spoke, looking as wretched as he felt. He asked to go to the English camp, to meet the commander in charge of the invading army, and hoped to be denied, even punished.

But no, the earth would not stop moving, would not give him any time to collect himself. It swept him into Tipu's inner chamber, then out of it, put him astride a horse, took him across fields and groves, then straight to the edge of the English camp. The English soldiers would not grant Francis entry, but the earth was still moving for Richard, his story again believed by someone, taking him through the labyrinth of tents, back among his countrymen. He could talk to the world again without his English being filtered through Francis into another language; if only, if only the words would ease out somehow. And then the earth stopped suddenly, in front of General Harris's tent.

Richard was shown in. And then for an hour all stood still.

When he emerged from the tent, the earth lurched to motion again. Richard dropped on his knees in the grass and began to throw up. His head throbbed so wildly that he had to press back his forehead and eyes with both hands. He heard boots gather around him and felt the net close in, tighten and choke his throat. An end tainted by a public display of guilt in the middle of the English camp, this was to be his lot. He tried to stand up but could not feel his feet and dropped back to the ground. As the last bit of his strength ebbed out, he felt someone bend over him, grab his shoulders, say something. Despite his panic, he recognized the voice and smiled. And with that came the relief of a blackout.

The white roof of a tent greeted him when his eyes opened again. There was a stale stench in the air, of musty cloth and rotting shoes. Richard coughed and pulled himself up as the cot sagged creakily.

'So is it the heat or is it your nerves?'

'Jon Cole! So it was you! I was not hallucinating! How are you?'

Cole got up from his rickety campstool and grabbed his outstretched hands, 'I am guessing the Mysore weather does not agree with you.'

Richard looked down uncomfortably. Cole patted his hand and pushed the sheets aside to find a perch. 'Oh, there is no need to thank me for saving you. Fainting in the middle of the camp in full view of thousands of soldiers, I am so pleased to see that you haven't changed at all.'

'Maybe I was just trying to get your attention among the thousands. It worked, didn't it?'

'I heard you were here. To meet the great heroes of our army. How did the meeting go?'

Richard remembered every minute. He had been too bewildered, too nervous, and it seemed a miracle that he had survived the meeting in General Harris's tent. The faces and names of the men in shiny uniforms introduced to him as the Political and Diplomatic Commission were jumbled now – Wellesley, Close, Agnew, Malcolm, Macaulay – though he could recall Arthur Wellesley, a sad-eyed boyish officer, and only because he remembered to look twice at the man who was the Governor-General's brother. The men were polite, coldly polite, as if it pained them to have to believe his story. They asked him many questions about his life in Mysore, and more specifically of Srirangapatna, for the last six months;

questions upon questions, they made notes, watched every twitch in his face, studied his hands as they moved to explain. Why would any man offer himself up like this to be a double-crossing spy in a war where he had nothing to gain, and everything to lose if things were to backfire? How were they to know that he wasn't there to spy on the English army and take information back to Tipu Sultan instead?

That was indeed the agreement Richard had made with Tipu but not what he intended. He had tried his best to convince the Company officers. He was on their side. Our side, he had corrected himself.

'Well, in case you are wondering … the Commission has decided to believe you. I have it from a reliable source.' Cole got up to pour brandy in two glasses of different shapes.

'How do you know that?' Richard grabbed the glass held out to him and threw his head back to empty it.

Cole pretended to be hurt and refilled the glass. 'Is that how well you know me? The general has decided that you are telling the truth and that we will take the southern road, the one that Tipu Sultan does not expect us to take, while a smaller battalion will head for Bangalore to give the impression that we intend to spend a few days there amusing ourselves with the conquest of yet another of their forts.'

Why? Why had the general taken his word? And why had Tipu Sultan agreed to his plan within the two sentences it had taken him to propose it? Why had his truths and lies become equally convincing?

'A formal report is still expected from General Stuart but we heard what happened in Coorg and Harris is grateful for the timely warning sent to them. The officers think your story might explain something of it. But I have one question. Why are you doing this?'

He mumbled about not knowing and held his glass out for another drink. But Cole put the bottle away deliberately and Richard took the empty glass back to his lips to shake out a few droplets. 'I just want this whole war to be over today and if only there was some way to make sure of that.' Richard swung his feet to the ground. 'I should not take too long to get back. They will be waiting for me.' Richard's neck turned pink in response to Cole's searching gaze and nothing more was said on the matter.

Cole started to describe the month that the army had been on the march, much too slow and cumbersome, and endless troubles with the management of stock. He had just spent three days doing a new inventory and the provisions seemed alarmingly low. Thankfully, reinforcements were on their way. There were thieves among them but it was hard to nab anyone inside a gigantic city that constantly moved. All his findings were going into a report to be handed over to General Harris himself. The one thing he was sure of was that being a minor officer of the extensive administrative staff of a marching army any day trumped over a stuffy corner in the old Customs House.

'I had not imagined I would be so glad to see you! How is the painting coming along? Have you made your fortune yet or are you thinking of becoming a professional army informer?'

Richard did not think that was funny and said so. But he was so relieved Cole was in the camp. The painting materials he had sent had been very useful. And the boy he had recommended, Francis, was an excellent choice.

'Oh yes, a very smart lad. Quite the talker too, isn't he?'

Richard's eyes twinkled in agreement. 'Hard to shut him up sometimes. I have an apprentice as well to help me around the studio. And I just finished a portrait of Tipu Sultan.'

'And?'

'He liked it of course, very much I think. And yes, I got paid handsomely as well.'

'Well, you seem quite settled…'

Richard abruptly asked if there were any letters for him. It had been so long since his mother's voice had played in his head. No, no letters, said Cole kindly. And just like that, something detached itself from Richard, something that had tied him to the parental tree, and floated away like an autumn leaf.

'Cole…' Richard hesitated, not sure of the words to pick.

Cole waved a magnanimous hand at him. Yes, yes, he would look out for him there, keep his ears pinned back, eyes peeled open and whatever else. He could count on him. 'Here, you can have another drink now and then be off on your way. You don't want to keep Tipu Sultan waiting, do you?'

The Company army was now only twenty-eight miles from Tipu Sultan's capital. A red banner with tiger stripes fluttered over the Mysore army as they waited at a vantage point outside the village of Malavalli, the enemy coming towards them like an unending tidal wave. The infantry charged first and with them exploded a cloud of dust so high and thick that even after hours of desperate fighting, it was impossible to tell which side had the upper hand.

Twelve miles to the west of this cloud was a camp with empty tents that awaited the return of the Mysore soldiers. A few caretakers and attendants walked around aimlessly. Nobody seemed to care or remember about the English artist in one of the peripheral tents.

Richard and Francis had not spoken to each other all day. Whether the Mysore army lost or the English army, their lives were dangling over an abyss with nothing but a favourable wind propping them up. They kept to themselves, ate the food brought to them, and sat gloomily in separate corners, Francis pretending to sleep and Richard staring at large fruit flies. From the battlefield they heard cannon shots and smelt the crop of death, fresh and bountiful. There was no escaping the part they had played in it.

Richard had lied to Tipu Sultan and Purnaiah had vouched for him, blaming the English General instead of giving misleading information to a poor unsuspecting fellow countryman. Richard's usefulness as an informer was over but he had not yet been ordered back to the capital. Whether Tipu Sultan suspected him was unclear, though he had no doubt that there would be voices in the council, led by Dewan Mir Sadiq, who would think the worst of the Englishman.

Knowing that they would be absolutely right about his treachery was making him feverish.

Dusk came very late and with it the terrible noises; feet and swords dragging rivulets of blood into the camp, screams of injured men being carried in, neighing of frazzled horses, shaky voices of men who still could not believe they were alive while someone they knew had a head blown off. Richard and Francis worried about the outcome of the battle but it was impossible to guess even though Francis had pressed his ear against the flap of the tent. They did not have the courage to step out and nobody came to talk to them.

The men sat in the darkness, not having lamps to light, in the company of the garbled sounds, trying to dissuade the insects that settled on them, anxious to keep sinking thoughts at bay. Richard thought of how frail and tired Francis looked this day, a boy worn out by his own bravado, utterly disillusioned by the life of adventures. He felt sorry for having dragged him through such misery and he felt sorry for himself. He would die in India, barely a year after arrival.

'Look, a light. Coming this way!'

The lantern sailed across the darkness, stopping once briefly to shine on a buttoned shirt, seemed undecided on where to turn and then continued towards them. The light pushed through the narrow entrance to their little tent and an officer in French colours stepped in behind it. His white breeches and long black boots were splattered with mud and blood, all dried into the same dull brown; a sleeve of his red overcoat had been ripped; a thick bandage ran from wrist to elbow of his left arm in which he swung a bottle of arrack. His hair was plastered with sweat.

Andre Surcouf introduced himself and shook their hands heartily. He was Mukunda's friend and was there at his behest. Surcouf had not seen Mukunda for months and had been shocked by his sudden appearance at the battlefield. Even then, Mukunda would not say much, except that he was in the employment of an English painter who needed help. 'I'm not sure I can be of any help, but I thought we could start by sharing a drink,' said the Frenchman.

Francis hurried forward with three cups into which Surcouf carelessly splashed the murky liquid. Francis showed off his smattering French and Surcouf politely complimented him for his linguistic skills, as also his Portuguese ancestry, which he silently preferred to the other's English.

'Where is Mukunda? He was supposed to stay back in the fort.' Richard grabbed the cup closest to him. 'Is he here?'

Yes, he had been there but had not been allowed into the camp. The anxiety of waiting for Richard and Francis had been too much for him to bear. But Surcouf had persuaded Mukunda to return to the island, promising to look into the matter. 'I have heard plenty about you, Richard Dawson, the audacious Englishman who won patronage from a man who hates all things English. I don't believe this story about painting commissions. Most of my colleagues argue you are an imbecile but I can see that is not true. Would you care to tell me what brought you to India?'

Richard's words were well rehearsed. A man tells his life story so many times to strangers and more so while travelling through strange lands that he begins to say the same words with little thought and much detachment. He tried to talk of his art with passion but it all sounded like lies even to his own ears. Surcouf took pity on him and swerved the conversation to Mukunda. They both agreed he was a fine young man with promise.

'I have to leave now for a meeting of commanders. Mukunda did not seem to want me to know why you are here, and I won't probe, but I would advise you to return to the capital at the earliest.' He swirled his cup with flamboyance. 'Can you believe they brewed this lifesaver just a mile away from here in the smelliest cowshed? Vile and divine at the same time, isn't it?'

'So what happened today? Did we win?' Richard could not help asking as Francis dipped his face into his drink with a grimace.

'We?' Surcouf taunted softly. 'Do you mean we the English or we the Indians?'

'Mysore, of course!' All the tensions of the day burst to the surface. Richard struggled to find the right words to assert his false innocence. 'That's why I am sitting here in your camp, don't you think?'

Surcouf looked at him curiously. 'I have offended you, it seems. But then it is just as surprising that you are sitting here in *our* camp and yet don't know what every child in Mysore does by now. We were forced to retreat. And with heavy losses. It would not be this painful if we had managed to do serious damage to the enemy but I don't think they lost as many men or guns. We had every advantage one can wish for in a battlefield and yet they were better prepared than us. It's a shame, a tragedy, a golden opportunity lost.' He smacked his lips broodingly. 'There might not be many more toasts to share if this continues…'

'Is Tipu Sultan safe?'

'His pride is hurt, the poor man! We are marching north tomorrow and then south-east to get behind the English army. We will attack them from behind as they ford the river at Arakere. It is likely to be a fight to the finish for they will have no place to retreat to if we get the upper hand which I am sure we will. Today was just bad luck but that is not likely to stalk us twice in a row.'

'Yes.' Richard nodded. 'Yes.'

'But you have had a turn of fortune already. It has been decided to send you back to Srirangapatna in the morning with some of the ministers and a fine battalion as escort. Far away from this smelly camp and filthy soldiers. I am sure you won't be sorry to miss more of the war action.'

'We are going home,' Richard muttered to himself, thinking of Suhasini. He had kept his side of the bargain, followed every instruction, and now she would keep hers. A strange stirring raced through his body. The smell of drying paint, the mahlstick sinking into a fleshy grove in his arm, the palette knife following a daring brush to scrap off every spot of excess. He felt restless to be back at the studio, to paint again, to paint her.

Surcouf was speaking meanwhile. 'Dawson, I would watch my back if I were you. There are some with unmitigated access to the

Sultan's ear who think you are a traitor. Be on your guard and stick to your paintings. You won't be sent out on anymore special missions considering how this last one has turned out. You are a lucky man, Dawson, to get out of this mess with your head still attached to your shoulders. Lucky.'

It is over, Richard kept repeating to himself, and it will save the lives of those poor imprisoned women. A war is what causes the death of people, not a little lie told with good intentions. He repeated the words till it seemed less and less like he had deceived those who had given him shelter.

Francis would not talk to him like before. The occasional brotherly familiarity and good-humoured bullying was gone. They had returned to the stone granary, trying to carry on by pulling as far apart as the corners of the shared space would allow. It helped to have Mukunda between them, oblivious to their strains, immersed in the painting that he had started on a square of canvas cloth that Richard had discarded. It had many of the lines that had started on the wall the other night but also had a new striking quality about it. Strangely, Francis was the first to notice for Richard had been too distraught, too anxious for the night to arrive with the possibility of Suhasini and some demonstration of her appreciation if not gratitude.

Francis brought the matter up by asking if Richard had looked at the boy's work. And so Richard did. He sat on the window ledge from where he had a good view over Mukunda's shoulder as his fingers coaxed the lines to recreate a face. The canvas had been prepared with a grounding that had the careful shading that Richard insisted on. Mukunda was working steadily, not in the manner of the Master at the Ganjam colony or his own quirky ways, but his hand was moving as though it belonged to Richard. The apprentice was copying him with unhesitating ease.

Francis was looking at Richard questioningly. Richard knew he was expected to stop Mukunda, distract him and give him some other work to do. That was what his own deepest instinct was goading him to do. He had taught his skills to someone with talent, something that had happened to him as well when he had been an apprentice. It meant nothing, he consoled himself, nothing.

Mukunda drew across the canvas as though tracing Suhasini's face on a dusty-looking glass. The men were so transfixed by the process that the first knock went unheard. The second time, it was sharper and clearly came from the backdoor. Francis rushed to open it, surmising one of his workers to be in distress. Instead, she had turned up again.

'Blow out the lamps!'

They quickly obeyed Suhasini. She left the door open for the crisp wind that followed her into the room. The men stared back into the darkness while she talked rapidly. From her voice they knew she was pleased and excited, even self-congratulatory. Her plan had worked without a flaw. The English army was closer and victory would soon be theirs. But it was early to celebrate and there was more work at hand.

Richard protested. He thought he had done enough. Her travails on the other hand might just be beginning. He told her about Tipu Sultan's meeting with his generals following the Malavalli battle and the decision to attack the English army from the rear as they forded the river at Arakere.

She thought about it briefly. But the English would not cross the river at Arakere. They might have done that in the last campaign, but they would not in this one. Instead, they would travel further east and cross the Kaveri at Sosale where her people had assured her the river was low and safe enough for a large army to wade through. Tipu Sultan would not expect it. And the English would safely be on the southern side of the river. All Richard had to do was write a letter. A man was waiting below the mango tree at the end of the lane to take the letter to the English General.

Richard had had enough of interfering with military strategies and so did Francis. No, he would not do it. Suhasini reminded him again that her life depended on this. The haughtiness was fading. She was pleading.

Just one last letter, Richard agreed.

The banging on the door would not cease. They had gone to bed for hours and daybreak was just a few heartbeats away.

Francis groaned. It was truly a night of horrors that would never end. What could she want now? But they knew this could not be Suhasini, slipping out of her house twice in the same night. Whoever was rattling the door was also kicking it angrily. During the few moments of hurrying out of bed, dragging clothes straight, lighting lamps and unlatching the door, they felt the weight of impending doom and feared the worst.

The man who was to be their secret messenger came sprawling into their room, his head smashed into a mangled mass of blood. In his fist was the letter that Richard had written to General Harris. Francis bit his hand to stifle his scream of terror. They just stood there, torn between wanting to rush to the fallen man and the dread of what might follow, for another person had just stepped into the room and calmly placed a foot on the corpse.

Mir Sadiq was staring at them with bloodshot eyes. This, he pointed to the pool of blood forming on the floor, this is what we do to traitors in our country.

They stood speechless with terror. Richard turned to Francis who was looking at the roof with a strange glazed look and knew he was close to a faint. All of Richard's fears were now coming true and the lives of these young boys were at stake because of his recklessness. If only he could somehow think of something, anything, to convince this man who had made no secret of his hatred for them that there was a mistake, a misconstruction of events; or perhaps drop on his knees and beg for whatever mercy could be scrounged. If only Francis would gather his wits and courage and speak up now, even if merely as a translator.

'You!' Mir Sadiq roared. 'You are still hanging around where you have no business to be.' He walked menacingly towards Mukunda who held his gaze but tumbled back a little nervously.

Richard quickly stepped forward. 'Francis, Francis, tell him that I would like to talk to him. I can explain and we can clear this matter up satisfactorily.'

Francis barely had a voice to gather the right words but he got the Dewan's attention.

'Explain? No, you don't get to explain. You only get to listen. Don't take me for a fool, not even for one misguided moment. I have had my eyes on you, Englishman, ever since you turned up here with that fake story of yours, getting sympathy from the Padshah, tunnelling your way into his trust, hoping to escape scrutiny because of the war. This spying favour you did for us paid fine dividends, didn't it? And yet, the Padshah believes you. I don't know what magic spell you have cast on him with your painting tricks. You deserve to die for this betrayal, all of you!'

Richard took a deep breath. Everything being said was true and the letter he had written was damning evidence. All logic dictated that they be killed instantly like their unfortunate messenger. Strangely, the Dewan, legendary for his impatience and depravity, was making a speech to them instead of drawing a sword. Was he trying to suggest a way out? If only Richard could be sure…

'So! I see you have nothing to say. If only the Padshah were here tonight and not so far away on the battlefield, I would have marched you straight to the palace. But in his absence, you are entirely at my mercy and I want to make sure you get the most efficient death, torturous and exceedingly slow.'

Richard instinctively knew then that a sliver of opportunity was being opened and that it would get smaller with every passing moment they stayed silent, till there would be absolutely no way out.

He and Francis struggled for the words in two languages. 'We acted in ignorance and are ashamed of ourselves. If only we could show you just how sorry we are.'

Mir Sadiq calmed down. A calculating look came into his eyes. 'Some crimes are too dastardly, undeserving of pardon…'

'Yes, you are right, we understand … perhaps something would help you forget our unforgivable crime.'

'Not now, Englishman,' Mir Sadiq lowered his voice and stepped very close to Richard, towering over him, pushing his face directly in line with his.

'But soon, I hope your English General will generously reward the lapse of memory that I am going to have about this night. I have no doubt about how this battle will end. And I have a family to think of, many people who are dependent on me. I want to make sure they are well provided for when the English have taken over. Can I take the word of an unworthy worm like you?'

'Yes, yes of course, well provided for. I will personally recommend to General Harris, the invaluable service and concern you have shown towards the interests of the Company, and…'

'Enough!' Mir Sadiq held up his hand and turned to go. 'If anybody else hears of this, you can be sure to meet the same fate as this friend of yours on the floor. We have an understanding and that is good enough for me for now.' He bent down and plucked the letter from the dead man's hands and dusted it. 'I will make sure this is delivered. You are lucky I caught your messenger tonight. But if you are careless again, I will not be able to save your skins and you will forget all about our understanding. Is that clear?'

'There won't be a next time, you can rest assured.'

An unconvinced Mir Sadiq banged the door on his way out.

DANCE OF THE PLANETS

The night swayed slow and sultry. The suffocating heat of the day slowly trickled out of the stone walls, across the stone floor, into the feet of the wooden easel. The scent of blooming parijata flowers wafted in through closed windows. She would not allow more than two lamps to be lit in the room, one on the ledge beside her and the other beside Richard's unsteady hand. Francis sat glumly on his cot and pretended to be absorbed in the contents of the moneybox. Going over his accounts and drawing up grocery lists remained his only shield against the moody easel that lorded over the room.

Richard felt her laughing eyes on him as he hopped to shift his weight, charcoal poised between his fingers, white canvas waiting for its first smudge. She had kept her promise and turned up for the portrait and had patiently rearranged herself to suit his changing whims. She had even worn the blue sari he had wanted to paint her in, to recast her as she had appeared by the riverbank. After requesting her to shift from one position to the other, he had finally caved to her exasperation and asked her what she would rather be doing.

'Read,' she said at once, she liked to read. So Richard handed out one of his sketchpads for her to look and her eyes softened in an unusual way. Like lightning it came to him, the painting he had imagined during his journey to Mysore. A waiting Penelope, the look of endurance, of faith.

'Our women have been shut outside the world of books, a world they would most be at home,' she was saying. 'Do the women in your country read?'

'Yes, yes, certainly, if they want to, they can learn to read but most have to work hard to earn a livelihood and look after their homes, just as they do here. There are many who never learn to read.' He did not tell her that she would be at a loom when he was finished.

She continued to look at the sketches curiously while he readjusted the lamp beside her to let the light hit her profile from behind, placing her sharp features against a mellow halo.

'It is unfair to never be allowed to read,' she said, 'perhaps because when we get knowledge it is the one thing they cannot take out of us.'

Mukunda refilled both lamps with oil, tweaked the swollen wicks into place and went to his corner to watch Richard work. He seemed uninterested in his own drawings and had even stashed away the sketch of Suhasini he had been started in such earnest. The lines on the wall that were once her face had also been scrubbed out as much possible. Richard had decided to ignore his moodiness and attributed it to having exiled himself from his home again, but did not suggest a return for fear that he would disappear for good.

'You don't talk much, do you?' Suhasini turned towards Mukunda. 'Perhaps your wife has domesticated you a little too efficiently.'

He looked away.

'I heard you moved out of the house again. Your mother had come visiting and she is wrought with grief. Poor woman!'

'Don't move so much,' Richard interrupted and then tried gestures to explain the words. Please. Try. Stay. Still.

Her attention back on his sketchbook, she did not look up as he continued to work. Richard was pleased at how easily he was able to get her likeness. But his breathing was becoming laborious, making him feel quite wobbly and long for the cool outdoors. Only his fingers continued to work as if the rest of him did not matter.

She arrived late the following night but appeared to be in a happier state of mind. They knew she must have had some news from the battlefield that had pleased her. Richard waited for her to settle down and then asked from behind the canvas. So how did she get to know all these informers?

Why won't he let her look at that drawing he was making of her? She pushed her question against his.

'It is just my professional way. You will have to wait till it is completed.'

Then she supposed she was allowed her professional secrets too.

'Aren't you afraid of the consequences?'

'I am more afraid of the consequences if our mission were to fail. The young prince needs to be back on the throne of his forefathers, restored to his subjects, and all the women in his kingdom deserve to feel safe.'

Richard wondered if there wasn't anything else she thought about him, or wished to share, apart form politics – this kind of revolutionary life belittled everyone else.

Richard continued to sketch, Francis grumbled about the heat and Mukunda's eye lit up in sympathy. Suhasini fired up the stone room with her presence and their minds hovered around her like suicidal moths. They felt prepared to sit there for eternity while she looked at the sketchbook, while the painting continued to grow, as if it had no intention of being completed.

But Suhasini did not turn up for the rest of the week. That was when the fort was paralysed by terror, finally accepting that a defeat was likely. Their reliable army led by the valorous Tipu Sultan had failed to crush the English army. Only a wide rocky stretch of the evaporating waters of the Kaveri lay between them. Tipu had not only miscalculated the road the invaders travelled but had scorched the land beyond the north and east walls of the fort to deter them from setting camp while they had headed straight for his own army's pastures in the south. Even the last full-frontal assault that Tipu and his generals wished to make was foiled when the English army altered their march without warning.

Every gateway leading out of the Srirangapatna fort had been sealed. In a few days cannonballs would be flung at them from across the river. If the residents had wished to escape they ought to have done it sooner but now a heavy price would be paid for their complacency. How had it come to this? Tipu had to consider that there were forces other than fate and providence helping the English get the better of him at every turn. This was the unmistakable work of a traitor.

When Suhasini finally appeared at their doorway, she seemed thinner, her eyes glazed with feverish distraction. The blue sari was crumpled and she frequently looked at the windows. They had never seen her so edgy before. She knew she was being watched and followed. There were spies outside who would report exactly how long she sat on a stool in front of the English painter. And yet, nobody had stopped her from coming or said anything untoward. This strange complicity was unnerving.

'Is it beginning to look like me?' she asked about the painting that was decidedly turned away from her.

'Yes. But it also going to be what I see of you. But please, you must settle down now. Unless you don't want me to paint today.' Richard used his wrist to push back his hair, now grown long and unkempt down his nape. It made him look more impetuous than his nature allowed.

'We have to work when we can. I am not sure how much more time we have. Aren't you happy about the war, Englishman? Your countrymen are here and soon you will be reunited with your friends and they will be in charge of the fort.'

All the friends Richard wanted were right there in that room.

'Will you send another message to the English General for me? An important message.'

'No,' said Francis for Richard who reiterated it. No, it was not possible, under no circumstances. They had got into enough trouble and one did not even want to consider what might happen if that bully Mir Sadiq sold his conscience to a higher bidder. Richard tried to explain that he was likely to be more trouble than help for the women now. No.

Mukunda saw more than ever what Suhasini was up against. How had she managed to be an exception? Everything in their upbringing had taught them to be docile, fearful, hesitant. Even more for a girl. How was she able to disobey families that insisted they stay sheltered?

'I could do it if you asked me,' Mukunda spoke up. Francis and Richard looked at each other. Would he?

Why would Mukunda do it? Suhasini stepped away from her position and faced to ask him again. Why?

Because she would.

Was that reason enough to do something on which the lives hung of other people in balance? And especially when his father was one of the court astrologers? She was looking at Mukunda with new interest.

'What my father does is my father's affair, and mine is of no relevance to him.'

Suhasini would have liked to hear that her cousin believed in her cause, that he would do a heroic act with the sole intention of saving the young Wodeyar. But no, Mukunda said it did not matter who ruled them. Ordinary people would continue to struggle with their lives. The powerful, on the other hand, needed the war to stay powerful.

'He really is mad!' Francis laughed. Mukunda was as bereft of malice as he was capricious and had grown on Francis.

'Will you please get back into position? We haven't made any progress today,' Richard snapped.

But Suhasini was restless. She could not stay in her seat, worry and sleeplessness slackened her body, wrinkled her face, turned her into someone else. She seemed to want to talk. Her hands would not stop moving, waving through the air, touching her sari, her hair.

'Okay.' Richard put down his brushes. 'Let's not work tonight.' It was futile to even try. But they did not want the night to end or for her to leave. She was saying something about the seasons, about the fruits ripening on the trees, the flowers she picked as a child, the warm dessert that nobody makes like her favourite aunt. And then that time when she got separated from her parents at the village fair, only ten years old, she had crawled under a banyan tree and cried for hours till they found her. Before their eyes she turned into a little girl and they ached to hold and console her. No, no, your parents will be here soon.

'Come, come, see yourself, see the portrait. A long way to go to completion, but still, it is already starting to be you.' Richard invited her to the canvas.

'Really?'

The other three were taken aback. Richard had been a stickler for keeping his canvases safe from the scrutiny and feedback of his models till the project was completed. But he was being enthusiastic, making room for Suhasini in front of the easel. She looked at the emerging lines of her body in black lines, looked at it for long, and smiled encouragingly at an anxious Richard. 'Very nice.'

Richard was embarrassed, apologetic. The work was in its infancy, this was just a starting point, the seed of the idea. For now, the lines are falling into place, just creating a composition…

She was not listening, but thinking deeply, and then addressed them. 'Two people could see the same thing and yet not the same way. Did that make the painting about the model or the artist? It would make an interesting experiment to see who emerges … maybe … probably … if only … easier to tell if one subject had two interpretations … worth a try, didn't they think?'

The men were not sure what she meant.

'Perhaps,' she said, 'Mukunda should draw me as well, that is if his master did not object.'

It took Richard a few moments to understand. What was she trying to do? Was she trying to start a competition?

Mukunda nodded at her, at Richard. He wished he could.

'Fine,' Richard felt compelled to concur. It might be fun, he told himself. To paint together. It will give the boy a chance to try his new skills and improve. It might keep her in better humour or at least bring her back again and again till his painting was done.

Suhasini stayed longer than usual, and the rooster in their yard was starting to clear his throat when she headed for the door. She appeared reluctant to go or perhaps the world awaiting her was frightening. It had been a night for friendship but it was going to be a day for hard bargaining.

Mortals have played their part, but the outcome of this war now hinges on the gods. Both sides look at the skies and try to read it. Every cloud that drifts in, every tint of the horizon, they gamble on the coming of the monsoons this year. Varuna is a busy and temperamental god, to say the least. His duties are far ranging, too many water bodies to monitor, and water too messy to manage. We pray he does not forget about our little fort in the middle of dusty nowhere or our river that cuts between the foe and us.

On that side is an army that is reeling from the fatigue of a great march, rationing supplies that will barely last eighteen more days, digging trenches deep in the river bank, building a giant battery of great guns all turned at our walls, and worrying that if they cannot force an outcome before the onset of monsoon, they will have to go back in shame. The rains will make the river impossible to ford and the water currents will fight fiercer than our soldiers to keep the fort out of the invaders' reach.

On this side lies a strange mix of panic and fortitude. No matter what we do, the English seem to be a step ahead of us. All sections of their army have reached and gathered around us. Our Sultan decides to fortify the southern wall but their general decides to focus his guns on the bastion at the joint of the northern and western walls. Military confrontations in small pockets take place every day, the

English continuing to gain ground. And our men continue to retreat towards the fort, till we are all sealed inside its gates. Repairs and reinforcements to our fort defences are constant. Our panic stems from the bloodshed ahead and our fortitude is an abiding faith in the moody God of rain.

Will it rain? Will it not?

Two paintings grow together. Two rectangles of canvas cut to equal length, backs to each other, faces open to infinity, they grow together but with different personalities.

The nights arrive slow and depart too soon. The painters wait restlessly, endlessly. Suhasini has a way of making time skim. Sometimes she is there before they expect her and sometimes she comes for just an hour before the sky is ablaze again. They try to understand what is different in her that night that had not been there last night or any other time in the past. She dips within herself, like a fathomless well, and their eyes fall on her like pebbles that never hit the dark ground. She brings fresh mystery with her every night, and leaves it behind with the dawn, unsolved.

The painting to the right of her sits upon an experienced easel. It looks at her as if through a window. She is framed with exacting elegance, long braid curling down her arms like a serpent about to strike. She radiates power like a closed fist. Richard has come to accept that he will never really know her, only love what he sees and experiences – the little he knows has to suffice for that. The charcoal on his fingers rubs passionately into her contours. The lamp is the other thing he has thought about much these days. Its flame licking upwards to reach the light in her eyes, drawing her out as if a secret lover. The edge of a wooden loom sticks out at one end of the frame, one finger stretched to straighten a skein of thread, she is Penelope daring someone to walk into her solitude. Her waiting. All that Richard has ever thought about the pain of waiting has now effortlessly become hers.

The painting to the left of Suhasini rests against a stack of wooden blocks. She fills it up and there is no room for either lamp or the book in her hands. Her body is no longer an oyster for her brilliance, it is a glass case that both contains and spills it over. Mukunda's fingers are not seeing the same things as his eyes. Her hair is untied and tumbling down in curls, her lips twisted into half a smile. The woman on the canvas does not even look entirely like Suhasini but that does not stop her from inhabiting her spirit and looking straight at the viewer. In the artists' colony they said one who saw typically was closer to the truth than one who saw objectively. A painter has no ego, no self. There is only the divine spirit, the gift of the fingers and then there is this woman who is now within him.

Two paintings. The strokes on both paintings have the same elegance and strength, both dark and confident, almost drawn by the same hand, but they are not the same. And there are no interruptions except for the ticking of the night.

Their home is becoming insulated from the anxiety of the war that contaminates the rest of the fort. Suhasini is no longer allowed to see their work, but the two painters match their progress in the light of day and nod appreciatively at the other but never say what they really think. Pouches of colour lie scattered between them. Mukunda's defiance in depicting his model extends to the colouring as well. There are a few bright red strokes on his canvas, and Suhasini's blue sari is not going to be blue. His mind wishing to see her again as she was in his mother's kitchen, not so long back, aflame in vermillion. Richard is generous with his tools and pats Mukunda's back encouragingly. But his face has that cornered look again, anxieties slow his painting hand, his eyes dart repeatedly to his rival's canvas.

Francis does not like what he sees on Richard's canvas and he cares even less for what is on Mukunda's. His instincts are on the prowl. There is something in that cage of stone that makes him nervous, for he can neither see it nor name it. He wishes the project finished, wishes to have no part of it. He pretends to sleep whenever Suhasini is there and seethes in anger because they do not miss him, or need him. Words have no place between the two paintings.

'I was wondering how long it would take them to figure out that you needed to be shut in here with the rest of us,' said Lakshmi with a sad smile.

The guards showed Suhasini through the door and closed it behind her. She stood undecided, clutching a bundle of clothes, her anger white in her knuckles. Lakshmi indicated to the attendant woman to put away the bundle and took both of Suhasini's hands between her own, as though a dove with a broken wing. The loss of freedom she understood; the humiliation too, of being judged and condemned by one's own people.

All the other women had slowly inched out to see for themselves the new addition to the prison home. They stood at a distance, afraid of Lakshmi's temper, their eyes hostile, filled with communal hopelessness. The house of women – and one little boy – still waiting for their deaths would have to make room for another woman in their cramped prison. Lakshmi ignored them and drew Suhasini into her room and settled her against a wall. Suhasini slumped down, stunned at being physically shut away. She had known that she was being watched but when nobody had moved ahead to either stop or accuse her, it had been easy to believe she had been considered harmless and not as important as the war efforts.

'Do you want to tell me about the Englishman and the nightly meetings?' Lakshmi sat down beside her, expecting to be told what she had heard from other informants.

Suhasini looked up sharply and bit her lip.

'Did you think I would not find out if you did not tell me? I have known all this time but am asking you today because you have been sent here to live with us. Visiting this strange man every night ... I don't know what to say, and to someone as wise and sensible as you … It is not what good women do,' said Lakshmi, struggling to speak as a well-meaning older woman, not the Queen.

Suhasini did not reply. She wiped off the tears of anger streaming down her cheeks and stared back. Lakshmi lowered her eyes in apology. She had not meant to accuse. She was both a queen and a widow shackled to a dependent family, everything done was for their welfare, nothing for her own comfort or desires, her authority was feared, but her goodness rarely acknowledged or perceived in the right light. As the dowager, she was a hunter in the political jungle, a woman taking decisions without a man's sanction. Any desperation had to be carefully concealed.

Lakshmi patted Suhasini's hand. Perhaps all the decisions involving the Englishman had been taken for the good of the state and its prince, even if Suhasini's heart might have sneaked into the situation with its own undercurrents. These were not normal times and they were not women who wished to be unheard.

Tipu Sultan was rounding up everybody he suspected of treachery. The vigil outside the house of the Wodeyar family had been intensified, and communication with the outside world drastically slimmed down. They had heard that the war was driving to a resolution and the not-so-distant gunfire created a demonic rhythm through the hours. Their hearts trembled at the approach of any footsteps to their door. Tipu could easily decide to have them all killed to vent his frustration and announce his own invincibility to the subjects and the enemy at once. The women crowded in that little locked-up house prayed through the day for deliverance from their captor and for the victory of the English army.

Lakshmi gathered Suhasini in her arms and held her as the rage flowed in tears. Their dreams were like dust thrown into a strong wind, scattering to the needs of the state they served. Both had known the yoke of marriage, and it had left them tied to a life of limited choices. Lakshmi understood how the young woman felt. Life was long, much too long.

Richard was wondering where he had seen the grey-haired man who walked through the door tentatively and then remembered. Mukunda's father. Had he come to drag his son off again?

The old man stood moodily in the middle of the room, his shoulders folded from fear of being polluted by anything he might touch, and avoiding eye contact with Richard. He hates me, Richard thought, I have stolen his son. Richard picked his coat off his chair and pointed it to the visitor who did not move or look at the chair. Richard walked to the backdoor and yelled out for Francis who was in the kitchen supervising the lunch preparations for the day.

Mukunda appeared instead. 'I am not coming home. And I am not going to be dragged away this time,' he told his father.

'I am coming straight from the palace. The Padshah had called all the astrologers for a consultation. There isn't much time left,' his father pleaded. The configuration of the planets had given a verdict about the war. And so had Tipu Sultan's chart, a man who had been predicted for greatness. The sun at his birth in Aries, his life was a vessel for knowledge and strength. But Mars had decided to challenge that in Tipu's fiftieth year. This year, this coming month, and it would all culminate on the fourth day of May, a fortnight hence, when the moon turned its face. It was a time to dread, for both kingdom and ruler. If Tipu managed to appease the disgruntled planet of war and find shelter from his wrath till sundown of that day, he would go on to be one of the greatest emperors of the world. Between this battle with the English and the lordship of the world, stood one planet and one fateful day.

Mukunda's father feared what the future promised to unleash and had arranged for a quiet exit from the water gate of the fort, paid for with years of savings. He would take his wife and his daughter-in-law to Nandidurga to stay with relatives till the dust settled. And now for that son of his. Would Mukunda be sensible enough to leave with them? Would he spare a thought for his innocent wife? Why was he punishing her like this, for no fault of hers?

Mukunda hid his face in his palms. He did miss Meenakshi, her gentle ways, those shy unspoken requests. She smiled so rarely, but when she did … Yes, he missed her. He rubbed his face and looked into his father's pleading eyes. No, he could not go with them. He had work to complete and he was needed here. The truth could not be said aloud, that he had to choose, that it was not possible for him to leave Suhasini behind in the fort.

The old man trudged out with a heavy heart. He had done his best for the boy, tried everything from pleading to force. Now he left him behind to make his own pact with the destiny of a ruler hounded by Mars and an island bombarded by the English.

The Question of Love

The palace was softly humming as they were ushered through long corridors into dim chambers that merged into darker ones. Francis strode ahead with their messenger who nodded to all the whispered questions of urgency but spoke little. Richard walked a few paces behind, his hands curled deep in his pockets, marvelling at how the core of the fort could reflect almost nothing of its punishing siege.

The trenches of the invading army were extending along the river and every assault by the Mysoreans in the vicinity was being foiled. With the rains still elusive and summer stretched to its limit, the Kaveri was flowing as feeble streamlets. The vegetation had shrivelled, turning the fort naked. Crops abandoned both by clouds and farmers formed little barriers for the English army's twelve-pounders to hide behind as they inched closer to the Srirangapatna fort. By now the pattern of the battery fires had announced the location of the intended breach. An attempt had been made by Tipu Sultan to open negotiations with the Company but the terms offered to him were deliberately kept so harsh as to get turned down. The Wellesley family's political future depended on waging a successful campaign that ended with Tipu's death.

Richard and Francis were shown inside a library sealed from daylight and lit up like a chandelier by long flames that burnt bright within countless glass lanterns. Stacks of books and manuscript rose from the floor to touch all four edges of the ceiling. Tipu Sultan was alone. He appeared to have been contemplating his portrait when they walked into the room, the one that Richard had painted. The messenger disappeared after making an announcement.

It was common knowledge that Tipu had given up the comforts of his palace and lived among his soldiers in stone pavilions along the ramparts since the start of the siege. Their being summoned to his private library without anybody else in attendance was unusual and deliberately arranged.

Richard bowed but Tipu indicated that he wished to shake hands and the surprised artist took his warm hands, jolted to feel the flesh he had created in paint.

'I hope your stay with us has been good, Englishman, and not as barbarous as you expected perhaps.' Tipu spoke in a soft friendly voice. Richard was aware of his painting looking down on them, mocking him for having entirely missed out this melodic quality to the man, this coaxing pensive man.

'I am very grateful, Your Highness. It has been a privilege.' Richard heard Francis's tense breathing intersperse with his words and understood there was cause for worry.

'My men tell me that I am not to trust you. But I disbelieve them. Tell me why.'

Richard waited to find out. He knew they had been under surveillance, shadows darting past their windows day and night without discretion. Suhasini had stopped her visits. But both men continued to paint each night as if she were there. The days were hot, meant for lying in bed and battling with furtive thoughts, hiding their passions behind close eyelids and hoping she would slip in through the door somehow that night. Mukunda seemed angry and unhappy with his painting, even more than Richard was with his own work. They both attacked their canvases with ferocity, the melting blue of this one holding its own against the other's flaming red. They reached out for the palette knife often, and usually at the same time, their fingers skimming past each other, to scrape off layers that did not obey their hearts, the fabric beneath wearing so thin that the grounding had to be patched in carefully. Not only was she there in that stuffy room, locked in with them all the time, but they had two of her, and they felt more crowded than ever before.

Richard, dressed in his high-collared shirt and coat, giving up comfort for formality, now worried that the sweat gathering on his forehead would be mistaken for fear or, worse, guilt. And Tipu Sultan was saying something about traitors and deserters.

'It was for a painting,' Richard explained the nocturnal visits of a respectable priest's married daughter to his bachelor quarters. 'A special painting I was hoping to present to Your Highness, something to celebrate your impending victory.'

'I know about the painting and you don't need to explain about this woman. She has caused enough trouble and is now locked up with those she takes orders from. As soon as this war is over, they shall be tried for treason and sentenced to death. I can't fight the savage English and these witches in the fort all at the same time. If only the rains would come sooner!'

Richard's heart thumped as Francis softly translated Tipu's words. What was expected from him?

Tipu had decided to send Richard back to the English camp and persuade General Harris to hold fire, tempt him to wait a bit longer for an opportune strike. 'Tell them any lies you want.'

Enemy guns were hammering away at the walls and it would not be long before a breach was made. The Mysore troops would fight to the end but if the English were delayed till the monsoons arrived in a few weeks, victory was assured.

'Why will they listen to me?' Richard protested. 'They are experts in military matters and I am a humble painter. I am inconsequential.'

'Maybe you were inconsequential among your countrymen. Here, you are a friend, Tipu's friend, and I am trusting you with my life and the future of my children.'

'I may fail.'

If Richard failed, Tipu Sultan would rather die in the battlefield like a soldier than turn into a servant to the English. His words were unambiguous. He would not sign any treaty and he would not compromise the kingdom's sovereignty.

Richard remonstrated as respectfully as he could. He would gladly be of service, but not at the risk of the lives of the Wodeyar family, the imprisoned women. He needed a promise.

Tipu Sultan raised his hand in silent assurance. Richard would be his emissary and the lives he cared for would be safe as long as he was trusted. An infantry escort had been arranged to take Richard across the river in the morning, bearing another letter of negotiations from Tipu to Harris. The southern gate to the Periapatna bridge would be opened to let Richard out. He had to be back before dusk. If not, the gates would never open for him again.

The audience declared over, Richard and Francis were led out to the deserted streets that shook with gunfire from across the river. They were safe and out of range from the fire but the smoke and debris in the air hung low. Richard stood with his back to Tipu's palace and gazed into the west, at a little white house shaded by a gigantic banyan tree and surrounded by patrolling soldiers. Suhasini was locked in that house and he had just learned something new about himself, in the way he had thought of her well-being without any concern for his own.

'I know what you are thinking,' Francis told him, 'and I don't like it.'

Francis would not have liked what Mukunda was thinking either. While they were visiting Tipu, he had gone looking for Suhasini. Her house was empty. The neighbours would not talk to him. One did not talk about someone locked up on charges of treason. A kindly woman next door who thought highly of the good priest, Suhasini's father, leaned over the wall to whisper that they had fled. That cannot be right, Mukunda said, they would never leave their daughter behind. But the daughter had insisted, the woman said, and persuaded her old parents to go to a place not disclosed to anybody else, just before the guards came for her.

Mukunda's parents and wife were also among those who had left the fort to avoid the war. He thought of taking his uncle Purnaiah's help but the woman who opened the door would not even extend a cursory greeting. The minister was away with the army was all she said before slamming the door. His only hope now remained the French camp. He borrowed a horse cart and reached there only to find it desolate. The soldiers he met were either dying or preparing for death. Tired servants were carrying stretchers with figures wrapped in bandages. Men drank alone in their tents, anxious about the next call for arms, for one last thrust towards the war front. The few who stopped to answer his questions did not know Surcouf's whereabouts. The attack on the English camp the previous day had wiped out almost half of the French regiment. Those missing were also counted among the dead. Mukunda did not wait to ask about the list. He had a feeling he would not be seeing his friend again.

General Harris and his commission sat around a large collapsible table, little silver teacups clinking solemnly into saucers, as they listened to Richard. He outlined Tipu's proposal for calling off the whole battle with a pact less humiliating to the Mysoreans and then he elaborated his own ideas. The officers listened in amazement, even admiration. They found it hard to believe that this diffident artist had survived Tipu, managed to win his trust, and now was volunteering to gamble his life on a proposed plan that was audacious, almost impossible to execute. Richard wanted their word that there would be something in this for him. They continued to be baffled, for he did not ask for money or spoils, he wanted an assurance about giving some people in the fort their freedom and rightful property. He also wanted to be the first one to step into the house of the Wodeyar family when the fort was under their command. It would be an expensive mission, but only because his informant from Tipu's council of ministers was expensive and he needed to be sure that a suitable compensation would be offered to that man. The officers discussed it over and finally nodded in agreement. They might have acted with more caution if circumstances were different and if they could carry on the siege for another month – surely the fort could be tamed before the monsoons arrived – but they had neither the stocks nor the energy to last that long. As many men were crumbling to the heat and the fever as from bullets showering into the trenches. Soon they would have deaths from malnutrition as well.

'That man guarding my tent,' Harris had pointed out to one of his personal guard, 'is so weak that a sepoy could push him to the ground with a finger.'

Richard understood. He gave them a date not too far away. Tipu Sultan believed he could lose, possibly die, before sundown on that day. His trusted court astrologers had told him so. To strike then would be to strike at the darkest fear of this man. That gave them a week to prepare, soon enough to have the force of an unexpected assault.

Later that evening Tipu Sultan would hear from Richard that the English would not receive any ambassadors from him unless accompanied by hostages and money with his seal on the treaty. These conditions were on offer only till three o'clock the next day and no longer. Naturally, Tipu would reject them.

General Harris instructed Richard on their storming plans, pointing the intended breach on a map rolled out between them. It would take two days of turning every battery on the bastion to be able to create an access for their troops and it would not be done any sooner than necessary to prevent the Sultan from carrying out repairs or alternate plans. They knew there was a second rampart inside, certain to be lined with musketry, and a large cavalier likely to be constantly manned by experienced snipers. They needed to know the strategic position of forces along the entire ramparts of the fort and the quickest way to reach Tipu's palace as well as the security arrangements there. Richard scribbled as they spoke and stuffed the scrap of paper into his shoes. When he was ready to go back to the fort, he solemnly shook hands with each of the men.

As soon as he had stepped out, Cole quickly took him away to his own tent. There they talked for long and in subdued voices. Richard started by telling him about the meeting just concluded and then his voice started to waver as he began to confide about all that he had been unable to share with the uniformed strangers in there. About Suhasini, about the two paintings, about not knowing what was the right thing to do anymore, about everything except his double-edged lies.

Cole soaked up every word sympathetically. He had nothing to say. Richard did not need advice. He needed a friend. And friends were the hardest to come by in a war where every resource was at a stretch. Cole had intended to talk about his own troubles, trying to keep track of the military supplies and patching up inexplicable differences in the stock with clever figures. The price of rice and spirits could match those of precious metals elsewhere. But Richard was not listening.

Cole reminded Richard as he stood up to go: Every man had to fend for himself when the system broke down outside him, and more so when it did within. There was no shared compass between the morals of men. There was courage or cowardice. And then there was survival.

What about love? Richard wondered. Cole shook his head sadly and did not reply. In his world, love did not merit dying for. They embraced as brothers, wishing each other caution, hoping to stay alive and to meet again when the war was over.

Francis was worried. Both paintings had not been touched with fresh paint that week. He had known of the rivalry and the simmering jealousy even before the artists themselves did. It was a matter of interest to him, amusement too, and had seemed inevitable. Emotions had been aroused without intent, raw and primal, important to resolve, fortunately with paintbrushes, rather than pistols. Francis had watched the duel, like a benevolent arbitrator, secure in knowing that only hearts would be broken, not bones. And then Richard had been sent to the English army Camp, returning a different man. He would not tell Francis anything, except that the nightmare would soon be over.

Francis tried to talk to Mukunda but found him depressed. 'I cannot paint the rest,' he moaned. He was painting Suhasini from an image in his head, just as the Master had taught him, but without her in the room it felt as though holes were being hammered through his solitude and into his soul. He disappeared during the day and returned late at nights, refused to eat, and slept with his face to the wall.

Richard would not paint either and Francis found his smock stuffed into a large rat hole in the room that they had not bothered with all these months. He would not look at his own painting anymore, staring moodily at Mukunda's canvas that had not made as much progress but blazed its hues even when the lamps doused themselves.

'I don't need an assistant anymore, Francis. Tell him to leave,' Richard finally said that morning when they were alone, even though he dreaded that Mukunda's painting would leave with him.

There was no reply from Francis, just a searing glance that challenged Richard to do the telling. Mukunda, never hearing of his dismissal, stayed in his corner of the room, nursing his unhappiness. Richard would not look or talk to him, and the silences in the room grew grey and dense.

The more Francis looked at both the incomplete paintings, the more his spirits sank into a morass. What could he possibly do to salvage them from this disaster? The artists would not listen to him and he could not leave them to their fates.

At sunrise on the previous day, the second day of May, all the English guns on both the western and the northern side of the river had directed to the north-west bastion of the fort; twenty-nine cannons and six howitzers, all firing at the same time, to make the final breach. One of the shots went well over the fort and landed on a store of rockets resulting in a deafening explosion. Pandemonium broke out in the streets of Srirangapatna. Everyone believed that the enemy had landed. People wailed, running around with their families and possessions. It was hours before their soldiers could reassure everyone that the English were still on the other side of the river and that the shattered walls of the fort were holding out.

That night, General Harris sent one of the lieutenants to cross the river in the night and make his way to the breach to gauge its feasibility for the troops. The water in the river did not go higher than his chest, mostly staying at his waist or knees, and the retaining wall before the fort was not as discouraging as it looked. A leap of seven feet would take them into the ditch that ran around the fort, now holding about twelve inches of stagnant water. The debris from the fort walls was already starting to create a rough bridge towards the rampart.

As the guns continued to widen the breach through the next day, Tipu Sultan made a careful survey of the damage caused by the shelling. There was no doubt as to the spot from where the English planned to storm the fort. Two of his most trusted officers, Syed Saheb and Syed Ghaffur, were given charge of the area and the French commander Chapuis was stationed with his men in the large cavalier just beyond the bastion to gun down any enemy climbing over the rampart. Tipu's eldest son led a detached corps to fend with any northern attack and another prince was put in charge of the southern side of the fort. Tipu Sultan stationed himself in the shade of the water gate in the northern wall and prepared himself for the coming day. This was the day that his astrologers had warned him about, the last day of the lunar month when Mars would test his courage and endurance.

The guards gathered under the trees, dusting their hands and dipping into the baskets of sweets. The little boy who had carried the basket had scampered away without mentioning who had sent it. That did not matter much to them. Delicious surprises never hurt during bleak times such as these. The English guns were booming just a few yards away and none of the other guards stopped by to give them updates anymore; theirs was the cushy assignment, to watch over a house of ageing women and a prince who had not lost his milk teeth. They licked the sugar syrup on their fingers and bent down for more, waving sympathetically at the youngest among them, who had been left behind to watch the door and made sad faces at them.

The rustle through the flowering bushes went unnoticed, so also the leap from the wall to the roof, and then from the roof to the little space between the house and the outer walls. Mukunda crouched, his bare foot expertly sliding along the loose stones in the wall, trying to avoid crunching dried leaves; he prowled from one window to the other, raising his head a little to glance into each. The rooms were all unlit, a stench of sweat and illness firmly lodged inside. Someone was coughing very hard and gasping for breath. A few soft voices chanted prayers together elsewhere in the house.

He darted, from window to window, without lingering for too long. He did not want to be spotted, unless it was by Suhasini, and finding her was all that he could think about, his eyes scanning one corner to the other, seeking her.

The window at the far end was open and he heard her voice before he saw her untied hair shining against the wooden grills. She was talking, reading aloud, teaching something. He heard the young prince repeat her words. He sat down on the ground, pressing his back against the wall directly below the window. He was safe from the view of the guards, though making a getaway would become dangerous if he stayed too long.

He looked around and found a pebble with a flat shiny surface. The last rays of the sun were slanting down to him and he balanced the pebble on his hand to catch it, his hands trembling as though he were holding a live ember. The light bounced from his palms and caught her eye. He heard Suhasini calmly dismiss the boy from his lessons for the day and then close the door.

Mukunda was standing at the window when Suhasini had turned around. She hurried over to him, her eyes sparkling with tears of joy and anxiety all at once. 'How did you get in here? How will you get out?' she whispered. She did not need to ask why he was there.

'Are you well?' he whispered back, gripping the wooden sticks separating them, wishing he could pluck the window away from the wall, take her away from that humiliating darkness and smell of wasting bodies. A deep gurgling cough rang through the house again. Someone dropped a brass plate in the next room and cursed loudly.

She wanted to know what was happening on the war front. They had absolutely no access to any information. The cannons had not stopped roaring for two days and they sounded very close by.

The English were hammering the north-west bastion and would be in the fort very soon. The end was near. And it was Richard he worried about. Tipu had sent him again to the English camp a few days ago. 'But he won't talk about it, not even to Francis. I … I have been worried about you.'

His fists tightened into pale knobs as he rested his head on the window and blocked the light from her face. She leaned forward and kissed the clenched fingers lightly.

Mukunda touched her cheeks in reply and grabbed her hair in desperation. Suhasini did not pull away. He moved slowly towards her face, closer, as close as the unsympathetic bars would allow. She kissed his lips, her breath icy against his burning face. He sensed her reluctantly pulling away and tried to hold on, teeth sinking into her lower lip. He tasted her blood.

'Suhasini!' The voice was accompanied by footsteps and heading towards them.

'Keep an eye on the Englishman. Maybe he has changed his loyalties,' she said.

'I will be back for you,' he whispered and disappeared from the window, gone as quickly as a stealthy wind in that evening sky.

Mir Sadiq was disguised as a wandering mendicant and they would not have recognized him if he had not spoken, urging them not to waste time. He had come straight from a meeting of the commanders, brimming with details of defence placements in the fort for the following day. He grabbed Francis and on his trembling hands he drew a crude figure of the fort and hurriedly made various markings. Richard watched closely but only Francis understood what he was saying. Having finished, Mir Sadiq turned to Richard, slapped him on the back in shared confidence and rushed off.

Francis explained as much as he could recall. Mir Sadiq had promised to summon the soldiers guarding the crucial bastion during lunch hour on the following day with the excuse of paying salaries. A white piece of cloth would be waved from the ramparts as soon as the coast was clear. That would be the signal to the English soldiers to storm the fort.

'I have to take this message myself, Francis, across the river, and you have to wait here for me. It'll be over by this time tomorrow and I promise you that you will be safe. Just stay in here and wait for me,' Richard said, rolling his sleeves and grabbing his coat.

'Don't do it!' pleaded Francis. 'How can you trust this thug? Maybe he is setting a trap for us. This whole thing has gone far enough. Stay out of it. Please!'

'If I stay out of it, she will be dead, Francis. I can't let that happen. It will kill me too. I trust you not to say anything to anyone. I promise to be back here for you tomorrow. Just don't tell Mukunda. Not a word.'

Richard picked up his painting of Suhasini from the easel. To his eyes there were only inadequacies, too bland to even merit being sinful, so little of him in it and almost nothing of her. He flung the canvas to the floor with disgust. 'Get rid of that for me, will you?' he said.

He turned to Mukunda's painting. Now Suhasini was looking him straight in the eye and he experienced that same bittersweet pain he had been struggling with during those nights of painting. Time turned into water, first a trickle, then a wave, swelling to a deluge and submerging him. Time dragged him through many unlit walled alleys to a moment when it could all be turned around. His moment. His decision. It would change everything time had wrought and life could start anew. Through the window he saw the last drop of light soak into the evening sky. He had to leave at once.

Francis watched in horror as Richard grabbed Mukunda's incomplete portrait of Suhasini, ripped it from its wooden frame, laid it face down on the table, and hastily duplicated the diagram and markings left by Mir Sadiq on Francis's arm. When he had finished, Richard turned the painting around. Something was not quite right. He grabbed a paintbrush, took a deep breath and signed his name on the canvas. Dawson. He avoided looking at Francis, rolled the painting into a scroll, pushed it through the hollow of a bamboo stick, stuffed rags down the open ends, tucked it inside his coat and was gone.

The night was moving towards them, the blue above breaking into dark chunks of twilight. He could hardly feel his feet, yet Richard had made his way across the fort, sneaked through deserted doorways, ducked out of sight from armed soldiers, crawled out of a dry water duct, slithered down the bare rocky face of the fort wall. The dirt he had deliberately rubbed into his face and his hands had found its way across his shoulders, his shirtsleeves, into the pores of his skin.

The guns now went off sporadically, almost wearily, with frequent bouts of silence to revolt against the exertions of the day. Richard stayed close on the ground, crawling on his knees and hands. The rocky bank of the river cut into his skin, ants gathered around the smudges of blood he left behind on the stones. He dragged ahead blindly, towards the south, the flares of the smoking batteries signalling trenches leading to the English camp. Pain coursed through his folded back, but to be upright would be an invitation to be shot down instantly by bullets from both sides of the fort. He had to stay as close to the ground as he could, and he had to keep moving, sideways and ahead if possible, but to never rest, never pause even briefly. The batteries continued to boom and guns from the rampart answered back. Little bursts of dust and smoke around him hinted at missed death, and the candles flickering through the trees far in the distance offered a clean bed to lie in, the promise of life.

Richard had managed to reach the river. It was dark now and the waters perfectly still. He flopped into it and as the wetness seeped through his clothes, he pulled out the bamboo stick and held it between his teeth, using his arms to feel his way across. The water was not deep and his head easily stayed out of the water but it was hard to see where he was going. Tufts of prickly grass shot up unexpectedly along the way and frogs croaked close to his face. Even when the water was barely ankle high, he continued to crawl for fear of the whizzing bullets. A soft wet movement across his leg alerted him and he sat up despite his instincts to stay low. He knew it was a snake, perhaps a harmless water snake, but its slimy touch had jolted him into a sudden painful awareness of his surroundings, of being in the middle of the Kaveri, of the bamboo growing heavy between his teeth. And then he noticed that he had lost one shoe.

Richard pulled over a cluster of rocks in the middle of the river, still warm from the exertions, trying to calm himself. He held the bamboo close to his chest, remembering her face, her eyes upon him. Suhasini, the painting, all belonged to him. He no longer doubted himself. The sting of tears in his eyes made him turn instinctively towards the fort, disbelieving of his own madness. And a shadow blinked back at him.

Richard looked closely. The shadow nipped behind a line of bushes on the side of the stream he had just left behind. Richard held his breath and continued to watch. The dark shape was slithering towards the river. Richard knew it was Mukunda. Francis had given him away. Mukunda, wanting to stop him, to take away the painting that was rightfully his, to make sure he did not get to the English camp or do anything Suhasini would not approve.

Richard turned around angrily, bit back into the bamboo and slid down into the river. A small swirl of current took him unawares. He lost his footing and felt his head being pulled backwards under the water. He held the bamboo above the water, giving away his presence and his location, desperate to save the painting from any damage. The moment of panic passed and neither bullet nor shadow had reached him. He pulled himself back on his feet and looked around. It was all very still and dark. There were many lumps of greys around him but none of them moved or blinked. Had he imagined it? He was making his way across the water and pulling up on the southern bank when he distinctly heard a splash and gasp for breath not too far from him. Richard knew then for certain that Mukunda was close. He ran into the fields, hiding behind trees, hobbling along on his single shoe, not looking back. He heard footsteps soon after, trailing behind him. Shots exploded. Someone cried out. He panted his way across the rising slope, the painting clutched to his thumping heart, running blindly, no longer careful to stay low. He broke into a full gallop.

Suddenly the earth parted beneath Richard.

He was sliding into a deep gorge. The painting fell on top of him. He shouted and a hand clamped down on his mouth. Someone lit a match. He had landed in the trenches and a row of tired soldiers looked at him curiously. The match went off. Richard cried silently in the dark, relieved to know that he was safe, and that she too would be safe soon.

The Fourth Day of May

The morning arrived pale and tepid, rain clouds still missing from the western horizon. The river circled the island and bathed it in the tender light. A few exhausted guns on both sides sparred at random intervals.

Tipu Sultan woke up early and made his way back from his temporary lodgings at the water gate to the palace. Every minute of that morning was deliciously measured and beautiful to him, as only life can be. He washed and dressed with care, draping his favourite jacket with a bright red sash, the Quran around his neck in a silver case, an amulet of prayers tied to his arms, his turban carefully decked with jewels and placed firmly on his head. He was king, master of the fort, of all the land the eye could see from its ramparts, and further too. The vindictive English clawing at his fort did not frighten him. But Destiny was another matter. This was the day that Mars reached its zenith within the circle of his chart, this last day of the lunar month, and the red planet had to be appeased, at any cost. The astrologers were waiting for him in the outer chambers and holy heads of all the main temples and mosques had been summoned. They would join him in prayers. The kindling sacrificial fires were flared up with offerings of ghee as he walked out, and prayers chanted loudly in chorus. They had orders to try every remedy at hand to douse the wrath of the planet. His reflection in a pot of sesame oil was sent to light the lamps of the temple, gifts and cattle touched by him given away to poor Brahmins. His heart was calm. He was still king.

Along the western ramparts, Tipu Sultan's most trusted commanders stood in consultation. Syed Saheb and Syed Ghaffur, accompanied by a handful of experienced soldiers, surveyed the situation across the river. The enemy trenches were unusually crowded. There could be only one logical explanation. The English planned to assault the fort that day. Syed Saheb left his colleague behind to give instructions to increase musketry and rocket fire at the trenches. He needed to survey the other walls.

Across that north-western bastion, 5,000 troops from the English and Nizam's army cowered low in the trenches, unable to fire back, trusting their cannons to slow enemy fire till they were given orders for the assault. They had been wedged in there through the night, hungry and wretched, trailing a rifle in one hand and carrying spare ammunition in the other. At around eleven, a message was passed from man to man. The fort would be stormed at one in the afternoon. And before they did, each man would receive a dram of liquor and a biscuit, nearly the last of their rations. Their only hope of survival was the food and resources inside the fort. It was also their chance to future security; any treasures they could lay their hands on and keep from the eyes of the officials would be theirs to take back. Some men muttered prayers under their breath, but most of them sat silently, thinking about their lives, the possibility of being maimed, and the people who would miss them when they were killed.

The assault on the fort was put under the command of General David Baird and everyone agreed it to be the best choice. Baird had been imprisoned in the dungeons of Srirangapatna many years ago and was unmatched among them in his knowledge of the fort, as also his hatred for the Mysoreans. General Harris was to stay back in the camp to oversee the operations and arrange reinforcements.

Richard had argued and pleaded with General Harris to allow him to go with General Baird and the storming party. He had lived in the fort as a free man and knew it well. He claimed a responsibility to go in there after having put the lives of people he cared for at such great risks. They listened for a while and then pushed him out of the tent. It was too late to fuss over the consequences of his decisions and Richard would now have to learn to take orders when it was given to him. They did not want a bumbling artist to mess about in the business of soldiers and the best alternative on offer was that he join the reserve troops headed by Colonel Wellesley that would wait in the trenches and join the battle only in crisis or enter the fort after it had been captured.

Richard ran to Cole, convincing him to part with his own pistol, then crept through a patch of overgrown weeds and dropped into the nearest arm of the trenches. He wanted to be in the fort when the army stormed in and get to Suhasini before anyone else. The soldiers looked at him curiously but he kept his face averted from them. His guilt and shame were company enough; and the thought of the painting that now bore his name. He had begged Cole to retrieve it from the general's tent, burning with confused rage, wishing it had never come into being and yet loving it passionately.

In that moment it was as if Mukunda had never existed, never touched his life in any way. The English would take over the fort. Suhasini would be pleased when she found out how Richard had helped them, displaying unmatched courage and ingenuity. He warmed at the memory of how she looked at him, smiled, and radiated with empathy. She would love him as he loved her. He would take her away, to a world that would belong only to them and there he would paint again; his portrait of her would hang on his walls, where their children would ask yet again to hear the magical story of their romance in distant India.

In his palace, Tipu Sultan listened to the updates from the ramparts and trusted his men to defend the fort till he could complete the prayers. There was still time. He was certain the English would not be foolish enough to climb into the fort in broad daylight, or during its hottest hours. If his army could stall them till sundown, he would be invincible. His astrologers swore their lives on it.

Francis ate breakfast with Mukunda in their stone room. They chewed their food thoughtfully, as if to slow down time. Without Richard and the two paintings, the room was strangely altered, ghostly. They felt unreal themselves. On the bed, Francis had laid out a set of Richard's clothes, white shirt with sleeves and collar, dark breeches, darker belt. After breakfast, he persuaded Mukunda to get dressed in them. There was nothing he could say to keep the young man from venturing out into the heat of the battle today, as incapable of defending himself as of hurting anyone; Francis advised him to tear the jacket off any dead enemy solider and wear it if it would keep him alive a little longer, help him get to safety.

All rituals observed and completed to the satisfaction of the learned men, Tipu Sultan instructed the women of his harem to lock themselves in with his younger sons, and to continue to pray for the speedy arrival of the night, and with it his triumph. Sultana, his mare, was patiently waiting for him, and he rode towards the northern wall to see the situation for himself. Four men trotted alongside with an assortment of his weapons and two of his personal attendants kept up the rear.

General Baird and the officers went over the strategy again in their camp. The Forlorn Hope was in place, a detachment of twelve grenadiers who would be the first to go across the river. Their progress or failure would give the officers one last opportunity to change plans. Death was certain, but for any of the Forlorn Hope who survived the day, there was the promise of instant promotion to the next rank. They would be followed by thirty men, most of them officers who had volunteered, and had been placed at the head of various divisions.

The officers looked at their watches. The sun was directly overhead and the soldiers waited in shallow puddles of their own shadows. Their cramped limbs began to thaw a little as the alcohol came around. For most of them, it would be their last drink. When the bottle was passed to him, Richard pushed it away and the soldier next to him took the bonus swig. Sitting there between closing walls of earth, and waiting for the signal from the fort that he had arranged for, Richard knew he had become a stranger to himself, and that there could possibly be no greater tragedy a man's soul could suffer.

Tipu Sultan walked the northern ramparts, talking to soldiers along the way. They were overjoyed to see their ruler there, treating them as if they were his close military advisors. Their spirits rose and the fort felt invincible all over again. Tipu straightened the tiger-striped uniform of one young soldier, fondly calling him a cub, and continued onwards at an even pace. To look at him, smiling and striding, it would be impossible to say that he was at the threshold of the most crucial battle of his life.

Syed Ghaffur was still organizing the troops, in anticipation of an attack, ordering the construction workers to create an obstruction towards the southern wall. He had a sinking feeling about the eerily inactive trenches across the river. He left the men to their work and decided to report to Tipu Sultan in person. Just then he saw the cannonball come his way, too fast to avoid, and was slammed down to an instant death.

Getting closer to one o'clock, the English guns fell silent. Up in the battered bastion it was nearly time for a change of guard and the weary soldiers waited eagerly for their lunch. Mir Sadiq appeared instead, unescorted. He ordered the soldiers to collect their salaries from the killedar and dismissed them from their duties for the day and the men left, grinning, hardly believing their luck. As soon he saw the last of their backs, Mir Sadiq stepped up to the edge of the rampart walls, close to the hundred-foot-wide breach that the English batteries had carved out, and held up a white square of cloth. Now.

General David Baird stepped out of the trenches, pulled out his sword and held it high about his head. The Scotsman was one of the tallest and bulkiest men in their camp and he had never looked more of a giant than he did now, and the men gaped in awe. He roared out to them to follow him and prove themselves worthy of being British soldiers. Three cheers resounded from the trenches.

In seven minutes, the men of the Forlorn Hope had made their way across the 300 yards to the fort, through the river, past the damaged fort glacis, into the watery ditch and then up the staggered edges of the bastion. The Mysore troops on the southern wall had spotted them and commenced heavy firing. Soldiers continued to rise out of the trenches and rush wildly towards the fort, unaware that the river had suddenly turned treacherous. They slipped down deceptive shallows, sank into clinging clay, tumbled into hidden holes, lay trapped on exposed rocks that scorched their skins. A rain of grapeshot from the fort shattered into the riverbed and splinters of stone flew all around them. Those wounded and trapped screamed, pleaded for help, but their colleagues were stepping over them, unable to stop or help. Each man had to find his own way to survival.

As the men pulled themselves over the edge of the ramparts, wet from river and sweat, General Baird directed them into two columns. The right was led by Colonel Sherbrooke and went down the southern wall. The left under the command of Colonel Dunlop would head north. The plan was for both columns to encircle the ramparts, clear all resistance along the way, and to meet at the eastern gate. A small detachment of soldiers went over the wooden board that had been laid out by Mir Sadiq to cross the watery depths that separated them from the inner ramparts and they headed left as well, knowing that was where Tipu Sultan would confront them.

The island reverberated with cries of distress and alarm as the townsfolk saw the invaders' uniform flash past their walls. They grabbed their children and ran towards the nearest exit, willing to break down gates if need be, anything to get away from the angry enemy. Mukunda was caught in the stampeding crowds as they surged ahead in different directions and did not pay any heed to his pleas to be let across. He had to put his shoulder against that moving human wall and push through with eyes closed, till he somehow extricated himself from the chaos and raced towards the Wodeyar residence, now frighteningly close to the breech, screened only by the tall towers of the temple and the ancient banyan tree.

The door was wide open and the rooms empty. Mukunda dashed around, trying to find signs, any clues to where all its inmates had vanished. In one of the inner rooms, sitting blankly in a corner was a young soldier, still a boy, who had been left behind to guard the place. Mukunda had to shake him till some words tumbled. The Queen and her family had moved into the Sriranganatha temple for safety, and to pray for the well-being of their subjects as well as a quick end to the carnage. Mukunda knew Suhasini would be there, staying beside her Queen till the very end. Nearly every Brahmin family in the fort had decided to seek shelter in the temple, packed with people from the courtyard to the inner sanctorum where the more privileged families conducted special prayers. With room neither to stand nor find a way through its many chambers to reach her, Mukunda turned around and began running towards the old stone granary. There were other lives he cared for just as much.

The trench that Richard had been occupying now received orders to rush to the fort, nearly the last to do so. Their view of the fort was masked by a screen of dust and smoke but the right column could be seen moving steadily along the southern wall where Mysore soldiers were letting themselves down with their turbans, or grappling with the stones, falling into a pile of colleagues dead from bullet wounds. The fort guns in that direction had been nearly silenced. Richard wanted to join the left column, to be closer to the little white house. He was pushed ahead by impatient soldiers, soon going down the same path he had taken the previous night. This time the wetness seeping through his boots was not water from the river but blood. The arms of dying men reached out to grab him as he passed. He shaded his face with the crook of his arm and ran blindly.

The left column was not faring well. Starting with Colonel Dunlop, every European officer taking command of it had been injured or killed. Tipu Sultan had not walked too far along the northern ramparts when his men caught the first sight of the charging English uniforms. The Mysore troops put up a determined resistance, energized at having Tipu Sultan fighting beside them like a common soldier, pushing the invaders almost all the way back to the bastion.

The detachment of English soldiers that had sneaked down the inner ramparts now emerged from one of the inner gates and began to fire at the Mysore troops from the flanks. Caught in the unexpected crossfire, the defending troops floundered and fell into disarray. Raza Khan, Tipu's attendant, slipped through them and began to hustle his master back towards the waiting horse. An enraged Tipu grabbed his neck, wanting to fight on, when he realized why they were concerned. A big patch of blood was spreading on the right side of his tunic. He had been shot.

Astride his horse, Tipu rushed back towards the next water gate, closely followed by his attendants, wanting to get into the inner fort and establish a defence at the palace. The gateway was swarming with people from nearby houses attempting to force their way out towards the river. Tipu struggled with the reins as he goaded his horse to find a way ahead when he felt her legs buckle. She came down with a loud neigh and a black curtain fell across his eyes. Both horse and master had been shot at the same time. The left column of English soldiers had reached the gateway and began firing indiscriminately. Raza Khan grabbed Tipu by the collar, dragging him free from the dead horse and people falling down over them. Tipu was still breathing. They placed him in a waiting palanquin to one side of the gateway and watched tearfully. Tipu bit his lips to hold in the pain and talked to his men about the next battle strategy. Soon, yes, as soon as he collected himself.

A few yards away, Richard was running in their direction with the last of the storming soldiers. The sun had flipped sides and now burnt on his neck. The only Mysore soldiers now visible were either dead or dying. Richard was more frightened of the men he had sat in the trenches with, who having started the slaughter could not stop. Some of them were jumping off the wall and breaking into the more prosperous-looking houses, hunting for valuables before the officers raked in everything in the Company's name.

Francis jumped up when the door burst open, pistol shaking in his hand. Behind him huddled all the servants that had travelled with him from Madras. They were counting on Francis to get them back safely. Mukunda ran in. Francis rushed ahead and held him in a tight embrace. What was happening outside? Had he seen Richard? What were they going to do now?

Mukunda had nothing to say about Richard but he had seen enough of the happenings around the fort to tell them to try as best as they could to leave. The main gateways were no good. The English had set most of them ablaze, muslin clothes and cartridge papers quickly catching fire and engulfing entire crowds. The only way out was now through the smaller openings in the fort, either unguarded or not known to many. They would have to wait till all the soldiers had entered the fort from the breach and then head in the same direction, for it was unlikely anyone would be stationed there. Francis and his men could head towards Bangalore and from there back to Madras. But Mukunda would not go with them. He would not leave the fort alone. Francis understood and agreed to the plan.

From the eastern gate, the regimental band started to play '*The Grenadier's March*'. Both columns had met and British flags were flying from every bastion of the fort. It was all over. General Harris heard the band in his camp and his men cheered loudly. Tipu Sultan heard them too.

How much longer to sunset? Tipu wondered. He had to keep breathing for a couple of hours, and then Mars would be powerless, and nothing would ever go wrong for him again. The sun was still in the sky and his strength was ebbing away.

Richard stood all by himself on the rampart wall and listened to the band. He could see the smoke billowing out of the eastern gate and men scurrying around the balconies of the big red palace. He wondered if Tipu was safely in there but only briefly because he now had a clear view of the little white house. There was not a single guard outside and the door was ajar. He pressed his hand against his chest to steady the throb and then started to lower himself down the side of the rampart.

Two grenadiers from the English army jumped upon the pile of human flesh between the water gate and began to grab anything that sparkled – silver, gold, precious stones – off the dead and dying. One of them noticed the palanquin at the far end and the man inside lying down with eyes closed, attached to a sword of gold encrusted with gems. He bent down to claim the sword when the man's eyes flashed open. It was Tipu. He grabbed a sword lying nearby and slashed it into the soldier who stayed alive long enough to aim his musket at Tipu's temple and pull the trigger.

Richard could not believe that he had returned only to find emptiness. Suhasini was not in the house, nor any of the other women, only some scattered belongings, as if somebody had hurriedly turned the place around looking for something. Richard had gambled with so many lives, most importantly that of Tipu and his family, and it was nothing to him till he was united with her. He ran out blindly. What could he do next? The evening sky was golden behind the temple and he noticed the English soldiers crowded around the main entrance of Tipu's palace. He found himself drawing closer to them, dreading and yet not able to resist finding out what had happened in there.

General Baird and his officers had searched the palace, accepted the surrender of the young princes and sent them with escorts to General Harris. There was still no sign of Tipu and the soldiers were growing impatient. They had survived a day of unspeakable horrors, only to be told that the battle was not over yet, not till Tipu Sultan had been found, dead or alive. Richard stood behind them and listened to the angry men. The killedar of Srirangapatna, a man he recognized, stepped forward with some information that one of his men had brought over just then. Tipu was dead at one of the northern water gates.

Torches were lit and passed around. A group of men selected by General Baird followed the killedar. Richard trailed behind.

The wooden gate to the archway had been pulled down and replaced by a stout column of dead people. The men started to clear the pile, children still clinging to their mothers, men entangled with each other, the light held carefully to each cold face in search of Tipu Sultan. The sun had set and the soldiers laboured at clearing the archway for nearly two hours. In the light of the torches it was a gruesome sight, an abattoir for humans now roasting its dead.

Richard shut his eyes in self-loathing. What had he done? Was he responsible for all of this? Could Suhasini possibly be among these people? No, no, no…

Finally someone yelled a discovery. They had found Raza Khan, heavily wounded, gasping for breath and pointing out to something. A palanquin. Inside was a man whose eyes were open, his skin still warm. The killedar bent over for a look and then drew back in fright. Yes, it was Tipu Sultan, undoubtedly so. General Baird took his lantern close, felt the pulse and heart of his old enemy who stared back sternly at him. Richard pushed his way through the men to see for himself. Tipu Sultan was declared dead.

Richard felt a pair of eyes on him, boring straight to his inner torment. He looked up instinctively and in the light of the lanterns, he saw two faces on the other side of the gathered crowd, passive as if part of the stonewall, steadily looking back at him. Mukunda and Francis.

General Baird walked in front of Richard, ordering the men to carry Tipu's body to the palace, and when he moved, the faces on the other side were gone. Had he imagined it? Richard could swear they were real. If so, why did they not wait for him, talk to him, attack him? Condemned by their silence, their absence, he felt abandoned, his heart a gaping hole that grew larger and larger. Richard started to sob, first in hiccups, then hysterically, unable to stop even though his fist was pressed against his mouth. One of the officers quickly herded him to one side and forced a flask to his lips. The whisky trickled out of his lips and down his clothes as he gulped his sorrow and wept.

The officers returned to the palace to raid Tipu's treasury and personal collection, trying to save it from falling into the hands of greedy subordinates. But there was nothing they could do about the rest of the town. The worst was just beginning to descend on the inhabitants, now that the battle was won.

Both the native and European soldiers of the victorious army were on the rampage. No house in the fort was safe. Family heirlooms were snatched, resisters were shot dead and roofs set on fire. The streets echoed with the shrieks of molested women. There was nobody to come to their rescue. Little rivulets of red trickled down the mud lanes. The women who escaped had gathered in the middle of the town square and clung together, believing they would not be assaulted in full view, while their homes were razed to the ground and their families annihilated, weeping together till the sun returned to shine upon their devastation.

Postscript

The young man was one of the survivors who had volunteered to clear the dead after the battle. He worked the hardest and he refused any payment except the mid-day meal doled out by the supervisors. And when all the other workers had gone home for the day, he continued to dig out bodies in the light of a lantern. If he got too tired, he collapsed in the open and slept among the dead. And then worked even harder the next day. Some of the men tried to speak to him but he would not reply. Somebody recognized him as the son of a learned man. They were horrified. A Brahmin reduced to doing this unthinkable job of an untouchable, touching the dead of every caste! But there was no time to fuss and nobody with the energy for it. So they let him be. He was clearly looking for something or someone. And each time he dug into the next pile of rotting flesh, he seemed to earnestly believe that his search was nearly over.

A few days later, an elderly couple came looking for him, clasped him to their bosom, called him son and gently took him back home. Mukunda had not found Suhasini. Neither did he speak again.

He stayed indoors for two years and let his family take care of him, feed him, bathe him and put him to bed. He settled to sleep only in the kitchen, alone, and refused to step into the room he had shared with his wife Meenakshi. She served him dutifully but her eyes were always swollen from frequent tears. And when she did not stop crying through days and nights, her sad-faced parents came to take her away to visit holy places and pray for her ill-fated marriage.

It was whispered that Mukunda had lost his wits. He spoke to imaginary people as if they spoke right back to him. And sometimes when those voices screamed at him, he screamed back as well. If he managed to sneak out of the house unnoticed, he was to be found back along the fort walls, searching again, tearing away at the rocks and grass with his bare hands till his old father came to fetch him.

Mukunda's parents tried many remedies to cure their only son. Despite strong reservations, they even took him down to the artists' colony in the hope that the painting work would cheer him up. At first he showed no interest but when a piece of tamarind charcoal had been pressed into his fingers, something stirred in him. He drew shreds, a finger or a nose, but never a whole face or person they could recognize or even appreciate. He kept drawing the same bits over and over again.

The battle inside the fort walls of Srirangapatna had lasted only a day but it left scars so deep and pain so crippling, it seemed impossible for life to go on as it did before. But somehow it did. Slowly. The people who had fled or survived limped back to rebuild walls and eke out a living. The Wodeyar queen had relocated the seat of governance from Srirangapatna to the town of Mysore, and instead of feeling a loss of privilege, the inhabitants of the old fort heaved a sigh of relief. They had paid heavily for being the citadel of power, all that their forefathers had gathered for years gone up in smoke. Tipu Sultan was already becoming a memory, a legend, the stuff that made up their songs and folklore. About that night, when they had been ravaged as spoils of war, they did not speak. It came up sometimes, in the tears in their eyes, or in the catch in their voice, or just in the way the sun lit up the sky on summer evenings. But in trying to recover and heal, more than anything, they wished to forget it had ever happened.

Mukunda's family had a distant relative visit them one day. In the course of the conversation it came up that a young Englishman was looking to hire artists. It was the first time they had noticed a reaction from Mukunda. On his face was a look they could not name. His father took his hand and went to meet this Englishman.

They were ushered into a tent filled with strange instruments and big boxes with white labels. The attendant told him that the man was a scientist, a man who liked to collect odd things, wrote down pages and pages about everything he saw.

A preoccupied Englishman entered the room.

Francis Buchanan was a trained surgeon who had decided to become an explorer and naturalist. The British administration had assigned him to investigate and document agriculture, minerals, industries, environment and customs of the residents of Mysore region. He spent most of his time collecting specimens, making elaborate notes and experiments. Travelling with him was a party of Indian artists who made accurate illustrations of objects selected by him as vital scientific data.

The interview was brief and to the point: Can he draw well? Does he draw from his imagination or from his eye?

Mukunda's father began to tell them about his son's great talent. The Englishman pushed forward a paper and put a leaf on the table beside it, indicating that the young man draw it. Mukunda seemed uneasy, and reluctant. His father coaxed him to try. He picked up the pencil and it flew around the paper. The Englishman watched closely and was satisfied. Yes, this he could use.

Mukunda had a job again. He travelled with the large party around the kingdom, collecting specimens and drawing whatever he was asked. His new master appreciated his work but often made him revise, for he looked at it with the eye of a scientist and tried to tone down the artistic flair in his young illustrator.

Mukunda still would not talk. And at times he would not even listen. He would often go wandering off without informing. A dead woman haunted him, said the men of the camp. As the days went by, his wanderings got more frequent and his drawings less acceptable. Finally, he was dismissed with some reimbursement and set off on the road to Srirangapatna.

He did not make it back home. The search parties went as far as they could but there was no trace of the young man, not a single person who claimed to have met him. He had disappeared.

Lady Miranda had taken three hours to get dressed that morning and her hair, carefully piled high over her head in the latest fashion, needed the assistance of three maids to fit into the carriage without damage. She was on her way for a portrait sitting, and though she had had portraits done before, this one was special and certain to be the delight of her winter ball. Quite a few strings had to be pulled to move her up the appointment register with the talented artist and she looked forward to being inside his studio. Richard Dawson was as much the fashion in London as her hairstyle and the cut of her gown.

The painter lived in an attractive part of the city, his large studio topped by two floors for a growing household. Sometimes in the studio, one could hear running feet overhead, and the frequent brawls of his six children. He liked that. It reminded him of the life that he had nearly given up on but which was now flourishing almost of its own accord.

Twenty years earlier, on Richard's return to Madras from Srirangapatna, everyone wanted to know more about the war and the great feat of their army. He had repeated what he knew they had wanted him to say, and being drunk most of the time had helped do that. His old host, Gilbert Forbes, had migrated to Africa with his wife to explore new business opportunities at the Cape. But Robert Havelock had been very willing to take a fellow painter under his wings and to provide a steady supply of arrack. Richard had stayed in Havelock's studio and ate whatever food was offered to him, sick of paints and all people. Havelock never questioned him and appeared to understand everything.

When Richard's body could not tolerate the drinking anymore, he had sobered up for a few days and with that found himself being invited to all the celebratory parties in the fort. He went out of sheer need to get drunk again at somebody else's cost. At one of the dinners he found himself seated next to a limp-haired and tongue-tied girl he remembered from a year ago, Doctor Wheeler's other daughter, Rose. By the end of the month he had married her, not because he particularly wanted to, but because he needed any reason, however shaky, to carry on. And he needed to push thoughts of another woman into a deeper vault within.

Richard had searched for Suhasini after the fort had been invaded and conquered, every hour of that dreadful night, every place that he could think of. He did not find her. After a few days of pleading and pestering General Harris, he was given a private audience with Lakshmi Ammani who was busy gathering the reins of political power for her adopted son. She received him very warmly but with regal detachment. She was aware of how much he expected from her.

No, he could not meet Suhasini. And no, she could not say anymore. Every woman is entitled to her own aspirations and had her own limitations, especially the married daughter of a respectable priest.

Richard dropped to his knees and begged for her mercy. He could not go without Suhasini or at least without hearing the rejection from her own lips.

The audience was declared over. But he was not ready to give up. He raised his voice in the hope that it would break through the formality. How could Her Majesty take such a drastic decision with other people's lives? And after all that he had done for them?

The Queen spoke to him sadly. He did not really know Suhasini if he thought she would let someone else decide for her. No, this was just the way she wanted it to be.

Then Richard knew that Suhasini was there, listening to them, and that it had all ended. Two kindly guards led him out by the hand for he could barely see through the tears. There was nothing left on the island for him. Francis and his entourage of men had left without leaving any message. Jonathan Cole, preoccupied with precious stones he was pocketing while cataloguing the Company's loot from Tipu's palace, had little patience with his moping friend but was able to persuade Richard to travel to Madras with one of the regiments. Richard could not bear to look over his shoulders as they rode past the fort walls of Srirangapatna. He could not stay in Madras either, not even with a new wife and an influential father-in-law. He travelled to London with Rose and used some of her inheritance to buy a house and start a modest business as a portraitist. But there was no joy left in his heart. He painted with manic energy, all his skills now had a certain instinct and creative recklessness that he had always wished for before. Some of it, he knew, came from watching a gifted apprentice at work, but he never spoke of it.

Richard's initial attempts to find Francis in Fort St. George had not yielded any leads but many years later he heard that Francis had opened a tavern in Black Town and was flourishing at it.

The painting that meant so much to Richard, Mukunda's vision of Suhasini, that carried the claim of his name, had been misplaced and he never managed to recover it despite frantic efforts and repeated requests over the years to many Company officials.

The painting was lost, they said.

The painting was returned to her.

If the general's secretary thought it was an unusual request, he did not say so. The Wodeyar queen had sent a personal note requesting that any artwork that might have crossed enemy lines during hostilities be sent back to the fort at once. The Secretary knew exactly what she wanted. It would have made a wonderful memorabilia to take back to England, the portrait of an Indian woman by a young English artist that had also served as a map to win them the greatest war fought on Indian soil. Just the sort of thing to brag about in political circles and bequeath to one's heirs, but the situation was too delicate, the letter too sharp, and the painting was returned reluctantly.

Lakshmi Ammani refused to see the canvas. It lay at her feet, wrapped in a white sheet, like a shroud. She sent it across to join the departing caravan of carts, to she who had chosen to leave. What would she do with a cold image when she would rather have Suhasini standing by her side at this moment of shared triumph? Lakshmi walked into the dark inner chambers of her old home, closed the doors behind her, lay down on the cold floor. The throne had returned to her family but the suffering had long outweighed the rewards. She closed her eyes tight. What had happened to Suhasini the night that the fort was stormed? She was with them one moment and the next she was gone. For two long days, Lakshmi had barely time to think about anything, so pressing had been the needs of her state, to make sure the British accepted her family's claim to Mysore. She had heard Suhasini was safe in her parents' home, she had heard the family was leaving for Kashi with all their belongings, but nobody had come to meet her.

She had then sent word for the young woman. Don't you dare leave without seeing me, your Queen, your sister in strength, your deepest self.

Suhasini did come, gaunt, closed, fatigued. All of Lakshmi's questions fell around her like rain on parched land. She said little, only that she wanted to go back to the banks of the Ganga. She had played her part, she said, and now she had nothing to offer anyone else. Not even her family. Her life was now finally hers to own.

That's when the English artist had arrived, seeking an audience with Lakshmi. Suhasini had stepped behind the wall and listened which he talked about her, before Lakshmi turned him away.

'What happened to you? How could I have let this happen to you? I have failed you. Forgive me, forgive me.' Lakshmi held Suhasini's hands after the Englishman had gone.

The younger woman had something else on her mind. 'There are two paintings, of me, and I don't want the English to have them.'

'I will get them back for you.'

Suhasini bent down to touch the Queen's feet for blessings, and then walked away without wasting anymore words or glances.

In response to Lakshmi's request, just one canvas was received from the English camp, the one wrapped up like a corpse that Lakshmi sent across to Suhasini. It was promptly returned to the palace. The past cannot travel into the future.

What is to be done?

Lakshmi did not want the painting seen, but it was much too precious to be destroyed or given away. Leave it somewhere, she said, the more important thing is to forget.

Two hundred years of forgetting would follow.

During the bi-centennial celebrations of the war, the painting is found in the storeroom of an art gallery owned by the royal family. A curator who authenticates the canvas as an original Dawson swears it to be a rare glimpse into the great portraitist's early career, priceless even though it is incomplete. The painting is promptly put on display.

Untitled. 1798-9 (?)
Richard Dawson (1774–1845) Oil on canvas.

The violent aftermath of the storming of Srirangapatna on 4 May 1799 continued till the following morning when General Harris sent Colonel Arthur Wellesley to take over as commander of the fort. The town streets were swarming with their soldiers, intoxicated with liquor and power, pockets stuffed with newly acquired wealth, and mere orders had no effect on them. Wellesley's troops rounded the culprits, four of them executed by hanging in the town square, and dozens flogged. With that began the monumental task of disposing of the dead and restoring normalcy to the island. Over 11,000 bodies of its inhabitants and soldiers lay scattered all around the fort, buried under debris, floating in the moats, half-eaten by vultures in the middle of streets, charred inside burning buildings.

On receiving General Harris's written report on the victory, Governor-General Richard Wellesley appointed a second commission with specific briefs. Four sons of Tipu Sultan who had surrendered to General Harris were sent to Vellore under military escort. Their families would soon follow them. In 1806, following a mutiny in Vellore, they would all be relocated to Calcutta. They never regained any royal privileges.

Tipu Sultan was buried with religious and military honours beside his father Haider Ali in the mausoleum at Lal Bagh on the river island. During this ceremony a violent storm burst over the island of Srirangapatna accompanied by thunder and lightning that felled two men of the English army. Even though the monsoons would not arrive for weeks, it rained heavily that night and the river became unfordable for forty-eight hours. Many inhabitants of the island claimed it to be a sign of divine retribution and of Tipu's martyrdom.

Mir Sadiq, whom Tipu Sultan trusted to be his Dewan, was killed the same evening as Tipu. He was fleeing for safety from one of the gates during the storming of the fort when soldiers from his own army, suspecting his betrayal, attacked and stoned him to death.

Krishnaraja, the five-year-old Wodeyar prince, was proclaimed ruler of Mysore. Purnaiah was selected to be the Dewan and Colonel Barry Close became the first British Resident to the court. Lakshmi Ammani ruled as the regent till the prince came of age. She died in 1810 with the satisfaction of having restored her family to the Mysore throne.

King Krishnaraja Wodeyar III, popularly known as Mummadi, reigned over Mysore for seventy-four admirable years, building a reputation as an able ruler, patron of the arts, scholar of many interests and skilful administrator. The Mysore kingdom would never again go to war against Britain and remained a loyal ally till it joined the Union of India in 1947.

Richard Wellesley aspired to an English marquisate as reward for his success against Tipu Sultan but had to be satisfied with an Irish one and the title of Marques Wellesley. Though he turned down any share in the prize money, he accepted a badge of the Order of St. Patrick made from Tipu's jewels and an annuity of 5,000 pounds. He had arrived in India to run what was primarily a trading company. Seven years later he returned to England leaving behind an imperial power that would spread across the entire subcontinent in a few decades.

His brother Colonel Arthur Wellesley went on to become the famed first Duke of Wellington and the hero of many English battles, most notably the one that ended Napoleon Bonaparte's career at the Battle of Waterloo.

Nearly all of Tipu Sultan's treasury and personal collections made their way to the royal collection and several personal collections in England. One hundred and fifty thousand gold coins found in Tipu's state treasury were divided among the troops soon after the battle. Tipu's extensive library comprising thousands of books and rare manuscripts, his journal of dreams, swords, firearms, clothes, shoes, armour, ornaments and jewellery, guns and cannons, carpets, as well as three of his trained cheetahs accompanied by trainers were all shipped to England.

The gold throne that Tipu never ascended was cut up and melted into small pieces for distribution as prize. The jewel-studded Huma bird atop the throne was presented to Queen Charlotte and its tiger head became footstool to King George III.

As for the infamous wooden tiger-man-organ, said to be made by French engineers and local carpenters, it was dispatched to the Company's museum at India House in London and is now displayed at the Victoria and Albert Museum.

An obelisk at the north-west bastion of the Srirangapatna fort commemorates the successful storming of the fort by the English army and the sacrifices of its soldiers. A modest memorial marks the spot where Tipu Sultan's body was discovered. His famous red palace has been reduced to its foundations and a few broken walls. It stands right opposite the Sriranganatha temple that saved many lives during the storming of the fort, though only the lives of the upper caste and more privileged citizens.

There is no memorial to honour the soldiers and inhabitants of Srirangapatna who died during the Fourth Mysore War of 1799.